"Ellen Shanman gets right to the center of personal disaster, and understands disaster the way it ought to be understood: as the focus for a continually expanding radius of big laughs."

—Katherine Taylor, author of *Rules for Saying Goodbye*

"Look, Edwards," Oliver said, "we have a problem. We've had this conversation before. You're a damn good writer. Which makes it all the more difficult for me to do what I have to do now." He sighed and Mike waited. "I've been reassigning Blackwell's accounts.... Nobody wants you on their team, Edwards. You don't play well with others."

"What others?"

"I'm not going into it—"

"Is this about the tampons? Because—"

"It's about a lot of things, although while we're on the subject, it was probably inappropriate to refer to the consumers as 'bleeders' in front of the ad manager."

"It slipped out."

"Edwards. You're icy with your coworkers and you argue with clients. And, unfortunately, you no longer have a champion in this office. I've gotta let you go, Edwards." Oliver looked almost embarrassed. Almost. "I'm sorry."

"Believe me," she said slowly, "I bet I'm sorrier."

"Can I give you a piece of advice, Mike? Wherever you land next, try to act more like a ... person."

As the elevator doors slid shut on the life Mike knew, and she began a literal descent to match her figurative one, Mike realized that this bothered her.

Also by Ellen Shanman
Published by Bantam Dell

RIGHT BEFORE YOUR EYES

EVERYTHING NICE

ELLEN SHANMAN

A Bantam Discovery

EVERYTHING NICE
A Bantam Discovery Book / August 2008

Published by Bantam Dell
A Division of Random House, Inc.
New York, New York

Book design by Lynn Newmark

Bantam Books and the rooster colophon are registered trademarks and
Bantam Discovery is a trademark of Random House, Inc.

Library of Congress Cataloging-in-Publication Data
Shanman, Ellen.
Everything nice / Ellen Shanman.
p. cm.
"A Bantam Discovery."
ISBN 978-0-385-34053-3 (trade pbk.)
1. Single women—Fiction. 2. Risk-taking (Psychology)—Fiction.
3. Women teachers—Fiction. I. Title.

PS3619.H3548E94 2008
813'.6—dc22
2007052119

Printed in the United States of America
Published simultaneously in Canada

www.bantamdell.com

BVG 10 9 8 7 6 5 4 3 2 1

FOR JON

WHEN YOU GOT IT,
FLAUNT IT

They say the truth will set you free. They never explain that with an insouciant thwack, the truth will shove you out into the cold, dark forest of self-awareness, to be pursued by the hungry wolverines of doubt and loathing. They never mention that part. And when it happens, you can only hope that somewhere in the woods you will find a bar that's still open.

Luckily, at six-thirty on a Friday in Manhattan, all the bars are open. Mike sat at one of them with her heels against the brass foot rail and sipped slowly and deliberately at a double Jameson neat. She stared into the glass after every sip and willed the alcohol to seep into her veins. She'd been drinking for too many years to rush foolishly into intoxication as though there weren't a long evening ahead. She had all the time in the world and an open tab.

The Town Drunk was a filthy cesspit in the Meatpacking District with a splintering bar and perpetually sticky floors. The jukebox played Merle Haggard and Bob Dylan and sometimes the Charlie Daniels Band. A few long-forgotten bras were tacked around the mirror behind the bar, mementos of the nights when young professional women got a little too amusing and lived out their sad *Coyote Ugly* fantasies on the bar top. Mike had never been one of these women; Mike was a regular.

"Guy at the jukebox is tryin' to work up the nerve," the bartender said quietly as he wiped up the bar in front of her.

Mike glanced into the mirror briefly and caught the outline of someone feeding the jukebox and trying to stare at her out of the corner of his eye.

"Good tip, Jimmy," she said.

"Don't worry." He chuckled. "I don't think he's gonna get there." Still smiling to himself, he moved down the bar to take an order.

Mike briefly mustered the energy to hope that Jimmy was right. She didn't have the reserves tonight to turn someone down politely, to make the obligatory six or seven sentences of conversation before excusing herself to pull out her cell phone or go for a smoke. And she didn't even smoke.

She was constantly having to turn men down, as though sometime in her early adolescence an evil fairy had come through Mike's window while she was sleeping and sprayed her down with some irresistible pheromone that she'd never be able to rinse off. Or maybe it was her utterly effortless and stunning beauty. One of the two. She didn't wear makeup. She cut her long, dark hair maybe twice a year. Fingernails, to Mike, were not for painting but for snapping open beer cans and taking off her stainless Swiss Army watch. Except it's hard to cover up a face that screams to be a portrait and legs that go on for miles. It's hard not to be noticed when you're nearly six feet tall and built like Elle Macpherson, but then, to each of us her challenges.

Mike hoped that Gunther would get there soon. They mostly left her alone when Gunther was around.

The door swung open with a shock of fading daylight, and as he frequently did when she thought of him, Gunther appeared. Like many Australians, Gunther entered a room larger than life, with the carefree warmth and goodwill of an entire continent blowing in behind him. How a ship of minor convicts and British undesirables spawned a nation of the world's most cheerful and gregarious individuals, we may never know. But nowhere is this more evident than in New York City, where the indigenous multitudes hurtle down crowded sidewalks just trying not to touch anyone. Gunther was Mike's equilibrium, a balance for her gruff pessimism, her best friend. And the only man to whom she wasn't related who'd never tried to sleep with her.

Gunther squinted when he saw Mike sitting at the bar, and consulted his watch. "Christ, Mikey, am I late?"

She smiled for a moment at the sight of his enormous, lanky form hoisting itself onto the adjacent barstool and tapping lightly on the bar with a smile at Jimmy to indicate he'd have the usual, which was a Guinness. Gunther always arrived first, as a rule. As the New York bureau chief for an Australian wire service, a title he considered perhaps too lofty as there was no bureau beneath him, Gunther worked from home, and occasionally from the Drunk, filing stories by phone to copy-takers in Sydney who would unfailingly get them somehow wrong. But the hours were terrific.

"No," she said slowly, "no, I'm early."

"Fess up." He smiled and sucked the foam from his beer. "You chuckin' a sickie?"

It had taken years for Mike to comprehend the variety of Gunther's vernacular, but she was now able to understand that he was asking whether she'd played hooky.

"Try again," she said. "Worse. Much worse."

"Hang on," Gunther insisted. He tipped his glass back and within four seconds drained the whole thing, slamming it down on the bar in triumph when he was done. "'Nother one, Jimmy," he requested with a grin and turned back to Mike. "Okay," he said. "Now I'm ready."

"That makes one of us," she returned.

"One's all we need then," he assured her. "Hit me."

Mike took a deep breath and sighed. "Brian Bentley was fired this morning." She listened to the words hanging in the air and felt like she'd tuned in to *Lost* midseason. Nothing made sense.

"Still waiting for the bad news." Gunther suppressed a smile.

"I was fired this afternoon." It was the first time she'd said so, and it sounded like someone else was talking. Since this morning, everything had felt like a day out of someone else's life. Someone who was vulnerable to things like humiliation and termination of employment. Someone who wasn't a winner like Mike.

It had all happened so fast.

One minute she'd been standing in the slim kitchenette of A. S. Logan Advertising, stirring Splenda into a mug that said "Nancy" in rainbow letters and thinking, nearly simultaneously, that she had no idea who Nancy was and that Splenda sounded like the name of a Vegas stripper. "Splenda's really working the pole tonight." "How does Splenda always bring in the big bucks?" She'd been pitching a paper towel account all morning and her mind was meandering, trying to keep from thinking anymore about toughness and absorbency.

"'Scuse me, Mike." Brenda from Research pushed past her, smelling strongly of something sweet and cheap. Brenda stole perfume samples from the cosmetics accounts and gave unsolicited lectures on the evils of coffee and had no sense of humor.

"Coffee break?" Mike asked her.

"Ha, ha, no," Brenda answered with a pinched expression that was probably intended to be a smile. "I have a peach in the fridge."

The women in her office didn't like Mike, she knew, but she reasoned that was their prerogative since she had next to no use for them. They were mysterious creatures she was obligated to see in the bathroom, and when she did they spoke in code words like "mascara" and "diaphragm" and "kick pleat." They trafficked in frivolous, clubhouse gossip and they pushed up their breasts and tucked hair behind their ears and dared her to pick through the minefield of their conversation. Mike had tried and failed to explain to her female coworkers that if they had to ask, they probably did look fat. That she absolutely did mind their pumping breast milk while discussing copy points. That crying was the lowest, most reprehensible form of game-ending, reprimand-defeating manipulation. They never seemed to take it the right way.

Men made sense. Men went after what they wanted and said what they meant, and usually what they meant was work or sex. Either way she always knew how to answer. But the women were impenetrable. So Mike always dried her hands and tightened her ponytail and fled as quickly as possible. Behind her back, she knew, they called her names. But everyone, *everyone,* acknowledged that she was one of the best copywriters around. It was the reason she'd been promoted so fast. It was the reason Brian Bentley had taken notice of her during her first year at the agency, and the reason he'd seen her up through the ranks at lightning speed. She'd landed her first television campaign at twenty-eight. She was a superstar.

All that was to be respected in Mike only seemed to make Brenda resent her more. It was Brenda who had started rumors about Mike sleeping with Brian, long before it had actually happened. And it was Brenda who now took immeasurable delight in delivering the bad news. From behind the refrigerator door where she rummaged for her produce, Brenda asked, "Are you hiding?"

"Clearly not well enough," Mike muttered. There was no reason to bother with false courtesy. There had been an unfortunate incident at an office birthday party during which Mike had failed to mention the lipstick on Brenda's teeth and she'd never been forgiven. They both knew where they stood.

"Oh-ho, as if I were your biggest worry. I don't blame you," Brenda answered and she suppressed a giggle behind the egg tray. "I think I would hide too."

"Yeah, well . . . have a day, Brenda." Mike turned to go.

"Did you wear denim to your pitch?"

Mike looked down at her badly beaten jeans and engineer boots. Creatives at A. S. Logan could generally wear whatever they liked, a fact that was probably deeply disturbing to Brenda.

"Turns out, the client wasn't there for a fashion show," Mike returned. "And by the way, I think it's great how you get all dressed up to sit in the cafeteria and read *The Rules* on your lunch break."

"Just seems like a shame that you'll be leaving such a disheveled impression. Today of all days."

"Maybe it's this dangerous, mind-altering coffee I'm drinking, Brenda, but I have no idea what you're talking about." Mike was going to give her thirty seconds, and then she was going to walk away.

Brenda gripped her cold peach tightly and stood up to say, "Oh, my goodness, do you not know yet?"

Mike had no time for this. She had twelve hours of work to get done in the next six. "Brenda," Mike said, "you're killing me."

Brenda carefully shut the fridge door. "Oh, that's right, you were in your pitch. Oliver just canned Brian."

Brenda smiled, because Mike looked like she'd been hit with a shovel.

"What are you talking about?" Mike managed.

"Mm-hmm. I guess he went to present to the Toreador distributors and they didn't like the campaign and Brian lost it. Word is he said some terrible things. It was lose the Toreador or lose Brian so . . . Tough break, I guess."

Mike stared with her mouth open.

Brenda moved past her toward the hallway. "P.S. Nancy really doesn't like other people using her mug."

Mike said nothing.

"And Mike?"

"Yeah?" Mike asked, without turning.

"Oliver's looking for you."

Mike listened to Brenda's heels clacking down the hallway. She wasn't going to take the word of the office gossip, knowing firsthand how often Brenda made things up just to amuse herself. She made her way quickly toward Brian's office, praying that she'd see his spiky gray head poking up above the back of his chair, see his expensive shoes up on the windowsill, and hear the familiar south London meter as he brayed into the phone. But there were two security guards in the office, cleaning out his desk, tossing Brian's Clio Awards into a cardboard box with framed photos of his wife and his beach house in Sag Harbor, acting as if there was no sacrilege in toppling an advertising legend in a single afternoon, all because a bunch of narrow-minded car distributors didn't know how to think outside the box.

It was then that Oliver found her, staring into Brian's office with a sort of conflicted fondness Mike didn't know she could muster for him. But she followed dutifully when Oliver motioned down the hall toward the corner office.

Oliver sank heavily into his chair before she was even in the room. "Shut the door," he told her and massaged his right temple. "Sit."

"I'd rather stand," she told him.

"Sit, Edwards."

She wanted to resist for the sake of resistance, but she wanted information more. She sat across the desk from him and stared hard.

"I appreciate the death ray, but he brought this on himself," Oliver began.

"That's a matter of perspective," Mike said.

"No, Edwards," he continued wearily, "when you call the advertising manager of one of the nation's largest auto manufacturers a 'filthy cocksucking motherfucker' in front of a meeting of his distributors, it is no longer a matter of perspective."

She wasn't entirely surprised. Brian had said worse.

"He nearly cost this agency millions of dollars, Edwards, and you don't want to know how many jobs. There wasn't much of a choice to make."

"The campaign he gave them was perfect—"

"Edwards," he interrupted her. "It's over. He's gone. Quit fighting for him."

She wasn't fighting for him, she wanted to explain. She was fighting alongside him. You could give Brian twenty-four hours and a dry-erase board and he could come up with a way to sell kitten-fur tea cozies to every member of PETA. He had plucked Mike from career infancy and built his own beautiful advertising monster and in return she gave him loyalty and utter confidence. And yes, one time, one, single time she'd drunk enough to forget her better judgment and she'd slept with him. Just one time. Every day since she'd wished she hadn't.

"Look, Edwards," Oliver said, "we have a problem." She knew what the problem was. "We've had this conversation before. You're a damn good writer." She knew. "Which makes it all the more difficult for me to do what I have to do now." He sighed and Mike waited. "I've been reassigning Bentley's accounts . . . Nobody wants you on their team, Edwards. You don't play well with others."

"What others?"

"I'm not going into it—"

"Is this about the tampons? Because—"

"It's about a lot of things, although while we're on the subject it was probably inappropriate to refer to the consumers as 'bleeders' in front of the client."

"It slipped out."

"Edwards. You're icy with your coworkers and you argue with everyone. And unfortunately, you no longer have a champion in this office."

"I didn't realize I needed one." It was a lie, but she said it anyway.

"There's no room here anymore for the way Bentley did business. The reign of terror is coming to a close." He shook his head. "I've gotta let you go, Edwards." Oliver looked almost embarrassed. Almost. "You backed the wrong horse. I'm sorry."

"Believe me," she said slowly, "I bet I'm sorrier."

"Can I give you a piece of advice, Mike? Wherever you land next, try to act more like a . . . person."

"I'll deposit that in the bank," she said as she stood to go, "along with all the other gems you've given me over the years."

The two security guards who had been busily disassembling Brian's office were waiting for Mike in the hallway. And as they walked her to the elevator every head had turned. The carrion crows at the copiers and cubicles had smirked as she passed, junior art directors and account execs and secretaries, all glad to see her go. Mike wondered what she'd done to make these people dislike her so much. Where was it written that you had to be everyone's friend? Wasn't it enough just to do your job and do it well? Did you have to make small talk and go to Christmas parties and coo at photos of people's children? Did you have to be so careful not to hurt feelings that you couldn't point out an idiot when you spotted one? Didn't these people even begin to understand everything she'd accomplished?

No. They didn't. Or they didn't care. They were glad to see her dethroned. As the elevator doors slid shut on the life Mike knew and she began a literal descent to match her figurative one, Mike realized that this bothered her.

"Christ, Mikey," Gunther said when she finished. "I'm gobsmacked."

"Yeah." She sighed. "I'm . . . gobsmacked too."

"You talked to the mongrel?"

"Do you think, considering the man was just fired, that we could hold off abusing him for the rest of the day?"

"Sorry," Gunther said. "Have you talked to *Mr.* Bentley?"

"No. I haven't. I've talked to you and Mr. Jameson," she said and she swallowed the rest of her whiskey. "And so far he's the better conversationalist." She caught Jimmy's eye and pushed the empty glass away for a refill.

"You'll be okay. Of course you'll be okay. You're an ace. You're the darling of Madison Avenue. You'll get snapped up by Monday."

"Yeah," Mike said, "I know. Monday, we'll drink to celebrate. But tonight"—she hoisted her newly filled glass—"we drink to forget."

Gunther smiled and raised his glass to meet hers.

"Sometimes, my friend," Mike toasted, "the dingos eat your baby."

"Sometimes," he echoed, "an air conditioner falls on your mother."

They drank. They drank for hours, if not more than usual for a Friday night, then with more ferocity. They drank through four watered-down sitcoms on the TV behind the bar. Through the late news. Through *The Tonight Show,* which they ignored in favor of a recounting of the stories Gunther had filed during the week. They drank while men eyed Mike and Gunther stared them down. While women turned at the sound of Gunther's accent, hoping they'd see Eric Bana or Russell Crowe. (Gunther rarely made use of his accent to pick up women, though he might well have done, as being Australian in New York is almost better than being rich.)

They drank while Conan O'Brien gave his monologue and they watched Jimmy refill their glasses for what seemed like the three hundredth time.

And then a strange thing happened. Mike looked at Gunther, who was oddly silent and staring over her head at the television. "Hey, Jimmy," he said quickly, "can we get a channel change?"

Mike turned to see what Gunther was looking at, and in an instant the worst day of her life got worse.

It might have been the very first time a grown woman was loosed from her moorings by the stand-up segment on the Conan O'Brien show.

"Ladies and gentlemen," Conan shouted, "will you please welcome a very funny man, Jay Stadtler!"

Mike froze, because it isn't every day that the only man you've loved shows up on national television. Gunther stared guiltily at the former friend he'd sacrificed. Jimmy, seeing obvious distress on the faces of his two best customers, reached for the remote.

"No, no, leave it!" Mike nearly shouted.

"You sure?" Jimmy hesitated.

"Yeah, I'm sure," she mumbled.

"It's nice to be with people tonight," Jay greeted the audience. He looked . . . he looked good. His hair was shorter and he'd lost a few pounds. He was better dressed than she'd ever seen him, Mike noticed, even though it wasn't something she'd ever particularly cared about. She waited for him to roll out the same old bits.

"This is the two-year anniversary of breaking up with my girlfriend."

"Oh, no," Mike heard Gunther say.

Jay's math was off. It had been longer than two years. The audienced "awww"-ed their sympathy.

"Thank you, yeah. But on the upside, I finally get custody of my balls back."

The first laugh sent shock waves through her.

"It was sad, they barely recognized me." Another laugh

and Mike twitched. "I guess you could say my ex kind of wore the pants in our relationship, but she was really nice about it. Like she never made me go out and buy tampons."

They chuckled.

"I did get the periods though."

They guffawed.

"Yeah, I was surprised too."

They loved him. Mike wondered if she was actually shaking or only felt like she was.

"Steady, Mikey," Gunther whispered.

"It's tough dating a woman who's more of a dude than you are," Jay told the studio audience. "You know, I'm a sensitive guy, right? We would fight and I would want to talk about it. She would want to arm wrestle." Live audiences will laugh at almost anything. "Which sucked because I never got to win an argument."

Mike had no idea he'd been doing well enough to land a spot on Conan. She'd avoided comedy clubs like the plague for more than two years. For two years and seven months. And eight days. Since he'd moved out.

"But surprisingly that's not why we broke up. Actually, it was because she didn't wanna have children." He paused. "She wanted me to have them."

The audience erupted again. "Thank you very much, you guys, you've been great." He replaced the microphone and Conan appeared to slap him on the back. "Jay Stadtler, everybody!" Conan repeated. "We'll be right back."

Mike stared at the screen as NBC cut to a commercial produced by A. S. Logan. It was as if an entire network were out to destroy her. Her mouth was gaping, fishlike, and she just stared. How long, she wondered, had she been his material?

"Don't you two know that guy?" Jimmy asked, completely innocent of all their horror.

"I need another one," Mike said.

"No, you don't," Gunther told her quietly.

"Yes, I do."

"No more," he said gently.

"Well, I need . . . something," she seethed.

She spun around on her barstool and spotted the soft-focus figure who'd been wanting to talk to her all night, the one Jimmy had warned her about. He'd been there for almost as long as she had and looked like he didn't hold his liquor nearly as well.

"Mikey," Gunther said.

"What," she said, still staring toward the jukebox.

"Look, I'm gonna take a piss, and when I come back, we'll go. We'll take a walk, okay? Do you good."

"Sure," she said. "Okay."

She sat alone and stared until she wasn't looking at anything anymore, just staring into space.

"Hey, you leaving?" Jimmy asked from behind her as he cleared their glasses. "Mike?"

There was a loaded question. When she had come home to find that boxes had been packed and a rental truck was parked outside and Jay's friends were sheepishly ferrying his belongings into the freight elevator, this was the question she'd asked. "What, are you leaving?"

"No, I'm going away for the weekend. But I'm taking *all* my stuff," he'd answered. This was the problem with dating a comedian.

Most women would have cried. They would have begun to shriek or sob or at least begged for one more chance to talk it through, but Mike just stood there.

"You have anything to say?" he demanded, and he held a pile of clothes above a suitcase like a challenge.

"What am I supposed to say?" she returned. She wasn't trying to fight. She was just asking.

"That's what I thought." He jammed sweatshirts and jeans into the suitcase and smashed the lid shut. For another half hour she stood and watched. She watched him emptying the books off the shelves and the silverware from the kitchen drawers. She watched him taking pictures off the walls and towels from the racks in the bathroom.

"I'm leaving you a set of sheets," he said.

"Why?" she asked.

"Because you don't own any, Mike."

"Okay," she said.

"You're fucking welcome." He threw a nylon pack over his back and picked up two suitcases. "If I forgot anything I'll get it next week."

"Okay," she said again.

He headed for the door, but stopped just short of the threshold and turned back to her. "You know, I used to think you just weren't like other women, but that's not it. I mean, you're not, don't get me wrong. You bear no resemblance to other women in any fucking way, but really it's that you're not even like other human beings. You're a fucking stone. I don't even think you know what regular people feel like—oh, wait, I shouldn't say 'feel.' Let me try to think of a word you could understand—"

"I thought you were going," she interrupted him, so calmly that he couldn't continue.

"Fuck you, Michaela." He'd slammed the door and he was gone.

Mike had been too overwhelmed to notice Gunther's

absence that day. She'd never asked why Jay's best friend had refused to help him pack. It had just seemed natural when he'd arrived at her door with a cup of coffee and taken her to buy new forks and spoons. But she thought of it now as she realized that Gunther should rightly have been in some other bar tonight with the rest of Jay's friends, celebrating his broadcast triumph. They never talked about how he'd started out as Jay's friend and ended up as hers. It made her uncomfortable in places she liked to pretend she didn't have.

"Shall we?" Gunther asked as he returned from the men's room. "Mikey?"

"I think I'm gonna stay," she said.

"Come on, it's late. Better to get out of here."

"Probably. But I just…I just want to sit for a while. Alone. Okay?"

Gunther sighed. "You know that's got bad idea written all over it?"

"Come on, big guy." She smiled wanly. "I'll be fine. We both know I'm the toughest son of a bitch in this bar."

He smiled because he couldn't argue with her. That was how you managed to stick around with Mike.

"I'll be fine," she repeated.

"Ring me tomorrow," he insisted.

"I will."

"G'night, Mikey."

She felt a tightness in her chest dissolving as the door swung shut behind him. And this feeling, this terribly frightening unnameable feeling was the reason she didn't just make six or seven sentences of polite conversation when the stranger by the jukebox finally worked up the nerve. Had she not just been knocked off her stellar career trajectory, had she not been subjected to a cruel dose of barely comedic reality from her once and only love, had she not been reminded multiple times in a single day of the ever-widening chasm that lay between her and the rest of humanity, she would never have made real the stranger's fantasy of taking the beautiful woman at the bar home with him for completely mediocre sex. When he awoke the next morning, she was already gone.

I'VE FALLEN AND
I CAN'T GET UP

In times of adversity, some human beings have a natural grace, an indomitable spirit that lifts them from the depths of despair and gives them the courage to fight another day. They pick themselves up, dust themselves off, etc. You run into them on the street and say, "Gee, I've been worried about you." And they tell you, "No need! I've got a great new job, my cholesterol's down, and I'm coaching a soccer team of orphans! That wrongful murder conviction was the best thing that ever happened to me."

And then there are people like Mike. Six months after losing her job and frankly, her selfhood, Mike awoke with her face pressed against the leg of her coffee table. The table was early-generation Ikea, and therefore only a reminder of how little she'd accomplished in the world.

She was lucky to be hung over and unable to take the aerial view; it wasn't a pretty picture. There was a buzzing in her head. She tried to close her eyes and slip back into unconsciousness, but the buzzing persisted. Finally she recognized the ring of her cell phone, and she stretched an arm underneath the coffee table to claw it from her bag.

She squinted at the phone, which insisted that whoever was calling was "unavailable." Just as well, she thought.

She flipped the phone open.

"Yeah?" she croaked.

"Missus Edward?" a man with a Russian accent demanded.

Shit and a half, why had she answered the phone?

"It's Edwards," she whispered. "With an *s*."

"Missus Edward, today is for the rent."

Mike had been successfully avoiding her super for the better part of three weeks. She'd kept intentionally odd hours, let her mail pile up in the building lobby to suggest she was out of town.

"Okay, I'll write a check."

"Missus Edward! Three months you say writing this very check! Where is check, Missus Edward?"

"It's Edwardzzz," she repeated, "and I told you I'll write it today."

"No, Missus Edward. Is no more telling Yuri 'today, today, today.' How you would say, time is up!"

Okay, that one she had to give him. Time was most definitely up.

Mike had coasted by on savings for the first three months. Brian had promised over and over again that he'd have a new position in no time, that every agency in America was clamoring to snag him, that he'd take her wherever he went. He'd called her repeatedly after their common dismissal, trying to coax her to meet him at the apartment he kept solely for the purpose of trysting with women who weren't his wife.

So many times she'd almost asked him if he'd known it

was coming; she would never be sure whether Brian had had any idea of the precariousness of his situation within the advertising world, but unbeknownst to her he'd somewhere made the leap from brilliant adman to raving madman. His inquiries at other agencies in the days following his dismissal were all politely rebuffed. Several times Mike had heard him through the phone, shredding or burning cards from his Rolodex, muttering about "those bloody fucks. Bunch of bloody hacks. Fucking fucking fuck. Come over tonight?"

As her bank balances dwindled and the days ticked by, Mike tried to build increasing distance between herself and Brian. Partly it was the growing awareness that he wasn't getting anywhere, that perhaps the well really had been poisoned and she should stop lowering the bucket. But more than that, without the glass walls of A. S. Logan to give them safe definition, she and he seemed to be hovering in a dangerously nebulous relationship, one whose terms he was constantly trying to negotiate in favor of sex.

She didn't want to be his minion, and frankly, if his ship was sinking she wasn't going to go down like a rat. Unfortunate water metaphors aside, she began to make her own inquiries. She sent e-mails to the firms that had expressed interest over the years, to the creative directors who'd tried to poach her. She reached out to former colleagues who had moved up and out, and to everyone who had ever said, "Someday, we'll get to work together."

She was in entirely new territory, and she hadn't exactly arrived prepared. The Monday after she was canned, Mike gathered a bag of Fritos and a six-pack of Red Stripe and waited by the phone watching old episodes of *American Gladiator* on cable. She waited for the polite inquiry that would begin, "Listen, Edwards, heard about that bullshit over at Logan. Tough break. But I'm hoping their loss will be our pot of gold." She would entertain a series of offers and then play them against each other. She would mastermind a quiet bidding war and to the victor would go Mike. She would send Oliver a fuck-you note.

When it had not rung by Friday, the phone accidentally on purpose landed in the toilet.

She sent resumes. The few responses she got were almost too polite. As if she were some kid just out of college, as if she didn't know any of these people. It took weeks to get e-mails answered. Every ad exec she knew was suddenly in a meeting or on the phone. The only loop she was in existed between herself and Brian and there were a million reasons not to ask him what was going on, but something was wrong. Mike was a star. She was all over *Adweek,* people knew her name, and suddenly she couldn't even get a meeting.

Eventually, when a creative director at Barron, Petrie & Klein who'd once courted her refused to take her calls, she squeezed the secretary.

"Lauren, I need you to tell me something."

"I didn't know you knew my name."

"I've been talking to you on the phone for seven years, Lauren. Of course I know your name."

"But you've never used it."

"I've used it."

"Not really—"

"Lauren! Focus. I need to know what the hell is going on."

"Um—"

"It's like I have plague, Lauren! It's like I'm covered in locusts. I can't get an interview. I can't even get a fucking phone call through!"

Mike could hear Lauren shifting uncomfortably on the other end of the line.

"Lauren." Mike swallowed hard and used a word she didn't like. "Woman to woman."

"They call you the Bride of Bentley!" Lauren sputtered.

"They what?"

"The Bride of Bentley. They think you've been damaged. That you're all brainwashed or something and—"

"There's an 'and'?"

"And they don't like you."

Mike tried to take it all in.

"They don't *like* me? Who the hell said they had to like me? It's work, not eHarmony!"

"Everybody kind of thinks you're difficult to work with and . . . cold."

"Oh, my God." How was she supposed to win this game? When she'd started, nobody had used words like "cold" and "difficult." They'd used words like "genius" and "winner" and "money."

"Sorry, Mike," Lauren whispered. "Go get yourself a pedicure. You'll feel better." Clearly, where Lauren was going, Mike could not follow. Mike didn't do pedicures, even when she could afford them.

"Oh, hold on," Lauren added hastily, covering the mouthpiece so that Mike could only hear a muffled warbling of conversation.

Lauren returned to the phone sounding confused, even for Lauren. "Okay, Mike? Um . . . Dana wants to speak with you."

Dana Petrie remembered her. Dana Petrie knew what was up. Bride of Bentley, nothing. Mike was in.

"Mike Edwards." The smoky voice on the other end of the line took its time unfurling her full name.

"Dana," Mike said, her confidence rushing back and propelling her to her feet. She heard Dana exhale what was probably a long plume of smoke. An earring clinked against the phone.

"Mike Edwards," Dana repeated. Mike's confidence began to waver. "I hear you're pounding the pavement."

"I am," Mike said tentatively. There was something strange in Dana's tone. "So how's tricks? Congrats on landing Ocean Spritz, by the way. That campaign is gonna be hot." The schmooze made her teeth hurt.

"What can I do for you, Mike?" Dana drawled.

"You know I've always loved what you guys do over there, Dana."

"Mm-hmmm…"

"I don't want to work for just anyone."

"Of course you don't." Dana was unconvinced, Mike could tell. She scrolled through her memories of Dana Petrie for something specific, a hobby, a passion, something she could use to hook this woman.

There had been a luncheon, two or three years ago. Dana had invited Mike, what was it? *American Businesswoman* magazine or something…

"You know, Dana," Mike took a shot, "it would mean so much to me to be mentored by a woman working at such a high level in the industry. We, ah…" Mike swallowed. "We have to stick together, right?"

A low, rolling laugh broke quietly from the other end of the phone, and Mike suddenly felt chilly.

"Dana?"

"Mike Edwards, you have some nerve." The laugh had stopped.

"That's what you like about me, right?" It might have been just a tad too late for flippancy.

"Do you remember, Mike, three years ago, I sent you an invitation to a networking lunch for Women in Corporate America?"

"I do. Absolutely—"

Dana cut off Mike's response. "I still have your response card. I keep it in my desk drawer."

Mike sat down. She bit her lower lip and winced. "Oh, yeah?"

"'Thanks for the offer, but I'm washing my hair,'" Dana recited. "Does that ring a bell?"

"I have a feeling that was really funny at the time." Mike laughed gently as she spoke.

"Hilarious," Dana hissed.

Mike cleared her throat. "Listen—"

"No one agrees more than I do, Mike, that women in business need to support each other." She paused. "But unfortunately at the moment... I'm washing my hair."

There was a click and suddenly Mike was listening to the arrogant hum of the dial tone. She sat with the disconnected phone in her lap and tried to process what had just happened. She couldn't get a meeting because... what, she'd alienated the popular girls? This was not real. This could not be how it worked.

The world over, this is exactly how it works.

Alas, it seemed that word, that little slut, had gotten around: Mike Edwards was tainted meat. She got two first interviews. Neither requested a second. Fewer and fewer of her phone calls were returned. A disturbingly large percentage of her industry had apparently been waiting years to enact a passive-aggressive revenge fantasy. And while they got their probably well-earned kicks, little by little, Mike's savings escaped through the expanding crack in her foolproof life. So she stopped paying the rent and started hiding from her super.

"Yuri," she now whispered from underneath the coffee table, "I'm working on it." She hung up when Yuri began to curse in Russian.

Mike inched gingerly from beneath the furniture and tried not to regret drinking so much. It was eleven-thirty AM. She used to have a rule about not sleeping with free-lancers because they never woke you up in the morning. And now look at her.

She was down to the bottom of the prospect pile, contacts she thought little of and never intended to use. And today she was supposed to have lunch with some junior art director she'd gone to college with, hoping he might get her an interview at Stern/Fuller, an operation she'd said many times she'd never work for. Stern/Fuller were re-search hacks. They didn't care about the creatives. They didn't get the *art* of advertising. Brian would scoff if she even interviewed at Stern/Fuller. But Brian was no longer in a position to scoff and neither was she. Oh, how Mike longed to scoff.

Brett Horowitz was married with two children and his wife was in fund-raising with the Brooklyn Symphony. They lived in New Jersey. Mike met him at a trendy east-Midtown restaurant she couldn't afford, hoping in equal measure that the smell of the fusion cooking would cover her stink of desperation, and that she wouldn't run into anyone who knew her.

From the moment Brett walked in, everything was un-comfortable. He fidgeted in his chair and would barely look at her over the menu. He wanted small talk, she sup-posed. Mike hated small talk.

"So," she attempted, "what do your children...do?" She had stalled out in mid-sentence. What were you supposed to ask about children?

"Sorry?" Brett looked confused. "What do you mean?"

"Oh, I just wondered what they...how they...spend their days," she said.

"They don't...*do* anything," Brett said. "They're children."

Surprise, surprise, she thought. If they didn't do anything, why was she supposed to ask about them? Mike waited until they had placed their orders, then dove into the reason they were there.

"Look"—she leaned forward—"this is a little awkward." The enormity of the understatement almost tripped her up. They hadn't spoken since college. Her motives were obvious.

Brett looked uneasy. "Well," he stammered, "yeah. Yeah, it is a little..."

"I'm sorry. You shouldn't feel strange though. If I were you I would want to talk about the elephant in the room."

He coughed and required a sip of water to swallow his roll. Jesus, she thought, if anyone should be uncomfortable...

"I, ah...I guess I didn't really know how to bring it up," he said.

"It's fine. I'm bringing it up for you. I know what people are saying. I know I look like a dangerous bet right now. But I have a lot to offer, and obviously I'm willing to work on my...shortcomings. I'll bite the bullet. I'll start way down and earn my way up. I've done it before. I just really need somebody to give me a shot."

Brett squinted at her, his head pitched forward slightly,

like a curious turtle. He adjusted his tortoise frames and pursed his lips to speak three times before any sound came out. Mike bit her lip.

"Sorry, what are you talking about?" he spat gently.

This was perplexing. He knew about her bitter end at Logan. He had to, everyone knew.

"I . . . I thought you knew. That I'm a free agent, I just assumed—" This made things slightly more complicated.

"I . . . yeah, I knew you were out on your ass," he said.

Mike found this slightly hostile. "Oh. Okay . . . so, now I'm confused." She leaned back and tried to look innocent, pleased almost, to hear what he had to say. She just wanted another drink that would dim the glare coming off Brett Horowitz's shiny forehead.

"You . . . I guess . . . so what, you wanna talk about work?"

She smiled and hoped it looked real. "Brett, I wanted to talk about us working together. I've always thought it would be so great to work with you, and now I'm available. We might be able to get something together."

He shook his head a little as if something was unbelievable.

"Wow," he said.

Alright, what the fuck was the problem? He should have been panting by this point, at the very idea that he'd someday get to take credit for bringing her to Stern/Fuller. He should already have been planning what he was going to say to his boss. This was not working.

"You—I really can't believe this." He was starting to look annoyed. Annoyed was not good.

"Ah . . . okay, I'm mystified." She worked hard to contort her features into something resembling concern.

"Do you have any memory of college?" he asked.

"Big stone buildings? Books? Sounds vaguely familiar." She tried to smile again and felt the muscles around her jaw pulling.

"You really fucked me up in college."

Mike contained the overwhelming urge to turn her head and look for the waiter, because this was the worst possible time to have an empty glass; this uncomfortable dance was making her thirsty. "Okay, guy, you wanna fill me in here?"

Brett Horowitz gaped at her in wounded horror. "You don't remember this? How can you not remember?"

"I..." The less she said the better, she was sure.

"We slept together. I came over to help you study for organic chemistry, and actually, I basically gave you all the answers to the test, I really don't think you would have passed—and we slept together."

Oh, Christ. Mike tried to reach back through the haze for some memory of Brett Horowitz's pale naked ass in her dorm room. It was completely possible. She just couldn't seem to conjure anything specific. He was waiting for an answer.

"Oh..." What exactly was the etiquette here? She gave it a shot. "Of course! Of course I remember. My God, I wouldn't forget that...night?"

"You never spoke to me again."

Well, that was just super.

"I...that can't be right."

"Um, I think I would remember being completely crushed and demoralized and humiliated to the point where I couldn't sleep with another woman for almost two years. I think I have a fairly accurate memory of that." He was getting agitated. People were starting to turn.

"Of course you would," she managed. She cursed her

nineteen-year-old self for getting anywhere near Brett Horowitz in the first place. She should have known better.

"I mean, I was...I was crazy about you. You were my first!"

Nothing to see here, folks. Show's over. Please disperse.

"And I called you and called you," he went on. "I remember sitting by the phone and thinking, I'll call her at nine. Because I knew you'd be home around nine from the library before you went to play darts. But I didn't want to call you *at* nine, because then it would be so obvious that I had planned to call you at nine. So I called you at like, 8:53."

"Maybe I wasn't home," she offered.

"For three weeks? I called you for three weeks! I left you messages. I wrote letters and stuck them under your door and you just never talked to me again!"

People were definitely looking. From the corner of her eye, Mike watched the waiter start to arc toward their table and change his mind again.

"I mean, how could you do that to another human being? Just take their virginity and then blow them off. I mean, your first time is supposed to be special!"

It was more than she could bear. Six months without work. A bank account that was wasting daily into nothingness. And now this twinky, sad, little man wanted to dredge up a social faux pas from a one-night stand she'd had over a decade ago?

"I mean, I didn't even tell my wife that I was meeting you today, you know? That's how big a deal it was. I thought you were going to, like, apologize, or something, or tell me *why*, and you just, you want me to help you get a job?! I don't...how is that possible?!"

"Brett," she snapped in a loud whisper, "you wanna keep it down? It's a restaurant!"

She didn't see it coming. Suddenly his eyes were just pools of tears, tears that started to stream silently down his cheeks as if they, at least, were making a run for it.

"Oh, God. Okay, don't do that. I'm sorry. I'm really sorry. I . . . please don't do that!" she begged, but he couldn't stop. "I was a kid, Brett, and a stupid kid. I didn't . . ." His chest was heaving up and down as he slowly dissolved into something resembling a giant, bearded, little girl. "I just . . . God, it wasn't *my* first time, and I guess I . . ."

This was the wrong thing to say.

For a moment, Brett's eyes bulged in disbelief and horror, and probably because any sound he made would have been a wail, he bolted from his chair and ran, literally ran, for the door, his napkin tucked into his belt and flapping at his groin like a redundant loincloth.

The restaurant was silent. Everyone stared at her. Mike looked hard at the half-eaten roll on Brett's plate and thought that perhaps this lunch had been a bad idea.

"Check?" The waiter appeared beside her and gently slid it next to her plate.

She couldn't afford a cab home. As she trudged back uptown, she ticked Brett Horowitz off the list, and then realized there really was no more list.

Mike walked two extra blocks so she could approach her building from the rear. She opened the door an inch at a time, prepared to drop it and run if Yuri was in the hallway. All clear. She hugged the wall and tiptoed to the stairwell door, before huffing up twenty-seven flights of stairs. She bolted out of the stairwell, threw her key in the lock of her apartment door and ignored the astonished look on the face of the old woman down the hall who was returning from a walk with her toy poodles. Mike slammed the door behind her and leaned against it, sweaty and panting.

She looked at herself in the hall mirror, and for the first time began to wonder how long she could keep this up before they just evicted her.

She looked down to see that she was standing on an orange piece of paper. Though her heel covered half of it, Mike was just able to make out the word "Notice."

I'M NOT A DOCTOR,
BUT I PLAY ONE ON TV

Mike's mother always said that if one was going to die in New York, one should do it big. "Skip the peaceful, sleeping death," she'd say, "and do something extraordinary. Fall into an open manhole. Lose a wrestling match with one of the mythic alligators in the sewers. Wake up one morning to find that your building is being renovated and they've bricked you into your bedroom. You know, something that could only happen here." Caroline Edwards was a beautiful, long-haired, free-spirited, wit of a woman who wore peasant dresses and wrote children's books about a mongoose named Edwina.

She might have been pleased to note that her own end was to be hastened by a poorly installed air conditioner, loosed from a fourteenth-story window in 1979. Well, perhaps "pleased" isn't the right word.

If she'd had the time, Caroline might have left her husband a set of instructions for raising their four-year-old daughter. They might have mentioned important milestones like her first period or the junior prom. They would likely have covered inscrutable mysteries like the children's size 6X, or how to explain that a teasing classmate is usually hurting on the inside, or why it was normal to develop feelings for Michael J. Fox and Kirk Cameron during the '80s. But Caroline didn't have time. She would never know her daughter's growing pains, nor Kirk Cameron's for that matter.

To say that Dr. Gerald Edwards, one of Manhattan's top orthopedic surgeons, was woefully unprepared to raise a small girl by himself would be something of an understatement. Like all single parents, he did the very best he could. Exhausted and grief-stricken almost to the point of collapse, in the days after his wife's funeral, Gerry could barely summon the energy to speak to his child. The apartment that had seemed generous and grand now felt empty and cavernous. Days that had been perpetually too short suddenly stretched into tortured oblivion. Calling out his daughter's name when she needed to be fed or put to bed or kept from reaching for something sharp took almost more energy than Gerry could muster. And "Michaela" was such a big name for such a little girl. In the moments when he could manage only a syllable, Michaela became "Mike." The four-year-old learned to answer. The twelve-year-old couldn't remember being called by any other name.

When Caroline would have bought dresses, Gerry chose overalls. Ballet lessons seemed so unnecessary, whereas soccer practice with his brothers was one of Gerry's favorite memories. When she couldn't fall asleep at night, Mike listened to her father's stories of college football victories and fish so big they nearly yanked him into the sea. As the years went by, she became more and more her father's daughter. Her mother was gone and they couldn't bring her back. When no one was looking, and no one ever was, Caroline faded into one photograph on the mantel and four picture books on the shelf about a precocious mongoose.

Mike waited nearly a month before telling her father that she'd lost her job. She'd hoped to gloss over the unpleasantness and surprise him with word of her exciting new situation, but finally she'd cracked. They met for lunch on the second Tuesday of each month, at a deli near Lenox Hill Hospital. Eventually, she'd dropped the bomb over knockwurst.

Spearing a pickle with his fork, her father had simply said, "So you're a free agent. You'll get picked up."

They didn't talk about it after that. They talked about the stock market and sports medicine and how American beef was being devalued by high-quality Japanese meats. They pretended everything was normal, which had mostly worked for nearly three decades.

But this was five lunches later. She now had twenty-six days to leave her apartment, not half of what she'd need for a security deposit in the bank, a questionable credit rating, and no prospects for employment.

It was raining. Mike's father was in a foul mood, worn out and held up by a lengthy knee reconstruction. Mike picked at the peeling grain of the faux wood table and her father glowered as he attacked his pastrami on rye. Mike gazed into the huge glass jars of vegetables and vinegar and dill that lined the deli counter. She tried to think of a way to begin without using the word "failure." She peered at the old clock on the wall and realized that if she didn't say anything soon, her father would have to go back to the hospital. She couldn't go another month, which meant that she'd have to make a special trip to the Upper East Side and drop in on him one evening just to mooch and that would be much worse. She swallowed hard, ate a French fry, and tried to begin.

"It's not looking good for the Giants," she said.

"Hmph," her father answered. "They can still pull it out."

"They could," she concurred, "but with a couple of starters out? It's not even the same team."

"A team is the eleven men on the field. That's a team."

"Right." She kept pushing, trying to sound nonchalant, but hoping he would understand without her having to be explicit. "But what if the eleven guys aren't the right guys? What if they're not enough?"

"They can do it."

"I don't know."

"Now don't be one of these damned New York fans"— her father pointed an accusing finger with a gobbet of pastrami dangling from the tip—"who give up and turn on these guys at the first sign that things are gonna be tough! I didn't raise you to be one of those fans!"

"I'm not!" Mike began to turn red. "I am not one of those fans!"

"Good." Her father crunched a fry and squinted at her as though she were an X-ray showing bone fragments. Mike knew she couldn't stop now. She was out of options.

"I'm just saying, maybe the Giants don't recognize themselves anymore. Maybe they're feeling kind of lost and they're out of options. Sure, they're showing up, the rookies are trying, but maybe it's not working. Maybe, with so many guys on the bench, they're not sure how to keep going—"

"Mike, what the hell are you talking about?!" her father barked.

"I'm out of money!" she nearly shouted, and then more

quietly, "I'm broke. There are no jobs. Or at least there are no jobs for me. I'm screwed."

Gerry looked at her long and hard. "Spell it out. What are you asking for?"

"Five thousand. I owe back rent. They're throwing me out."

"Ah, Jesus." Her father sighed. Mike said nothing, but briefly considered changing her name and moving out of state.

"You're thirty-one years old."

"Is that going to affect my interest rate?"

"You're too old for a loan from your dad, Mike."

Under the table, she twisted the wrapper of her straw into an intricate and tormented pretzel. She felt like a gorilla was sitting on her chest. Bad enough to ask in the first place, but to ask and be turned down? She wasn't even sure where to go from there.

"Okay," she managed, but just that.

"You've dug yourself a hole."

"Yes," she concurred and tore the wrapper-pretzel in two.

Her father sighed again and looked out toward the rainy sidewalk. "This is one of those parenting moments." This was what Mike's father said when he didn't know what to do. It was filler for the period of deliberation that he didn't want her to mistake for unsteadiness. He'd said it the first time she snuck a boy into the apartment overnight. With a cowering seventeen-year-old lacrosse player searching for his pants in the corner of Mike's childhood bedroom, her father had said, "This is one of those parenting moments." Other people might have said, "Your mother would know what to do."

"If I gave it to you, it would be a crutch. What you need

is rehab." Thinking she was overhearing a drug intervention, a woman at the next table perked up. You have to live with an orthopedic surgeon to appreciate their metaphors.

Mike tapped her fingers on the plastic bench by her hip. When she could no longer take the silence, she said, "Look, I'm sorry I asked. I put you in a bad position. I'll take care of it."

"What does Gunther say?"

She wished he hadn't asked this, though she had known that he would. Mike's father looked to Gunther when he himself couldn't make heads or tails of her, and while a part of her found it endearing, the rest of her was thoroughly annoyed. They were like colleague zookeepers, consulting over why the tetchy rhino wouldn't eat. Because he's not hungry, she wanted to shout. You don't know.

"He said I should talk to you." Mike finished her Coke and the three-hundred-year-old waitress materialized with a creak to remove the pebbled plastic tumbler.

"You know what it is that's keeping you from working this out?" Mike's father asked. Diagnosis, treatment, prognosis.

"No one likes me," she said honestly.

He gave her a brief, disappointed glance. "Fine, I don't need to know the real reasons, as long as you know and you're fixing them." He chewed lazily on his pastrami while he thought. "I'm gonna make you an offer," Gerry finally said. "You can move back into the house. You can get yourself together, get a new job, and when you're on your feet again you'll go. No time limit, long as you're looking for work."

Mike opened her mouth to say thanks but no thanks, but her father wasn't finished.

"Only thing is, it's not just going to be the two of us and

you need to know that going in. I was gonna tell you. I'm . . . with someone. A woman. Of course. I mean, I'm . . . she's my . . . she's moving in."

Mike stared at her father's head, which began to look small and far away. She tried to digest what he'd said, but it made very little sense. She wasn't sure what to piece to-gether first—the unpalatable idea of moving back into the home where she'd grown up, or the concept of her father with a woman.

"You don't date," she said.

"Now I do," he explained.

"How?" she puzzled.

"The internet. The nurses showed me."

"Why?"

"In twenty-seven years," he said, matter-of-factly, "a man gets lonely."

Mike supposed that this must be true, though she had a hard time imagining her father knowing the first thing about dating and all its accompanying intimacies.

"Her name is Deja. She's a schoolteacher. Retired. Di-vorced. Two daughters. We've been seeing each other seven months. I was planning to tell you as soon as I knew it was serious. But it's a busy time of year."

"Deja? Like *'déjà vu'*?"

"There's no *'vu.'* Her parents were strange, but she's . . . she's special, Mike. She's moving into the apartment. And I feel confident that she'll be glad to have you with us. As I said, she's got two daughters. They're grown, so they've got places of their own."

Mike sat in stunned silence, not because she was dis-turbed particularly, but because it seemed as though all the rules that governed her world were suddenly invalid, and she needed to learn the new ones before she spoke. Her father had a girlfriend and they were moving in together. And her name meant "already" in French.

"So what do you say?" Gerry asked.

Mike blinked repeatedly and tried to make words fit together in her brain.

"Mike? You want your old room back?"

CAN YOU HEAR ME NOW?

Sitting before her father and saying with total conviction that absolutely, positively, under no circumstances was she going to move back home was about the first thing Mike Edwards had felt good about in half a year. Which made it even more shocking when she realized fifteen minutes later that she was once again completely and utterly stuck.

For the better part of the afternoon, Mike roamed the streets of Manhattan aimlessly, getting drenched and being gawked at by tourists and natives alike. She stopped at a corner deli to buy a Dr Pepper, inspiring the fourteen-year-old counter boy to sprout his first determined chest hair. Blithely unaware of the way that her soaking button-down shirt clung to her hips, Mike ignored the cab driver who ran up on the Park Avenue partition as she passed.

Gunther sent a text message around three-thirty asking, "How'd he take it?" Mike declined to answer. There were moments, and she didn't dwell long enough to consider them much, when he was too present. Sometimes a rhino needs her space.

By late afternoon, tired of walking and unable to think any longer, she found herself sitting with her head in her hands on the steps of the New York City Public Library. Determined graduate students trudged by shielding laptops and reference books under plastic ponchos. A Caribbean woman pushing a plastic-sheathed blond baby in a stroller hurried past her and then stopped, turning back with pursed lips. The woman pulled a dollar from her pocketbook, bent down, and pushed the dollar into Mike's hand before she could protest.

"Get to a sheltah, girl." The woman looked down at her pityingly. "Face like dat, you gonna get youself hurt on de street."

Mike just gaped at the woman, who pushed on with her charge, making a clucking noise that said, "Shame, crazy white girl."

Holding the dollar in her open palm, Mike watched George Washington's face bloat and twist under the pouring rain. Realizing she actually needed every dollar she could get her hands on, she quickly shoved it into the pocket of her leather jacket.

So this was what it was coming to, she thought. The creative ace who'd brought the world "Cyan Vodka: Worry about it tomorrow," was now being mistaken for a homeless runaway. She wondered for a second if she could actually sell this homeless thing, and just how much she might pull down in a year. Then she thought about actual homeless people, and realized probably not that much.

When she emerged from this reverie, the rain was letting up, and perhaps just to prove to anyone watching that she was a person with a cell phone, Mike checked her messages.

"I presume that you've dropped your phone into a puddle and are unable to retrieve my number because I can't think of another reason why I've not heard from you in nearly three weeks."

Bentley. Every time they spoke, things were a little more strained, a little less natural. Eventually he had had to tell his wife in Westchester that he'd lost his job, and now he no longer had a decent excuse to spend many nights in the Manhattan apartment. Lately, Mike had taken to ignoring his calls altogether and his messages had grown increasingly affected.

"Making progress, you'll be pleased to hear. Believe I'll have something very soon and of course you know there's a place for you wherever I land. Course you know that. Well, then. Ursula's on holiday for the week so I thought I'd pop down and enjoy the flat a few days. Drop by if you like. Right, then. Ciao."

He owed her. He owed her big. If she'd had any idea just how far down he might drag her she'd have rearranged her loyalties a long time ago. But the part of her that wanted to tell him what she thought always crawled back under the covers at the thought that he might someday save her. She couldn't afford to burn the bridge. She was too close to sleeping under it.

The call waiting beeped as she was about to delete Bentley's message.

"Get this one." Gunther's voice was unexpectedly comforting. "Aussie bloke in Texas claims he's captured the world's largest nutria rat, weighing in at a whopping thirty-five pounds! My editors are wetting themselves."

Mike couldn't help smiling. "What's that in kilos? You could be sitting on a Pulitzer."

"Tell me about it. It's just nice to know I'm making such

a bloody important contribution to the world of journalism. I'm changing lives, truly. You didn't answer my text."

"He wants me to move home."

"You're joking."

"Nope. He said it's that or nothing."

"Jesus, Mikey, what are you gonna do?"

She snorted. "Throw myself off a bridge?"

"Look," he said, "why don't you just bunk with me? You can stay as long as you need to."

"I can't do that, Gunther."

"You *can* do it, Mikey, that's what I'm telling you. It's not as if I pay for the place. The company pays my rent, why not yours?"

He waited.

"You live in Brooklyn," she said.

"And so could you."

She imagined for a moment what it would be like to fall asleep every evening to the sound of Gunther snoring, to wake up to the smell of his coffee in the morning. She needed to get off the phone.

"Hey, it looks like the sky's about to open up again. I'm gonna head indoors. Thanks for the offer, but...I'll just figure something out."

There was a pause on the other end of the line.

Then, "Right. Okay. I've gotta follow up on this giant rat and see if I can't come up with some actual news before the day is out. Can we make it a late one tonight? The Drunk at nine-thirty?"

"See you then," she said, and snapped the phone shut. She felt guilty for the way that she needed to get away from him. The rain showed no sign of letting up, but it was warmish, so Mike got up and began to walk. She headed north for a while, then west. There was nothing and no place she needed to get to, and a handful of thoughts she needed to leave behind.

She wandered up Broadway, keeping her eyes on the traffic and the frenetic lights of the billboards and office towers to keep from seeing her reflection in storefront windows as she passed. But for reasons that escaped her, reasons that some of us might refer to as fate or destiny, Mike looked up as she neared the orange and green harlequin pattern of the sign on Caroline's comedy club. Staring out of a black and white photo on the side of the building was Jay Statdler's toothy, smiling face, right above the words "TONIGHT" and "TICKETS AVAILABLE."

Angelenos may be familiar with the street where Ashton and Demi live or the coffee shop where Lindsay Lohan sucks down soy lattes, but New Yorkers are more likely to map the city according to their past relationships. You avoid 44th Street west of Broadway because your ex owns a one-bedroom above that Italian place. You walk ten extra blocks to take kickboxing because your old flame does free weights at the Crunch on Lafayette. You skip the Museum of Natural History because you split up in the shadow of the Rose Center after viewing the Darwin exhibit. You amputate whole neighborhoods as you move through relationships, because how else are you supposed to maintain your sanity? How else are you supposed to achieve the minimum distance required to get over somebody, to forget that they humiliated you and broke your heart and made you believe you weren't fit to love or be loved by anyone? This is another good reason not to get involved with anyone in the entertainment industry. You can't triangulate their locations and they're more likely to pop up where you least expect them.

Ever since she had seen his Conan segment on the night

Mike had come to think of as the lowest of her life, she had known Jay was going to appear again. Like some angry sprite's curse, his flimsy jokes had been haunting her since she'd heard them. Partly it was the simple and understandable shock of showing up as fodder for his weird, self-loathing shtick. She remembered well Jay's reluctance to include intimate material from his life in his act; he'd almost bitten her head off for suggesting once that he make something of his neurotic mother's hypochondria.

"I don't mock the people I love," he'd told her in no uncertain terms. Apparently there was a whole different set of rules for the pitiful creatures who had once been loved and were now reviled. How nice to have such an unambiguous marker of his sentiments.

She never needed to hear it again, any of it. Especially that tampon crack, which was frankly beneath even Jay. But her aggressive attempts to forget had been counterproductive. Every empty afternoon that passed more fully demonstrated the deterioration of Mike's capacity to control her life, to the point where she had begun to take pleasure in the little tiny moments she could dictate. But you could spend only so much time choosing between the myriad available flavors of Diet Coke, and when you finally sat down to drink it you were liable to start replaying things in your head, like "I don't want to say she made me feel small, but by the time we broke up I was walking under doors."

She stood outside Caroline's and peered at Jay's black and white smile as if it might speak to her. It didn't. Suddenly, she was struck with an inadvisable urge, and before she knew what she was doing, Mike was yanking her wallet from the back pocket of her jeans and pulling open the door to the box office.

She slid into a corner, near the back wall, sinking low in a plush banquette and trying desperately to be invisible. Her very cells were screaming at the sheer stupidity, at the wrongness of being there. Over and over again she wondered what the hell she would do if he saw her. Would he call her out in front of the audience? Would he ask them all to give her a hand for providing him with such a rich subject for character assassination? Would he start to shake at the knowledge that she was physically stronger than he and could easily have knocked the shit-eating grin off his face? Or would he just look at her the way he had the night he'd left? Like a wounded animal that would get up and maul you if only it could.

She had to wait through five other comics, most of whom had no right to be torturing the public with their personal exorcisms of dysfunctional families and psychological ticks. One woman detailed her department store panic attacks and another poked fun at her boyfriend's fear of sex toys. Mike pondered queasily the forced intimacy of the whole exercise. Especially the popular school of "I'll be crucified for making fun of anyone else, so I guess I'll just dissect myself and you can all laugh and like me better for it." No wonder Jay was doing well.

Sometime during the fourth comic's set, the guy at the next table had leaned over and said something Mike didn't hear. She ignored him.

"Hey. You. I'm offering to buy you a drink," he repeated.

She turned her head slowly and stared at him, hoping whatever was on her face would scare him into evaporating.

"Jesus," he said, pulling back, "okay. Try 'no thank you' next time."

Wait five minutes, let me recite my CV, she wanted to tell him, and see if you still want to buy me that drink.

She had more than fulfilled her two-drink minimum by the time Jay took the stage. Only then did she feel the force of being in the same room with him for the first time in more than three years. When the host introduced him, Mike exhaled, so deeply that she had to remind her lungs to reinflate again. She wondered what would happen if they didn't, wondered if she'd just quietly expire against the banquette and whether Jay would go on to do his set, unwitting, in front of her corpse. There had to be some poetry in that. Retaliation for all the times she'd had to sit loyally by while he died on stage.

"Thanks for coming out tonight, you guys," he said. "Everybody drinking? Everybody happy? I know you've been sitting there a while. You've probably been lowering your expectations as time goes by. Well, you just wait, 'cause they're about to get a lot lower."

The crowd was lubricated enough to give him a tentative chuckle.

"I'm actually really glad I'm here because I was almost late tonight. I got caught up working on this comic book I'm writing that's based on my relationship with my ex-girlfriend. It's called *The Adventures of Ladyman*."

They threw him a bone and tittered reluctantly.

"Yeah, it's about this guy, Ladyman, who wakes up one morning to realize that he has sacrificed his entire manhood to this incredibly gorgeous, incredibly chilly woman. She's called Manlady. Don't worry, it's not her real name."

Mike couldn't believe that this shit had gotten him on television. But people were laughing. She looked around and they were completely with him. Completely with him and completely against "Manlady" which was maybe the most inane joke of all time. It was more of the same. More of what she'd seen on Conan, just longer. Pretty soon he was launching into the same "custody of my balls" bit and she could begin to stare at him without listening so hard. There were some new jokes about crying and mood swings and how she wouldn't have sex with him while there was a game on, but mostly it was all the same chaff.

"The thing is, she was *so* hot. I mean like, gold-medal, top-notch, you-couldn't-afford-it-if-it-was-for-sale hot. Luckily, my dignity has no credit limit."

Fuck him, Mike thought. Just fuck him.

"The weirdest part of all this," he riffed, "is that now that I'm with someone else, someone who actually believes that I have a penis, it's like I have to learn all this stuff over again, you know?"

She wasn't surprised. Jay had never known how to be alone, how to take care of himself. He was just the sort of walking wound that most women would be pleased to throw themselves over like a giant Band-Aid.

"Like when we first met, she told me her name was Nancy and I told her we couldn't go out. And she was like, why not, you know? And I told her it would just be too confusing because I was pretty sure that was my name."

More silly, meaningless laughter from a group of people who wouldn't know clever if it kicked them in the nuts, Mike thought. She did clever for a living. She had won awards for clever. She recalled the way Jay's comedy friends would try to talk advertising with her over a beer.

"I've always thought I could write that shit," they'd say.

"I'm sure you think so," Mike would reply, and inevitably Jay would come down on her for it when they got home. They were a bunch of whiners, as far as she was concerned. And Jay was their king.

"You guys have been terrific"—he waved at the audience—"and you've made me feel very masculine, so thank you." He replaced the mic, and as he turned to head into the wings, he winked at a table down by the front of the stage.

He winked.

It was quick and subtle. Mike knew she was probably one of only two people in the whole room who caught it, because that was the girlfriend wink. The wink he used to wink at her.

She followed the wink, craned her neck toward the table in the front where she could just make out a pert Indian woman in a red sweater with short pixie hair. She was grinning and clapping with her hands right in front of her face. The raised clap. The girlfriend clap.

She looked like someone who might carry a dog as an accessory.

Mike stared at this petite, beguiling creature who was giving Jay the girlfriend clap and who had certainly just guffawed the obligatory girlfriend guffaw through fifteen minutes of material on her predecessor. For the briefest instant she considered moving in for a closer look.

Then she remembered what it was like after the show. How he would trot out to join her in the audience for a drink as soon as the next comic took the stage. They were smaller, filthier venues then. Lousy bars, usually, where they would drink free for the rest of the night if the bartender knew Jay or liked his set, or felt guilty for hitting on his girlfriend while he was backstage. And Jay would sit and obsess for half an hour over whether he'd done okay and ask over and over what she thought of his jokes until she couldn't take it anymore and then she'd jokingly tell him to "man up."

She shouldn't have come. She should have walked by and just waited for time to convince her all over again that he no longer existed. It's no use hearing after the fact that you did everything wrong, that you broke a heart and beset a psyche. Chances are you already knew.

IT'S EVERYWHERE
YOU WANT TO BE

On the rare occasions during Mike's childhood when her father took her on extended car trips, he amused her by playing "If you were a _____." It was one of the ways he kept tabs on her as she grew and changed. At seven, if Mike were a fruit, she would have been a plum. By nine, she was a grapefruit. At fourteen, she refused to play and he told her she was a lemon.

At thirty-one, suddenly confronted with the question of where she might lay her head in a month's time, if Mike were an '80s hair band, she would have been "Bad Decision."

She couldn't picture moving in with her father and his new paramour. Couldn't face burdening Gunther, who would be only too happy to take her in. But there was one apartment she knew of that might just be available at a price she could afford. It was vacant, after all. Or nearly. And its occupant owed her big.

After several days had passed, she returned Brian's call.

She made an appointment to meet him at the apartment the following evening. Secretly, Mike had begun to ride rush hour subways whenever she could. For those few minutes a day, she blended with the harried commuters and tried to pretend that she was one of them again. One of the exhausted many being pressed uncomfortably against knees and shoulders, craning her neck to avoid chewing on the fur trim of a gargantuan parka, throwing an elbow against a rudely hoisted backpack. She had learned to look forward to the opportunity to dig her fingers into the spines of hoody kids inconsiderate enough to lean against the pole. She relished the shoving and loud "excuse me's" that accompanied the opening and closing of the doors. The shiny-shoed bankers and lawyers who ogled her didn't know that she hadn't worked in months. Weary secretaries and university professors and sanitation engineers admired her radiant skin and had no idea that her days were wasted. She could successfully pose as her old self, the illusion shattered only when the doors closed at 33rd and Park and Mike remained on the train. She didn't have a reason to trot off to Madison Avenue anymore. But nobody needed to know that.

She rode the D train up to Columbus Circle now and dug her hands into the pockets of her jacket as she strolled the few blocks to Brian's building. She gave her name at the concierge desk and was asked to repeat it.

"Mike," she said again, "like Ditka."

She tried not to dwell on whether the doorman remembered her. She rode the elevator up to the fourteenth floor and found the door to 14G ajar.

"Come on in," she heard Brian call. The sound of ice clinking against glass echoed into the hallway. She slipped inside and pushed the door shut behind her.

"What are you drinking?" he called from around the corner.

"Fine thanks, how are you?" she called back.

"Martini alright?" Stripped of his title he was more of a caricature than ever before.

"Whatever." She tossed her jacket over a chair in the foyer.

He had rented the apartment furnished. It had all the character of a spotless executive washroom. The carpets were gray, the tile in the kitchen and bathroom white. A single magnet hung on the stainless refrigerator, listing the phone numbers of the in-building health club, housekeeping service, and concierge desk. Brian could have his dry cleaning picked up and delivered to his door. His fridge and pantry could be stocked in his absence. He could probably have ordered out-call massage and flowers for his wife with a single call down to the front desk.

The living room furniture was sleek dark wood, the sofas leather. Mike followed the sound of the cocktail shaker and found Brian by the built-in wet bar. It had been nearly a month since she'd seen him, and he looked smaller against the backdrop of the skyline than she remembered.

"Shaken, not stirred," he said, pouring the martinis into glasses without turning to greet her. "Have a seat."

She sank into the corner of a leather sofa and hooked the heel of one boot on the corner of the Asian-inspired coffee table. He looked at it as he placed her martini on a coaster but said nothing. It wasn't really his furniture anyway.

"I was glad to hear from you," he said, sitting in a chair opposite her. "Cheers." He raised his glass and Mike inelegantly lifted hers, sloshing gin over the side and onto the carpet.

"Don't worry," he said, leaning back. "Girl comes in tomorrow anyway."

Mike registered with some distaste the way he said "girl" with no article.

"At least it's clear," Mike said, uneasily watching the drops soaking into the carpet but failing to disappear.

"How have you been keeping busy?" he asked.

"You know, this and that," she lied.

"Mm," he said.

"I submitted to White and Oglethorpe this week."

He made a clicking sound with his tongue. "Too big, both of them, you'd get lost."

"Have you talked to anyone? At either?" she asked.

"It would all be a step down," he said. "We have an opportunity here to break new ground. Now that my travel schedule has quieted, I should be able to get down to business."

They sat in silence. She didn't believe him, didn't believe *in* him anymore, and they both knew it. It was just a question of who found it more painful. Mike missed the old Brian, the one she'd been happy to buy into back when it served her. The one who never really existed.

"I was surprised you wanted to come all the way up here," he said. His eyes traveled over her body and she resisted the urge to squirm in her seat.

"Well, like you said, a visit to the big city is becoming quite an event for you."

"Ursula doesn't seem to think I have much reason to be here anymore."

"Is she wrong?"

He sipped his martini and stared her down as she'd seen him do with unruly clients. It was what he did when he couldn't formulate a comeback.

"I've missed your face," he said, and made her wince.

"I miss work," she said.

She hadn't anticipated being so uncomfortable visiting the apartment. But then there were ghosts here that she mostly chose to ignore. The nights when she would accompany him up for a drink after long work sessions. More than once she'd been introduced to some lithe, willing model type who was coming as Mike was going. "This is my friend Sascha," he would tell her, laying a possessive hand on an available flank as they all stood awkwardly in the foyer. She could remember meeting at least three or four of them. Naomis and Thereses and Gretas, a parade of young things he would pick up in bars, at cocktail parties. There was a certain kind of stunning girl in Manhattan who wouldn't ask too many questions, who understood what was being asked of her and didn't seem to mind. Mike wondered what they got out of it, whether he bought them presents or dinners. Maybe it was just cocktails and compliments and that was enough.

For her, being with him had been revenge. Brian had to have known it and certainly didn't care. He had never made a move, never laid a finger on her in all those long nights of working too late and drinking more than was advisable. He had just let her know, in a million tiny ways, that he would always be there if ever she were interested. That he wondered about it, thought about it, envisioned sleeping with her. He was just too cautious to risk rejection or a sexual harassment complaint. He wanted her to want it. And in the end, when she'd arrived at his door ready to give him exactly what he'd hoped for all along, he hadn't cared that she was thinking of someone else. He'd been happy to be the parting shot she fired as Jay walked out the door. Brian wasn't much for questions either.

Sitting in his living room now, back for the first time since she'd committed that cardinal sin, she couldn't imagine asking the question she'd come to ask. Did she expect herself to sleep in that bed every night? To wake up in the morning staring at the same view she'd taken in as she'd lain in bed realizing that she'd done something she couldn't take back? Had she really planned to walk barefoot on this carpet and to drink coffee from the mugs that Brian used to offer her water in in the morning? This wasn't a place that anyone lived.

"I had hoped to have you up to Scarsdale," he said now, jarring Mike back to the present.

"To meet your wife?"

"Ursula's been traveling." He smiled a James Bond–villain sort of smile. "Aren't we both a bit old to play that game?"

"You certainly are."

He ignored her. He leaned forward and carefully set his glass on the table. He stood and she knew he intended to join her on the sofa, but she sprang up before he could get close. All of a sudden she had to go. She had to be out of this place and away from the ghosts. She kicked herself for ever thinking she could ask to stay here.

"I have to go."

"You've hardly touched your drink."

"It's a little strong for me," she said.

"For you who drink right out of the bottle." He chuckled as he said it. "I thought we could chat some more."

"We chatted," she said. "I'm having meetings. You're having meetings. Nothing new."

"I'll behave myself, I promise," he assured her and she knew he was torn between disappointment and amusement at seeing her lose her composure. She ignored him and headed for the door.

She shrugged quickly into her jacket and as she reached the door he said, "Stop by anytime then."

"Thanks." She didn't slow down though she could feel his irritation swelling in the air.

"Keep your feet off the table next time. It's not a bloody stable," he said, as she pushed the elevator call button.

"Call me when you hear anything," she said. She smiled nervously to herself as the doors closed between them.

She was late to meet Gunther. He was waiting for her at the Drunk, nursing a Guinness and vigilantly guarding Mike's whiskey, poured in advance. He looked her up and down without saying a word and she realized he could see her jangled nerves.

"I won't ask," he finally said.

"Strange couple of days," she said.

"What exactly did you spend this strange couple of days doing?"

"You said you wouldn't ask." She was buying time while answers formed in her head five different ways. She still hadn't told him she'd seen Jay; he was the one subject they simply did not discuss. There had been a life in which they'd shared him, but it was long over and best forgotten. And she didn't want to ruin a much needed escape from reality by darkening Gunther's mood with talk of Bentley.

"I don't know," she said. "I walked. I looked for apartments."

"Okay," he answered, because although he always knew when she was hiding something, you couldn't push Mike any further than she'd go.

"How 'bout you?" she asked.

"The nutria rat turned out to be wild boar."

"No."

"D'you know there was a moment when I was actually disappointed? This job may genuinely be ruining me."

She popped him gently on the knee with her fist. "What can I tell you? Sometimes the dingoes eat your nutria rat."

He cleared his throat. "Listen, about this housing issue—"

"I'll work it out."

He paused so she would know he wasn't pushing.

"I know you will. But why rush? You can stay as long as you like. It's not as if I haven't got room."

"I'm taking my father up on his offer." Until she heard the words she hadn't even known she intended to say them. But she knew somewhere that being at home was safer than any of the alternatives.

He answered carefully, listening to make sure he didn't sound disappointed. "Fair enough," he said.

To Mike, he seemed relieved. She reddened slightly at the idea that Gunther thought he had to take care of her, to manage her.

"But I need you to do something for me," she said, banishing the idea almost as soon as it had come.

"Name your poison." He smiled, signaling to Jimmy. "I'm buying."

"This'll cost you more than a couple of bucks," she said. "I need you to come with me when I meet my father's new girlfriend."

IT KEEPS GOING,
AND GOING, AND GOING

Moving house, as Bentley would blithely have referred to it, is a punishing task in New York City. There are the narrow streets to contend with, making any attempt at large-vehicle parking nearly impossible. There's the general every-man-for-himself attitude which necessitates constant vigilance; you can't leave a two-hundred-pound sleep sofa unattended for a moment or it's likely to walk away. And then there's the general sense of real estate desperation, making it so difficult to abandon hard-won booty, even if the booty has hissing radiators and vermin.

Just when you're certain that you'll never be done, that there will always be one more box to haul down three hundred steps, that you'll never erase all traces of that hole you accidentally punched in the wall during that mad episode with the pogo stick (and don't even think about reclaiming your security deposit after that), it's over. You close the door one last time, hear the lock clicking behind you, and close the book on years of your life. Better not to imagine knocking on the door in a decade and asking to look around for old times' sake; if your building is still standing and hasn't been turned into an NYU dormitory, the new tenants will be more likely to break out the Taser than invite you in.

The night before she said goodbye to Apartment 27D, Mike sat with her back against a packing crate and thought that only a Buddhist could be delighted to discover that the sum total of her worldly possessions could be packed into fourteen boxes and stowed in a cargo van. The apartment had always felt crowded and untamed, but she now supposed she'd just been spreading out the clutter.

She took in the feeling of her bare feet against the uneven floorboards and ran a finger over the popped nail by her bedroom door that had shredded so many socks. The sound of a spoon ricocheting off the side of a ceramic mug carried through the paper-thin walls, which meant that Mrs. Arnulfson next door was taking her evening fiber therapy. Soon the coughing would begin. Wet, hacking sputters would echo through 27D as if Mrs. Arnulfson were bringing up a hairball in Mike's bathroom. It happened every night.

It happened the night she and Jay moved in. Both fleeing sub-par sublets, they'd set up a home with little more than two butterfly chairs and a futon mattress. Jay said that it was all very Eastern and minimalist. Sitting on the futon in the living room that first night, eating McDonald's out of paper bags and sharing a six-pack of Brooklyn Lager, their first exposure to Mrs. Arnulfson's post-prandial phlegm expulsion had sparked a fit of laughter so uncontrollable that Jay had spit a Chicken McNugget across the room and under the radiator. Mrs. Arnulfson and said McNugget, hastily abandoned, would alternately be blamed for the mice that moved in soon afterward, prompting the revelation that Jay would scream like a little girl at the sight of a rodent.

In those early days, the hysterical laughing always led to sex. It was the sex that held them together for so long, maybe because it lasted longer than the laughing. The sex lasted until the day she'd asked him, during an argument, "how someone so fucking insecure could be so great in bed?" That was pretty much it. He was gone a week later.

Mike would really have preferred to stick to the older memories, but as Mrs. Arnulfson ceased to expectorate, a quiet descended over her paltry belongings.

"You have a good night?" She heard Jay ask as if it were yesterday. He had been sitting in their darkened living room, facing away from her as she came in the front door. There had been too many nights like this toward the end.

"Hey," she said. "Turn a light on or something." She could see his silhouette against the city lights coming through the windows. He didn't move. "What are you doing?" she asked.

"I asked if you had a good night," he said.

"Well, it's eleven-thirty and I'm just getting home from work, so what do you think?" Since she'd started working with Bentley he'd been like this. Sensitive about the long hours, picking at her when she walked in the door. Mike dropped her bag in the hallway and walked past Jay to get a beer from the fridge. She flicked the fluorescents on in the tiny galley kitchen, twisted the top off the bottle and turned to face him, leaning against the doorframe.

Jay squinted in the light and turned his head away.

"What are you doing?"

"What do you mean?" he asked. There was a passive tone he used when he wanted her to get angry first.

"I mean I know I get paid in nickels, but we don't exactly have to worry about the electricity bill." She took a swig from her beer.

"Did you eat?" he asked her, but it was an accusation.

"Yeah," she said.

"He buy you dinner again?"

She sighed. "He doesn't buy me dinner, the firm buys us both dinner." She was tired of saying it, tired of telling him there was nothing going on. "And by the way it also bought dinner for an art director and two other copywriters, so you can stop making things up in your head."

There was a silence. Mike sipped at her beer.

"Great. It was great. Thanks for asking." Jay finally spoke.

Mike took a minute to retrieve from her crowded, tired brain what it was she was supposed to be asking about.

"Oh, crap," she said quietly.

"Yeah, good crowd. Tried out the new stuff. Went really well. Thanks for coming. Oh, wait ..."

"Crap," she said again.

"You didn't."

She had promised, she now recalled, to be at Gotham Comedy Club at nine. She'd remembered that promise at seven-thirty, sitting on a conference room table, throwing a squash ball against a wall and talking about margarine copy points. And at eight forty-five, looking at a Chinese takeout menu she had thought she should send a text message to tell Jay she wouldn't make it. But the margarine had begun to speak to her.

"I'm sorry," she said.

He just nodded.

"Shit," she muttered. "We had to revamp this stupid spot and—"

"You pretty much know I don't want to hear it, right?"

"I'm sorry, baby," she tried.

"I would love it if just once Brian got the 'sorry, baby' and I got you, showing up when you said you would."

She squeezed the bottle and tried not to get angry.

"Say something," he ordered.

She stared at him.

"If something is going on with him—"

"Jesus, Jay! You do these fucking shows all the time! Who the hell cares if I miss one? Are you doing it for me or for you?"

"Miss one?!" he exploded. "When was the last time you came to see *anything* I was doing, Mike? Huh? Do you even remember?"

"I'm going to bed," she said and she threw her beer bottle into the recycling bin so it landed with a clamor against the others.

"Are you fucking him?" he asked.

Which wasn't fair, because she wasn't. And then she'd said what she'd said and they stopped sleeping in the same bed. One week later, he'd left.

Mike dug the heel of her hand into the popped nail to shut off the memory. She looked at her watch. She should sleep. Gunther would be there at ten AM to walk with her to a parking lot in West Chelsea where they'd pick up the rental van.

Gunther was always there.

He had found her at the Drunk the evening after Jay had left. She'd skipped the bar in favor of a corner table in the back behind the pool table and the dart board. Her foot kept sticking to a spot on the floor and she'd just stared at the crusty linoleum and left it there.

He'd taken the chair opposite her. And he'd said nothing,

just sat there and let her feel his presence so she would know she wasn't alone.

"I slept with my boss last night," she said.

"Okay," he said. Just that.

"Why get punished for it if I wasn't doing it?"

He said nothing.

"Does Jay know you're here?" she asked.

"Not exactly," he said.

"You should go," she told him.

He stayed.

"I wasn't cheating on him." When another woman would have cried, Mike refused.

"I know, Mikey."

"Okay," she said. "As long as you know."

Next door, Mrs. Arnulfson began to sing to her cat.

WE'LL LEAVE A LIGHT ON
FOR YOU

Her life was on rewind. Moving her meager belongings from the old apartment to the new old apartment had taken Mike and Gunther a surprisingly long time. In fairness, there had been a three-hour pizza break in between carting Mike's furniture down to the curb and returning the rental van. When they finished, a shocking eleven hours after they'd begun, they stood in the lavish foyer and stared down the hallway into the darkened rooms where Mike had gone from princess to tomboy to whatever the hell she could be called now.

"How did I get here?" she said out loud.

"Don't whinge, I've got rats," Gunther said.

"I live with my father. I'm thirty-one and I live with my father."

"I live with rats."

"Are the rats learning to date again? Are they rediscovering their little rodent libidos around the same time they're receiving their AARP cards?"

"I don't know," Gunther mused. "We don't talk the way we used to."

"Don't leave me here," she said. "Take me to a shelter."

"It's a deal. You'll be very popular."

"Come on." She moved toward the kitchen. "He's usually got cookies."

They sat on high stools by the kitchen island, dunking Oreos into tall glasses of skim milk.

"Where is the good doctor this evening?" Gunther asked.

"On call. Or on Deja. Hard to say..."

Gunther squinted at a note on the refrigerator. "Mike, at the hospital. Portobello fajitas inside. Heat in the oven twenty-five minutes at 350. Welcome."

"He left me takeout. How thoughtful." She brushed crumbs onto her jeans.

"It is, actually."

Mike was already wandering down the hallway. Gunther followed. He took in the many paintings purchased at hospital auctions and the black-and-white photographs of faraway places.

"Hey, where are all the humiliating snaps of you with braces and bad clothes?" he called to her.

"Holy crap, this is new!" she shouted from the den and ignored his question.

Gunther caught up to find her staring at a forty-five-inch plasma screen. "Game night," she breathed, her eyes bright.

"The rats don't even get premium channels," he said.

Within minutes they were glued to the Discovery HD channel, and a series of undersea adventure programs about large-scale predators like sharks and killer whales. Gunther looked over to see just a hint of a smile creeping across Mike's face as a giant orca escaped human capture and swam on to shred a colony of smaller marine mammals.

"You're a sicko," he said.

"Am not!" she protested. "It's just a really great picture."

Gunther laughed.

"Go eat a rat," she said.

They sat quietly in the blue-green glow until he fell asleep watching a barracuda gliding through crystal waters off the Caymans. Careful not to wake him, Mike shut the TV off.

She padded down the long hallway, past the living room where Caroline smiled broadly from the mantel, even if her daughter never stopped to look. Mike flicked the light on in her bedroom. Nothing had changed. The walls were still lined with field hockey and lacrosse trophies. A poster of the 1986 Giants hung above her bed. It was like a shrine to some awkward teenaged girl Mike could barely remember. She untacked the poster carefully, then rolled it up and tossed it in the closet. She paused to listen for the sound of a coughing neighbor, for signs of anyone else rattling around the building, but remembered that the more expensive construction here included some measure of soundproofing.

Mike tugged a fleece Michigan University blanket down from the top shelf of her closet and took it back to the den. She unfolded it over Gunther, realized that it only covered him from knees to chest, then gave up and returned to her room.

She tried not to look in the mirror while she brushed her teeth, and was grateful to find she was exhausted as she fell into the twin bed. She had to lie on her side with her knees pulled up to her chin to fit right. This wasn't her bed anymore. Her bed was lying on a street corner waiting for the garbage truck to haul it away. She didn't have a bed anymore. Within minutes, Mike was asleep.

She awoke late the next morning to the sound of Mel Tormé, crooning "You and the Night and the Music." She could smell bacon mixing with something sweet, and was sure she heard male laughter coming from the kitchen. Gunther and her father were both morning people, which was wildly unfair.

She stumbled slowly, her knee stiff from sleeping with her long left leg dangling nearly to the floor. Her ankles cracked and her shoulders ached from carrying boxes and clinging to the tiny mattress. It had been years since she'd spent a night here.

She pulled the plaid flannel robe from behind her bedroom door and threw it over her T-shirt and boxers. She made some attempt to shove her long hair into a ponytail, but gave up and left it bunched in a tangled topiary somewhere near the back of her head.

The first thing she heard when she opened the bedroom door was a woman saying, "It's turkey bacon. We compromised."

Deja. Fucking Deja. Why, Mike thought, couldn't her father have waited a single day to stage this little episode of *The Brady Bunch*?

It was too much, too soon. Mike wasn't ready for this. She took one giant step backward toward her bedroom door. She would just go back inside and lie down until Deja had gone.

The parquet beneath her feet groaned its disapproval.

"Mike?" her father called from the kitchen. "I think she's up," Mike heard him say.

"Ass floor," she muttered.

Her father popped his head out from the kitchen. "There she is! Hurry up, brunch is almost ready."

"Who's making brunch?" Mike feigned surprise.

"I am!" her father called, retreating into the kitchen. "Who else?"

"Marie Callendar? The Hungry Man? You don't cook..." Mike muttered to herself as she dragged her feet along the hall. She had grown up thinking Eggo waffles were labor intensive.

She arrested when she reached the kitchen doorway. Sunlight streamed through the windows over the sink. Gunther sat hunched over the table, cradling a mug of coffee. Mike's father smiled at her from across the room, wearing a surgical smock that bore evidence of vegetable detritus. And next to him, holding a tray of cinnamon rolls between giant oven mitts, was Deja.

She was a good deal shorter than Mike, and had shoulder-length gray hair with a few traces of brown left. Her eyes were bright, and she wore an apron with a giant baby seal face staring out from her midsection.

Mike stared at the huge glassy seal eyes.

"Oh, my gosh, it's silly, isn't it?" Deja smiled. "We won it at a benefit for the World Wildlife Federation."

Mike stared like an idiot.

Deja hastily dropped the cinammon rolls and the oven mitts on the counter and extended a hand to Mike.

"I'm Deja," she said.

"Mike," said Mike.

"Zucchini frittata!" Mike's father proclaimed, pulling a cast-iron skillet from the oven.

Mike shot Gunther a desperate glance that said, "I'm still asleep and not nearly equipped to deal with this alien scene of domestic bliss which bears no resemblance to the household in which I was raised."

Gunther shrugged and smiled.

"Coffee?" Deja asked, already pouring a cup for Mike. "How do you take it?"

"Sugar. A lot of sugar," Mike murmured.

"I'm learning to cook, Gunther," Mike's father announced. Gerry had always shown a boundless enthusiasm for Gunther's company, as if Gunther were the enormous Australian son he'd always wanted. "I'm no expert, but hopefully it won't make you *chunder*!" Gerry laughed heartily, his ongoing need to prove his command of the Aussie vernacular momentarily satisfied.

"Very good, Dr. E!" Gunther humored Mike's father with his usual grace and gusto.

"Sit, Mike!" her father barked. "You look like a stone statue."

Mike sat and allowed him to serve her a slab of frittata.

"Alright." Deja announced the arrival of the cinnamon rolls at the table. She took a seat between Gunther and Mike's father. "They're Pillsbury," she said, "but I think they're better than the bakery kind."

Mike agreed, which irked her. One point for Deja.

"Gunther, go!" Mike's father leaned forward and stared, encouraging Gunther to take the first bite of frittata. "Enh?" he said.

"Excellent, Dr. E," Gunther assured him.

"You sure? Because I've got a jar of Vegemite if you'd rather!" He chuckled at himself once again.

Mike wanted to throw up in her mouth and prayed that her father would let the Men at Work references lie for the rest of the meal. She reached for a cinnamon roll and began to unravel the gooey spiral.

"So, Gunther," Deja asked, "Gerry tells me you're a journalist?"

"Masquerading as one," Gunther affirmed. "I used to be a journalist. Now I mostly report on American celebrities. Or if, say, an Australian does something notable in the U.S., like falling into a well or winning the lotto, then I report on that."

"You don't sound enthusiastic." Deja smiled. "Not exactly what you pictured yourself doing?"

"Not exactly," he agreed.

Very sharp, Mike thought. Most people immediately assumed that Gunther's job was glamorous and exciting, when she knew very well that he was hideously dissatisfied and demoralized. There was no news anymore. There was spin and commentary and entertainment, but there was no news.

"I heard an incredible story," Deja said, "about this journalist in London, I think it was, who spent six weeks with the people of this tiny Irish fishing village who were being pushed out of their homes by a huge pharmaceutical company that wanted to build a plant. So this guy spends all this time with these people and he writes this incredible exposé, and the day his story is supposed to run, he picks up his paper and he can't find it anywhere. And he's furious, obviously, so he calls his editor and he says, you know, what happened? And his editor tells him he's sorry but there was a woman in York who had trained her dog to howl 'God Save the Queen,' so they bumped him."

"I know that guy!" Gunther lit up. "And that's typical! People aren't interested in reading what you and I would call quality journalism anymore. They just want fluff, you know, crap pieces about Britney Spears losing baby weight. It's a fucking nightmare."

"I agree, absolutely," Deja said.

Well, there goes Gunther, Mike thought. Very shrewd on Deja's part.

"How'd you sleep?" Mike's father asked her.

"Not great," she said. "Bed's a little small."

"Yeah, I guess we've had that thing for a million years. Although I can't say I'm dying to go out and buy a mattress if you're only gonna be here a few weeks."

Mike declined to thank him for the warm welcome.

"Gerry, why don't you move the bed in from the guest room?" Deja suggested. "She's gotta have a real bed to sleep in. That one's a full."

"That's not a bad idea," he concurred.

Bed advocacy, Mike thought. Yes, Deja was good. Deja was a pro. Deja had not asked Mike a direct question yet, as if she could sense that Mike was not in the mood. Excellent strategy, Mike thought. It would never have occurred to Mike that Deja was always like this.

"I'll help you move it," Gunther offered.

"It's a deal. Extra cinnamon roll for you." Mike's father grinned at Gunther.

"So, Deja," Mike began, awakened by the surprisingly tasty frittata, "what do you do?"

"I'm a teacher. Former teacher, I guess." Deja smiled. "I worked for years at one of the first charter schools in the city. March Academy in Tribeca."

"What did you teach?" Mike asked.

"I was a classroom English teacher and then a reading specialist. I worked with kids one-on-one. It was an incredibly exciting place to teach, actually, because the state places fewer restrictions on charter school curriculum."

"Sure." Mike tried to sound interested.

"You don't always get to teach in the way you think is right. We were really free from a lot of restrictions there."

Mike noticed that as he wolfed his food down, her father was staring at Deja with something between pride and awe.

"That's great," Mike said, although she wasn't completely listening. "What do you do now?"

"I tutor, mostly. I do some volunteering."

"She tutors me," Mike's father said. "In vegetables."

"I'm a vegetarian," Deja practically apologized, which Mike thought was appropriate.

A particularly peppy rendition of "The Lady Is a Tramp" began to drift from the speakers in the living room.

"What the hell are we listening to?" Mike asked.

"It's the *Pottery Barn Cocktail* CD," Gerry answered matter-of-factly. "We bought a new sofa. It's coming next week."

"I hope you won't feel terribly cramped with me joining you here, Mike," Deja said.

"She won't even be around that much," Mike's father jumped in. "That job hunt'll be taking up a lot of time, right, Mike?"

"Oh, looking for jobs is horrible," Deja gushed. "Awful."

"Yeah," Mike managed. "Pretty much sucked, so far."

"Your dad tells me you work in advertising."

"Yup," Mike said.

"Tough business."

It was too early in the morning to catalog her failures. Mike chewed to avoid answering.

Before he could ask, Deja served another slab of frittata to Gunther, who beamed gratefully and hopped up to refill the coffee cups.

"You know my feelings on this," her father said sternly. "I don't care what you're doing, but you need to be getting up every day and going to a job. Any job."

"Good," Mike said, "they're hiring at Hooters."

"Well, there's a job that's all advertising," her father

quipped. Mike suppressed the urge to send the remaining frittata flying into the next room.

"We can't all be surgeons," she said.

"You know, Mike, I know it's not exactly in your line, but March is always looking for marketing staff. There are March Academies all over the country and the corporation that runs the schools has to sell them to the school boards in all these different areas. I could certainly send you down there to talk to someone. My good friend Grace still runs the place."

Mike's father gave her a "how 'bout that" look that she hadn't seen since she was sixteen and hadn't missed.

"Well, that's really...nice of you, Deja," Mike hedged, "but I'm going to stick with what I...do."

"Sure," said Deja, seemingly not offended in the least, "and it's always there if you change your mind."

Mike ignored her father's furrowed brow.

"Yeah," she said. "Thanks."

Gunther broke the tension. "Gotta tell you, Dr. E, I'm impressed." He patted his stomach, happily. "You got any more spare room around here?"

"Liked that TV, didja?" Gerry leapt at the chance to show off his new toy. "Did you see how you can adjust the picture size? Come here, I'll show you."

He jumped up from the table. "This thing has got features you wouldn't believe."

Gunther looked at Mike, perfectly aware that she would have done anything to keep from being alone with Deja, but said, "'Scuse me, ladies," and disappeared into the den.

Mike and Deja listened for a moment to the electronics convention down the hall.

"He's just lovely," Deja said.

"Who?" Mike asked.

"Your…Gunther—" Deja smiled, becoming aware in mid-sentence that for some reason she had said the wrong thing.

"He's not my…anything. I mean, he's my friend. Just a friend." Mike rose from the table in a hurry and began to clear plates.

"Oh, I'm sorry, I…." Deja searched for the words. "I just misunderstood."

Mike didn't say anything, but turned the water on to discourage further discussion.

"I'm so glad to finally meet you, Mike," Deja spoke up over the running faucet.

"Yeah, me too."

"You know your dad talks about you all the time."

Mike refrained from answering that she wished she could say the same. "Oh," she said instead. She scraped the few scraps into the garbage disposal.

"He's so proud of you."

Proud of what exactly, Mike wondered. Her unemployment? Her moving back home? It was just polite rhetoric, the thing you were supposed to tell an adult child when you moved in with her father.

"Yeah?" She didn't mean it to sound like such a challenge. She could feel Deja behind her searching for something to say.

"Did the move go alright?"

Mike flipped the switch on the wall and the disposal roared into action. She flashed Deja a thumbs-up over her shoulder. Her father would have been angry with this behavior. But then he should have stayed in the room.

She would have to find a job quickly, Mike thought. Or learn to make insipid small talk. Happy families were all alike, and Mike needed space to be unhappy in her own way.

THINK SMALL

When Caroline Edwards told her husband she was pregnant, he went for a six-mile run. Immediately.

"Don't you have a reaction, Ger?" she asked as he pulled on his running shorts.

"I will," he promised.

Because she understood him, Caroline didn't panic. She ordered Chinese food and waited for him to come home. When he did, she waited for him to shower. And when he'd showered and put on clean clothes and sat down at the kitchen table, she waited for him to pick up his chopsticks.

"Now, Gerry," she'd said, "react."

"I won't know what to do with it," he said.

"You will," she promised.

"I mean, I'll know the basics," he said. "I can do the right from wrong business, and long division, and don't run out into the street."

"Exactly." She smiled.

"But you're gonna have to do everything else."

Caroline understood that this did not mean, as some women would have assumed, that he would be unwilling to change diapers or host birthday parties or pick up groceries on the way home. He meant the difficult stuff. He meant the "What happens when you die?" and "Make me a Halloween costume," and "I only eat red foods" stuff. He meant the inexplicable, mysterious childhood minefield stuff that accumulated into "I only looked at colleges close to home" or "It's all my parents' fault." He just didn't want to screw it up.

"I will," she told him. "We'll be good at this, Ger. Between us, we really will."

And because he believed so much in her certainty in all things, Gerry said, "Then we're having a baby."

It seemed doubly unfair then, that just when he needed her most to guide Michaela around the world's trickiest mine, she was gone. When he needed someone to explain that sometimes people disappear in a day and they don't come back and it's nothing resembling fair but it happens, there was no one.

Michaela would ask for an Edwina the Mongoose story and Gerry would feel the unbearable weight of Caroline's absence threatening to crush him. He barely knew how to live without his wife, yet somehow he was supposed to see their daughter all the way from childhood to personhood. He didn't know what to do with the grief of a four-year-old girl.

But the flailing thirty-one-year-old ad creative with the sour expression and the sharp tongue, he knew what to do with her. He needed to get her working. Immediately.

Mike felt the enormous pressure of her father's concern. Gerry slipped the *Times* classifieds under her door on his way to the hospital every morning. He left Monster.com displayed on the laptop in the kitchen. He prodded. He pestered.

The truth was, Mike was getting nowhere and was no longer trying very hard. The attrition was getting to her. Somewhere along the way she had stopped believing that everything was going to work out. She spent most of her days watching nature programs and hoping no one would notice.

After two aimless weeks, Gerry had more than noticed. He took her out for chili dogs. He could talk to her when there was food between them.

"Deja stopped down at the school today," he said as if he didn't really care.

"Oh, yeah?" Mike answered as if she cared even less.

"Said they're looking pretty shorthanded."

"Maybe she should go back to work."

Gerry paused. He knew he had no one to blame but himself for her outstanding ability to stonewall.

"You know what happens when a guy sits on his contract for too long and misses the start of training camp?"

"Tell me," she said, because she knew where he was going and that there was no escape.

"First he gets antsy. Then he gets scared."

Mike chewed slowly, deliberately. "Are you implying that I'm sitting on my contract?" she asked with her mouth full.

"Any work is better than no work."

"I respectfully disagree," she said, in a tone that was hardly respectful.

Gerry sighed. "Mike, I'm doin' the best I can here."

Something about this last statement stirred in her gut. Either that or the chili dog.

Pressure, from anyone, anytime, always seemed like a

challenge to Mike. Push and she pushed back. But step aside unexpectedly in just this way, and she was very likely to fall through whatever door it was you were trying to open for her.

"You don't have to go down there," Gerry said, and then of course she had to.

Three phone calls and two days later, Mike was seated in the cluttered anteroom of an office inside the March Academy, listing in her head the places she'd rather be. Dentist's office. Traffic court. Hair salon. Stenciled on the door to Mike's right, in two-inch-high letters were the words "Grace Washington" and "Principal."

A small Latina girl with somber eyes sat across the room from Mike, her matchstick legs swinging wildly from underneath a green plaid uniform skirt and smacking against the metal of her chair. Mike twitched slightly under the odd intensity of the little girl's stare. She picked up a *Parents* magazine from the coffee table and tried to read a side-by-side comparison of breast pumps, but rapidly grew ill and had to put the magazine down. The little girl kept staring.

Mike finally looked back at her and smiled for a split second without opening her mouth. When the staring continued, she offered a terse, "Hey."

"You're not supposed to talk to strangers," the little girl told her firmly, with a trace of a Bronx accent.

"Agreed," Mike said.

They sat. Mike listened to the wall clock ticking and wondered how every school in America seemed to have all the same clocks. Where were they getting them from?

Grace Washington's door flew open with the force of a small hurricane. At five feet, three inches, Grace filled no more than the lower half of the doorframe, yet somehow she seemed to tower over the small room, changing the climate with her very presence. People were always comparing Grace to disruptive weather events.

She addressed the small Latina girl. "What was it this time?"

"A minus," the little girl replied with something of defiant pride.

"Then get out of here," Grace returned.

"Ms. Edwards." She turned her attention to Mike, who suddenly felt as if she were caught in some sort of tractor beam. "In my office." She held out a hand that somehow ordered more than it invited.

Mike obeyed.

"Talia," Grace barked at the little girl lifting her backpack onto a small shoulder. "Keep it up."

Mike thought she caught the phantom of a smile on the girl's face as she withdrew.

Grace's workspace was even smaller than the waiting room, but seemed to house the paperwork of an entire office park. Surfaces that weren't covered in paper were mired with plants in various stages of euthanasia. A bachelor's degree from Spelman College hung above a master's in education from Harvard.

"Talia is on academic probation," Grace explained before Mike could ask, which she wouldn't have done anyway. "So she reports to me. Every test. Every paper. Every day. B minus or above she gets to go back to class."

"What happens if she gets a C?" Mike asked and instantly wished she hadn't.

Grace glared at her as though she had just suggested selling Talia to the circus.

"Do I look like I'm worried about that?"

"Absolutely not," Mike said quickly. She could not re-

member, in the near decade she had spent climbing the
thorny ladder of the advertising world, ever being nearly as
intimidated as she was at this moment.

"So tell me what you're here for," Grace demanded,
glancing at her computer screen, never skirting stillness.

"I...Deja—"

"I love that woman," Grace said, looking up sharply as
though Mike were in some way attacking Deja.

"Oh, okay," Mike said.

"I. Love. That woman," Grace repeated. "It is important
to me that you know that. There is nothing I would not do
for that woman."

Unsure of the proper response, Mike said nothing.

"Continue," Grace said.

"Deja—who is...she's great—she said that you might
need people. Marketing people."

"I don't need marketing people. My marketing staff is
full."

Mike curled her tongue back in her mouth and bit
down on it.

"You see that empty desk out there? I need a secretary."

"Sorry?" Mike said, to avoid acting on the impulse to
get up and walk out.

The fossilized rotary phone on Grace's desk began to
rattle aggressively. "That's exactly what I'm talking about,"
Grace muttered, her hand shooting out to wrench the re-
ceiver from the cradle. "Grace Washington," she barked.
She leaned back in her chair and her eyes rolled back in her
head while she listened, holding up one finger as though
poised to interrupt. "No, it is not *Julius. Caesar,*" she said
slowly, speaking as one must to an idiot. "I need *Henry
Five. Henry. Five.* These kids are gonna fall asleep if they
have to look at *Julius Caesar* one more time. Pack the box

back up, send it out *to*day, and tell that sorry rep that if I do not have my books tomorrow morning I will personally come to his house, say 'excuse me' to his wife, and drag him down here to perform a one-man version of *Henry Five* in the auditorium." She slammed the phone down.

What had begun in Mike as utter terror had, during those few sentences, dissolved into respect. Grace was relentless and brutal and determined. This was a woman she could understand.

"I have a purchasing department that act like a bunch of monkeys on lunch break and my secretary has taken a job performing repertory theater for white-collar criminals at a minimum-security facility on Long Island. I have a marketing staff. I need someone to answer the damned phone."

Mike paused. She tried to find a nice way to say, "I'd rather eat hair."

"I'm offering you a position, Ms. Edwards, and now I am trying to understand why you do not look grateful."

Mike spoke slowly and deliberately. "Answering the phone is not exactly what I had in mind. I'm an ad copywriter."

"Then why aren't you out writing copy?"

Interesting point. Mike reached for the gilded frame in which she'd hung her recent predicament for display.

"There was an unfortunate shake-up at my agency."

"That's fancy talk for they canned you, correct?"

Mike clamped down on her tongue again. "Correct."

"You think I'm going to waste your precious skills here."

"I—" Mike had no chance to protest.

"You think the work we do here at Skunk Crossing is too simple for your complex and overactive intellect. You think you're too good for my school."

"I never said—"

"What *I* am saying, is that if you had any other offers you wouldn't be here." Grace answered an e-mail as she talked, jabbing angrily at the keyboard while Mike formulated her response.

"Listen," Mike finally said, "I really appreciate your taking the time—"

"You need a job?"

"Yes," Mike assented with a sigh of resignation.

"Now you have one."

Before Mike could say any more, the door to Grace's office flew open and a petite blonde woman who appeared to be draped in thirteen or fourteen silk scarves appeared breathlessly in the doorway.

"Grace!" the blonde woman cried.

"I don't wanna know," Grace muttered.

"Derek Luce didn't show up this morning!" the blonde woman moaned.

"He WHAT?" Grace barked.

"I just went to do a pull-out in his third period and he wasn't there! The kids said he never showed up this morning! They were just sitting there!" She looked at Mike. "Hi, sorry." She smiled wanly.

Grace exhaled sharply, pursed her lips, and shot an accusatory look toward the ceiling.

"Alright. You, get up," she ordered Mike, who obeyed before she even knew what she was doing.

"Cheryl Hershey, Michaela Edwards."

"Hi." Cheryl smiled broadly and swept a scarf-trailing hand toward Mike.

"Cheryl is a reading specialist. Michaela is our new substitute teacher."

"I'm what?" Mike nearly shouted. "I thought I was the secretary."

"You just got an upgrade. Congratulations, you're about to enter the world's second-oldest profession," Grace said, rapidly departing the office with Mike and Cheryl scrambling to follow.

"I don't think you understand," Mike protested with an urgency she hadn't felt in months.

"What in particular?" Grace continued to walk briskly through the waiting room and out into the hallway.

"I . . . I just . . . I don't do . . . children!" Mike insisted.

Grace stopped abruptly, swiveled to look Mike directly in the eye, and said, "Well, you know what they say, Ms. Edwards. Those who can't do, teach." She turned and strode briskly on, leaving a speechless Mike to try to keep up.

"You know," Cheryl-of-the-scarves whispered to Mike conspiratorially, "I hate that expression! I teach reading. What does that say about me?"

Mike just looked at her as though she were speaking Esperanto. They scrambled to keep up with Grace, who was barreling down the corridor like there was a fire.

"You can't really put me in charge of a classroom full of kids," Mike reiterated, hoping to sound confident.

"I can't?" Grace asked without stopping. "You have a criminal record?"

"No," Mike said and wished she did. "Don't I need a license or something?"

"Not in a charter school. You came from Deja. You can't be that bad."

"I'm not a teacher!"

Grace ignored Mike completely. "Derek Luce better be lying under a bridge somewhere. That's all I'm gonna say," she muttered.

They flew down hallway after linoleum-tiled hallway. Mike barely had time to peer through classroom windows as they went. She caught flashes of ponytails and head-bands and Peter Pan collars, all seemingly subdued at rows of uncomfortable plastic chair-desks. She smelled the long-repressed odor of too many sweaty little people in one space. Suddenly she was back in Mr. DiGiamo's third-grade class, ripping the bow out of Stephanie Noseman's hair. She was pouting outside of sixth-grade math, sent to sit in the hall for throwing a paste ball that stuck in Jordan Melsky's collar. She was kicking Beth Maxwell under the desk for looking at her English quiz because Mike didn't believe in snitching. She had always been edgy in school and not a thing had changed.

She had to do something, or surely in a moment Grace's breakneck pace would slow and they would be standing before an open door and Mike would be shoved inside, trapped at the mercy of those pint-sized lions who had been teacherless all morning and were probably growling for fresh meat.

"What do you expect me to teach them?"

"I don't expect you to teach them a damned thing except how to stay inside the building until three-thirty this afternoon. You do that, I'll find you a place here."

"I don't want a place here," Mike said before she could filter the thought.

"Well then you shouldn't have showed up this morning," Grace said, with very little irony. And then suddenly they were standing still and Grace had her hand on a classroom door handle and she was twisting it before Mike could throw her body in for a block.

There they were. Eleven of them. They were short. They looked mean. They were all wearing skirts.

Mike clawed at the air with one hand and managed to snag one of Cheryl's draperies.

"They're all girls!" Mike whispered fiercely.

"Of course they are." Cheryl smiled at her. "It's a girls' school."

Mike's stomach shriveled into a hard little raisin of terror. They stared at her, their little doll eyes drinking her in like the cherry cough syrup that probably coursed through their sugary pink veins.

"Listen up!" Grace barked, and every tiny coiffed head snapped to attention. Mike watched Grace move her finger in the air in a quick and silent head count.

"Mr. Luce has been detained and will not be joining you this morning and I apologize that you've been sitting here for twenty minutes waiting for him. The lovely lady to my left will be your substitute this morning and I know you will treat her with the same respect and deference that you normally show to Mr. Luce."

While Grace spoke, Mike took in the large windows facing the street and wondered how badly she'd be hurt if she threw herself out one of them. The windows didn't open, so it would have hurt very much indeed. She looked for additional exits toward the back of the room, and instead spotted a row of half-sized stoves and sinks, which appeared to be functional. They were just a room full of Hansel-free Gretels, weren't they, waiting to shove her into the oven. What the hell was this place?

"I trust you will fill her in on the work that you've been doing," Grace continued, "and I do not expect to hear of any further Mentos and diet soda fountains being constructed in this classroom. Are we clear?"

"Yes, Ms. Washington," eleven little androids answered as they had been programmed to do.

"Don't worry," Cheryl whispered to Mike, "they're a good group. Usually."

But Mike was worried. Sweating and starting to shake. Nearly apoplectic.

"Alright," Grace concluded darkly, "let's have a happy and productive day." She moved toward the door.

"You're not leaving me." Mike began to reach for Grace's arm but thought better of it.

"If I had time to babysit you, Ms. Edwards, I would not be forced to throw a total stranger in front of one of my classrooms, now, would I?"

"But wait a minute, I don't even know what I'm supposed to be teaching them! What class is this? How long are they here? What do I do with them afterward?"

Grace looked at Mike for a hard minute, as though perhaps she were doubting the advisability of this hasty arrangement.

"You have them for one hour and"—she consulted her watch—"one hour and four minutes. When the class is through, the bell will ring. You will not *do* anything with them. They will quietly rise, gather their things, and move to their next periods. This class is called Life Skills and I can only pray at this moment that you are in possession of at least a few which you have not demonstrated to me yet this morning."

"Life Skills?" Mike whispered. "What the hell is Life Skills?"

Cheryl and Grace smiled to each other.

"You may remember it," Grace explained, "as Home Economics. Good luck to you." She disappeared through the door before Mike had time to scream for sweet mercy.

"Don't worry about it," Cheryl said quietly. "Just get through the period. It's a short one today."

Mike's mouth repeatedly gaped and closed in carp-like desperation, but no sound came out.

"Talia?" Cheryl said, turning out to the class.

Mike recognized the girl who rose from a seat near the back of the class and rolled her eyes to her neighbor as she made her way toward Cheryl and the door.

"Where are you taking this one?" Mike asked.

"We're going to go read," Cheryl explained brightly, placing a maternal hand on Talia's shoulder. Talia looked at the hand sharply but did not remove it. She looked at Mike as if maybe Mike would understand.

"Well, wait!" Mike made one last effort. "Maybe I should go read and you should stay here. I could definitely read."

Cheryl smiled and beamed no small amount of pity toward Mike. "You'll be fine," she promised. "I really think you will."

The word "think" was not lost on Mike, who watched with the morbid certainty of her own doom as Cheryl exited the classroom with Talia, pulled the door shut behind her, and gave a sunny thumbs-up signal through the narrow window.

Mike was alone with the lions.

THE PENALTY
OF LEADERSHIP

Slowly, careful not to make any sudden moves, she turned to face them. They blinked at her from beneath a variety of wee ambitious hairdos.

She scanned each row, trying to size them up. It's just like a pitch, she thought. That's all, just like a pitch, except I have no idea what I'm talking about. She nodded at them silently for a moment.

One of them spoke, from the front row. "Hi," it said.

Excellent. Mike knew how to answer that one. "Hi," she said back. "Hi . . . everyone."

"Hi," they all chanted in one voice, which made Mike recoil.

She had to get it together. They would smell her fear, if they hadn't already, and then she would be finished. She had to act quickly. She reached back across twenty years and tried to remember what the hell it was that teachers used to do when she was in school. Her brain wasn't working. Crap. They were looking at her. What was the first thing a teacher did on the first day of school?!

A lightbulb appeared in her head, and with the sudden assurance that she was doing at least one right thing, Mike uncapped a fat green marker and wrote M-I-K-E in huge capital letters across the board. She sighed deeply.

"I'm Mike." She turned back to them and smiled broadly, this one thing accomplished.

"Hi, Miss Mike," they chanted as one.

She flinched again at their automated response. "No 'Miss,'" she corrected them. "Just Mike."

"What kind of a name is Mike?" one of them threw out.

"That's a boy's name," another volunteered.

"It's French," she said plainly, because it was just easier. She stared each of them down in turn, a social tactic she'd picked up in the fifth grade.

Her sense of accomplishment quickly evaporating, Mike was once again seized with utter uncertainty regarding the next step. How many minutes had she eaten, she wondered hopefully. Five? Seven?

They were staring again. She was supposed to do something. What was it?

"Don't you want to know our names?" It was the one in the front row with the glasses again. Clearly some kind of leader. She should get this one on her side immediately. She regretted not carrying more cash.

"Great," Mike said. "Yes, good idea. Let's start with you."

"I'm Asia," the one with the glasses said.

Asia, like the porn star, Mike thought.

"Asia, like the continent," Mike said.

"Exactly." Asia smiled proudly, as if she herself accounted for 60 percent of the world's human population.

"Great," Mike said again. "You?" She moved to the one with the bow on Asia's left.

"Makenzee." The bow quivered defiantly. "With an M-A-K-E-N-Z-E-E," she spelled.

"Of course," Mike said, "because there are lots of ways to spell Mackenzie."

"That's right," Makenzee nodded with absolutely no irony.

This gave Mike an idea. "Okay, one at a time, everybody come up to the board and write your name."

"Even us?" Asia indicated herself and Makenzee.

"Absolutely," Mike affirmed, theorizing that this might take as much as fifteen minutes to accomplish.

By the time the others had each taken a turn to write, Kinara, Sassafrass, Sadie, Brooklyn, Fenice, Dalwhynnie, Jahia, and Daisy, only six minutes had elapsed. They were still staring at her, and now she'd encouraged physical activity so they were even more awake. Mike was going to have to come up with something else.

"So"—she rubbed her hands together—"anybody know what life skill you're supposed to be learning today?"

Ten hands shot into the air.

"Ah, wow. You." Mike pointed at Dalwhynnie, a petite blonde in the third row who kept adjusting her red headband and was waving her hand wildly in the air.

"We're supposed to make healthy granola," Dalwhynnie chirped, but Mike read something sour in her small round face.

"You don't seem excited about that," Mike said.

"*Healthy granola* is an oxymoron."

"Oxymoron, huh? I bet you're not allowed to eat a lot of granola at your house," she said.

"Too much fat and sugar," Dalwhynnie confirmed, gratified to be understood.

Asia with the glasses raised her hand again, her shoulder twisting excitedly several inches above the socket.

"Asia," Mike called on her.

"Don't you want to collect our permission slips?"

"Your permission slips?"

"Saying that we don't have any allergies and are allowed to eat and handle healthy granola."

"You have permission slips for that?" Mike asked. When she was in grade school kids climbed forty-foot ropes in gym class. Nobody ever asked permission for that.

"I don't." Kinara spoke and raised her hand at the same time. "I have an oat allergy and my stomach is intolerant of cinnamon."

"Bummer," Mike said, to keep from saying anything else. "What grade are you people in exactly?"

"The sixth," Brooklyn answered helpfully.

Too old for dolls, too young for makeup. Mike hadn't half minded sixth grade. "I don't suppose anybody here knows how to make healthy granola, do they?"

"There's a recipe in Mr. Luce's desk," Asia offered.

They looked at her expectantly and with suspicion. If Mike could have conceived, in that moment, of a single thing to do with them for another hour and a half, she would never have looked in Mr. Luce's desk. But she couldn't. Giving them the falsely confident smile traditionally used in advertising for the moments when your notes get out of order, Mike moved to the desk to search for the recipe. She found it, without much trouble, clipped to a pile of papers in his top left drawer labeled "Lesson Plans." Mike had spent more time reading bathroom walls than she had reading recipes, and as she scanned a list of ingredients that included sunflower seeds and oat groats, she remembered why. What the hell was an oat groat anyway? It sounded like some sort of monster living under Fraggle Rock.

Mike riffled through the stack of lesson plans, hoping against hope that she might discover a hastily scribbled set of instructions for hypnotizing ten preteen girls for approximately an hour. No such luck. Derek Luce had carefully outlined weeks' worth of lessons for sewing, decoupage, and one-pot meals. There was one entitled "Lifesaving Dinners for Drop-ins" and another called "My Countertops, Myself." How this class had come to be called Life Skills was completely beyond Mike, who had never had a relationship with anyone's countertop, and couldn't think of a reason why a bunch of twelve-year-olds should be encouraged to do so.

The natives were growing restless. Mike caught a few anxious whispers and saw a note being passed guiltily beneath a desk. She was sure it said something like, "Who is this crazy person? I don't think she's ever been around children. Clearly we have the advantage here, so let's tie her up and braid her hair until her eyeballs pop out."

Asia raised her hand. "Miss Mike?"

"Just Mike," Mike repeated.

"Should I preheat the oven?"

Mike wanted to tell Asia to quit sucking up so much, but she was too impressed with the little girl's conviction that granola-making involved the oven, a fact which had taken Mike herself completely by surprise.

She looked around the room. Kinara was sucking on her hair. Dalwhynnie was examining her fingernails. Sadie and Sassafrass were exchanging dubious looks. Mike was rapidly losing any semblance of authority she'd automatically entered with by virtue of being taller and older than they were. If she attempted to execute healthy granola or any of Derek Luce's other cockamamie lesson plans, she'd expose herself completely. They would know that she had no right to be here, and then all hell might break loose. This freaking granola thing was getting incredibly stressful, which only made Mike angrier to have been shoved into this situation in which she clearly did not belong. She belonged in an office with other people in T-shirts and jeans who would snark at each other and conceive of humorous and innovative ways to make the average consumer buy flood insurance. And instead she was standing in front of a miniature tribunal who were just waiting for her to fail and humiliate herself. Well, she'd been humiliated enough for one lifetime already. She made a decision: fuck granola.

"No oven," she said.

"But—" Asia protested.

"We're skipping the granola."

Asia was clearly disappointed but said nothing. Sadie and Sassafrass consulted each other silently. Fenice raised her hand imperiously.

"What?" Mike answered the hand.

"I wanted to know why we're skipping granola," Fenice demanded in a quietly poised way that suggested she would someday run a large department at a major corporation.

"Because granola is not a life skill," Mike said, and this felt better to her. "I'm thirty-one years old and I have never once needed to make granola. If you ever really need granola, you can go to the store and buy it. But I can almost promise you that you will never really need it."

They gasped at Mike's radical ideas or perhaps at her advanced age. Fenice opened her mouth as if to make an argument, but closed it again when Mike cocked her head in challenge. She could feel her authority returning. This really wasn't so hard. They were just kids. She could handle them. She wasn't sure what she was going to do with them, but she could handle them. And with this renewed sense of her own power came an idealistic frustration at the knowledge that these small impressionable minds were being shaped around the idea that life skills were things like cooking and cleaning.

Sadie raised a cautious hand.

"Skip the hands." Mike decided as she spoke. "What's your name?"

"Sadie."

"Sadie, go."

"Where?" Sadie asked, terrified and bewildered.

"I mean, talk. Ask your question."

"Oh, um . . . are you really a teacher?"

Mike looked at them, and she didn't want to lie.

"No," she answered. "I'm not a teacher. I work in advertising."

They looked at each other. They were in the presence of a real adult. An adult wearing a plaid cowgirl shirt and worn denim and filthy shit-kicking boots. They chided themselves for ever believing that she was a teacher.

Asia raised her hand.

"I said skip the hands," Mike reminded her.

Asia yanked the hand down into her lap, chagrined. "Um, what are you doing here?" she asked quietly.

Fine question, Mike thought. She remembered all the useless lunches, the tense phone calls, the pretending that everything was fine and that she hadn't been humiliated almost to the point of a nervous breakdown. She was tired of saying that everything was fine, tired of trying to package her disaster of a life in a way that would make other people more comfortable. She didn't want to do it anymore.

She took a deep breath, sunk her hands into the pockets of her jeans, and rocked back on the heels of her boots for a minute. She wanted to tell them the truth.

"I lost my job," she said. "I was fired six months ago. I had to move back into my father's house and I need to make some money. I'm not supposed to be teaching you, and I'm only doing it today because I got pushed into it."

Because she never thought much about children, because she had fled childhood as quickly as possible, Mike was unaware that she had just executed the one and only maneuver that could have earned their undying and unmerited respect. Not only was she beautiful and young and oddly cool-looking in her total disregard for fashion and style, she was honest. She was speaking to them without pretense and this naked honesty in all its rare ugliness was the catnip of childhood. She was novel and strange and she just might tell them things that nobody else would. She was their hero.

Ten little hands flew into the air.

"No hands!" Mike nearly shouted.

Ten little girls began to ask ten different questions at one time.

"Okay, okay, okay, quiet!" Mike shouted over the din. "Here's a life skill. For the rest of the day we're going to learn to have a conversation without hand-raising. That means you look around when you want to say something and make sure that nobody else is talking. Think you can do that?"

They gaped at each other, wide-eyed. Asia shifted nervously. Nothing so revolutionary had ever been introduced into the Life Skills classroom at March Academy. Mike was like the Che Guevara of the sixth grade.

Sassafrass took advantage of the sudden silence. "Do you have a boyfriend and if not, why not and do you want one?" she spat out very quickly.

Mike couldn't suppress a chuckle. "No, it's complicated, and I don't know," she answered in order.

Sassafrass, who had expected to be told that she was being rude, smiled at her own bravery.

Kinara and Dalwhynnie both opened their little fishmouths to speak at once, and stopped immediately upon hearing each other.

"See?" Mike said. "Nice reflex."

Dalwhynnie bit her lips in an obvious and exaggerated way, to indicate that Kinara should proceed.

"My dad says that advertising is a disgusting business," Kinara said disdainfully.

"What does your dad do?" Mike asked, unmoved.

"He runs an HMO."

"Then he probably knows."

And this was how it went. For another hour and fifteen minutes Mike stood before ten endlessly curious little girls and answered every question they asked with as much candor as she could. It was nice not to try so hard.

"What do you want to be when you grow up?"

"I'll let you know," she told them.

"Do you have any siblings?"

"What's your favorite food?" "Where'd you go to college?" "Where do you live?" "Do you drive?" "Do you think Meredith and Derek belong together?" "What's your bedtime?" "Dogs or cats?" "Mickey D's or BK?" "Britney or Beyoncé?"

Mike drew the line at how many men she'd slept with. "Inappropriate," she said.

"Sorry," Jahia apologized.

"Not a problem," Mike said.

When Cheryl returned with Talia near the end of the period, Mike didn't even hear the door open behind her.

"What do your parents do?" Fenice asked.

"My father is an orthopedic surgeon."

"What does your mother do?"

"My mother is dead."

"I'm sorry," Fenice said, graciously.

"It was a long time ago," Mike explained.

Ten faces expressed their sympathy.

"Next question," Mike ordered.

"What's going on here?" Cheryl asked, smiling from the doorway.

Mike turned, surprised at the interruption. Talia, staring at Mike, wriggled out of Cheryl's grasp and back to her seat.

"Oh, ah . . . we're getting to know me," Mike said, not sure what the right answer was and not sure she cared what Cheryl thought.

"She's not a teacher!" Sadie crowed triumphantly.

"That is incredibly rude!" Cheryl scolded.

"No, it's not," Sadie argued, "it's true! Sometimes your life doesn't go like you planned and you don't have to be ashamed about it." She looked to Mike to make sure she'd gotten it right.

Mike kept her mouth closed and smiled at the floor.

Had she been on staff, Mike would have received endless grief from the various teachers who dealt with the Life Skills girls for the rest of the day. They no longer wanted to raise their hands, insisting that adults could speak without asking permission. Jahia told her math teacher that her weekend hadn't turned out as she'd planned and that she wouldn't apologize for not having her homework done.

By the time Mike arrived back at Grace's office after

class, she was confident that a positive report would be sent to Deja, and that her obligation had been fulfilled.

"I hear you made quite the impression." Grace leaned back in her chair as Mike stood before her.

"Well, they didn't run out into the street."

Grace nodded. "Cheryl tells me she saw no evidence of healthy granola."

"I told you, I'm not a home ec teacher," Mike bristled.

"And I told you I didn't care."

Mike waited, slightly confused.

"You can handle them," Grace said.

"Yeah, well, I feel like I need about nine hours of sleep now," Mike said.

"Welcome to the wonderful world of education."

"Call me if anything comes up in marketing," Mike said, turning to go.

"Derek Luce was walking by a deli during a delivery this morning and fell through an open loading hatch into their basement."

"Jesus," Mike said.

"He's not gonna be teaching for some time. So I'll see you tomorrow." Grace stared at Mike as if to suppress any argument.

"Whoa, whoa, wait a minute," Mike said. She'd been stared at before. "This was a one-time thing. I'm not a teacher. I just stood in that class and talked for an hour."

"What exactly do you think teaching is, Ms. Edwards?"

"Yeah, but I don't know this stuff. What he's supposed to be teaching them . . . I don't even use a can opener more than twice a year."

"Derek tells me there are lesson plans in his desk. Get me through this week while I hire somebody to cover the rest of the year. That's all I ask."

"Look, you have got this all wrong," Mike insisted. "I can't do a whole week with those kids."

She couldn't imagine it.

"It's one class a day. One unpopular, underattended elective class, which I am unfortunately unable to cancel. I've got Derek's cooking and crafting electives covered. You got something else going on?"

More disturbing than the fact that Mike had nothing going on, was the fact that Grace knew it. And if a total stranger knew that, it must be real. The future began to spill out before her like a bad tarot hand. One miss after another, a series of shit jobs. Agreeing to do this one thing would be admitting to the universe that she'd been beaten. She had to say no. She could explain everything to Deja, that she just wasn't a teacher. She could tell her father that she'd given it a shot.

"Ms. Edwards?"

But in two and a half hours she would be meeting Gunther at the Drunk. Since she'd stepped out of the classroom she'd been picturing the look on his face when she told him what she'd been doing all day. If she turned Grace down, what was she supposed to tell him? That she'd managed to get through an entire class with those little ankle-biters and now she was giving up? And then she'd drink too much and sleep too long and waste another day. The pointless, wasted days were beginning to make her queasy.

"One week," she told Grace. "One week and whether you have somebody or not, I walk."

Grace nodded. "It's a deal."

Son of a bitch, Mike thought. Gunther was definitely buying tonight.

A MIND IS A
TERRIBLE THING
TO WASTE

The smile on Gunther's face as Mike recounted her afternoon was worth the odd sojourn to Tiny Town. It gave her the strength to get up the next morning and do it all again. And the morning after that.

By the end of her third day, however, she was tired. She had never been this tired working at Logan, no matter how long the hours. Those little girls were hoovering away all her energy. When Brian called, insisting he had important news, Mike was unnerved to realize she hadn't looked at the job boards all week. She agreed to meet him right away.

"You're doing what?" He erupted into donkey-like laughter when she told him where she was spending her days.

"It's just for a week." She sipped her scotch and shrank back into her chair. She didn't need the whole bar to weigh in. "It's not like I'm off the hunt."

"Well, you'll have to forgive me." He tried to contain himself. "I'm just wrestling a bit with the idea that anyone would trust you with their children. I mean, have you met you?" He exploded again and his pale English features contracted to such a degree that Mike caught a tear rolling down his cheek.

The waitress approached to ask if everything was alright.

"I think he needs another," Mike answered, embarrassed.

"Okay, so instead of reading, writing, and 'rithmetic, you're teaching them to bake bread and sew buttons—" Brian was overwhelmed with another giggling fit and nearly choked on his chicken satay.

"It's only temporary! It's a favor, to this friend of my father's girlfriend. Oh, God, it's not a big deal. I shouldn't have said anything."

"Going to start making your own clothes then?"

"For God's sake," she muttered. "No, actually I'm mixing it up a little. I'm straying from the curriculum."

"Did anyone ever tell you that you are the world's most difficult employee?" Brian asked. It was more than obvious that he didn't give a hoot about what she was teaching, beyond the sheer entertainment value it provided. She couldn't blame him. Not like it was all that interesting.

"Not while you were around," she sniped and pushed away her crab cake, no longer hungry. "You want this?" she asked.

"Can't. Shellfish allergy, remember?"

"Vaguely."

Brian stared at Mike and she stared at the carpet.

"Would you take it wrong if I said I'd missed looking at you every day?" he asked, leaning back to gaze at her.

"What's the right way to take that?" Mike drained her

drink and gently indicated the empty glass to the waitress across the room.

"Well, much as I hate to think of derailing your burgeoning career in elementary education—"

"It's middle school," Mike corrected him.

Brian smiled at her, bemused. "Right, well, I think I may have something for us soon."

Mike's heart leapt unexpectedly behind her ribs. Brian saw her reaction before she meant to show it.

"I'm meeting with Legg, Stone & Gelding next week."

"You'd move to Portland?" She had never pictured him outside of New York.

"You wouldn't?"

Yes, she realized, of course she would. At this point she'd run home to pack a bag.

"They're thinking of a New York office. It's a growing firm, tremendously successful in the last few years. There are too many clients here."

"When?"

"Soon."

"Who's on top?"

"Not clear yet. But they're hungry for creatives. Fresh blood."

Mike took a deep breath and tried to imagine it. The two of them doing business again. Back where they belonged.

"I thought you'd be pleased," he said.

"I would be. If I thought it might really happen, I would be thrilled." She watched a marching band of expressions parade across his face and remembered the discomfiting feeling of having no idea what he was really thinking. They sat in silence. The waitress brought Mike another scotch.

Brian stirred at the ice in his glass and stole a glance at her breasts. "Keep me posted," she added, just in case.

"Where are you off to this evening?" He tried to sound as if he didn't care.

"Nowhere special," she said. She was heading home to work on a lesson plan. There was still the end of the week to get through.

"There's a write-up on Legg, Stone in the new *Adweek*. I've got it at my place. Come up and have a look?"

"I can't. I've got plans," she told him.

"I'm not in the city much anymore, you know. Seems a shame to waste the evening..."

She didn't have to think hard—she sent him home alone. Brian came through best when she left him hanging. And she could do without his groping stares. But Mike fell asleep that night imagining a new glass-bricked office, an igloo in a skyscraper, where she could begin to put herself back together.

When Mike arrived at school the next morning, Grace was waiting in her classroom. "I need another week," she said.

"Are you kidding me?"

"I don't have time to kid you."

"You said you were looking for someone!"

"I am looking for someone, but right this minute I'm looking *at* someone who has managed to survive for a week without losing any of the eleven children under her care."

"Grace, listen, I've been through Derek's lesson plans. I tried to teach them darning and sewed a sock to my own pants."

"Then I suggest you go through them again."

"Grace—"

"You have nowhere to be but here. Tell me I'm wrong."

"I might."

"Do tell." Grace stared up at Mike and gave her that shrinking feeling again.

"There's a firm in Portland thinking of opening a New York office." Out loud it sounded flimsy and thin.

Grace waited a moment. "You think they're going to get that all wrapped up by next week?"

Mike's nostrils flared, but she said nothing.

"I appreciate your help," Grace said more earnestly, "and I need it."

Mike couldn't find the strength to say she didn't care.

When Grace had gone, Mike sat seething at a chair-desk that was far too small for her, leafing angrily through Derek Luce's lesson plans. She was about to teach her last planned lesson and everything that was left on the pile was beyond her. She wasn't about to instruct a bunch of tweens in the preparation of a three-course brunch. There was no way in hell she could teach them to use a sewing machine or make lampshade covers. A party-planning seminar seemed wholly unnecessary. She decided to compromise on the finance lesson: she could teach them to write checks, hell, she could bring in her laptop and give them a lesson in online bill-paying. Maybe they could pay her bills while they were at it. Fine, she would get through this period, but she didn't belong there. She shouldn't have to serve an indenture in a charter school.

When the girls filed in moments later, primed to absorb a lesson on stain removal, Mike was gruff and quiet. She tossed piles of clean white T-shirts onto their worktables and grunted instructions. Sensing her mood, they did as they were told quietly and avoided eye contact. But there was something satisfying in watching them ruin the pristine cotton with indiscriminate splashes of grape juice and motor oil. Mike began to move around the room, encouraging Brooklyn to work the olive oil in with her fingernails, helping Asia to readjust her smock. She was unaware that she had started to smile as they pretreated and scrubbed like a fleet of mini Martha Stewarts. Kinara insisted on watching from the sidelines as any number of the ingredients involved might have sparked one of her numerous allergies and intolerances. And Talia, who had missed the interview portion of Mike's first class and was therefore not remotely in her thrall, poured grape juice on her T-shirt and didn't even try to remove it.

"Problem there, Talia?" Mike asked.

"No," Talia answered, sullen.

"You're not trying to get out the grape juice," Mike observed.

"I fight ring around the collar!" Sassafrass shouted from across the room, whipping the corners of her smock into the air like a superhero.

"So, what?" Mike turned back to Talia. "No interest in stain-fighting?"

"It's stupid," Talia complained quietly, as if she'd really rather be left alone.

"Okay." Mike shrugged. "No biggie." She left Talia to her own devices and was pleased to note that the girl seemed to relax by the time the T-shirts were gathered up and put away. Sometimes you just needed to quit poking people and let them be. Mike understood this.

When the room was finally clean again, Mike looked at the clock and noted happily that the period was nearly over. She'd managed it.

"Good job, you guys," she congratulated them, but they just sat at their desks and waited for her to say more.

"Shouldn't you all be packing up? Heading out? Moving on?"

They didn't move.

"Today is our long period," Asia said.

"How long?" Mike asked.

"Double."

"Three hours?!" Mike exploded, her mood destroyed once again. "I'm supposed to do another hour and a half?"

They looked at her uneasily. Mike was out of ideas. They already knew her life story and every household skill she could teach them. This, she wanted to scream, was exactly what she had been trying to explain to Grace. She wasn't a teacher and she could only do an impression for so long. But they were sitting there, staring again, expecting to learn!

"Fuck," she muttered.

Their eyes widened and Asia and Dalwhynnie leaned back.

"What do you guys want to learn? I'm out. I can't do this like your old teacher did. I don't know that stuff, and, frankly, you don't need to know it either."

They gazed cautiously at her, unsure if this was their cue to speak and afraid she wouldn't like their answers anyway.

"I'm serious, you guys! What 'life skills' do you think you need to know? Because I have to tell you the truth, no one sews anymore."

"My mom sews," Asia said carefully.

"Then she's the last one."

"Knitting is cool again," Jahia suggested.

"Who told you that?" Mike demanded.

"I don't know. People say it."

"Those people are lying to you, Jahia. Knitting is not cool. Knitting will never be cool. Rock 'n' roll is cool. Fast cars are cool. Even Mickey Rourke is still sort of cool, but knitting is not, has never been, and will never be anything remotely approaching cool."

"What about embroidering?" Sadie pressed.

"Are you kidding me?" Mike was incensed. "Embroidering? You guys, this class is called Life Skills! Embroidering is not a life skill! It's not 1890! You should be learning things here that are important, that you can use on the street!"

Mike's eye was drawn suddenly to the construction site across the avenue. Men in hard hats swarmed over the skeleton of a new building like ants. Something they could use on the street, she thought...

"You wanna learn some life skills?" she asked. "I'll teach you a life skill. Get your coats."

Within minutes, eleven little girls and one big girl were parading across Broadway. For construction workers on lunch break, Mike was the magazine spread they didn't have to pay for. They spied her dark hair and long legs from a block away, and though she was trailed by a gaggle of children, they began to holler and hoot.

"Oh, my God," Dalwhynnie whispered to Kinara.

As they passed, one particularly brave soul shouted, "Damn, girl, I'd like to get me a sweet piece of that!"

Like lightning, Mike wheeled on him. "You want a piece? Let me cut you a big hearty slice of shut the hell up! You think it's appropriate to talk like that in front of a group of twelve-year-old girls?"

The stunned construction worker nearly dropped his Pepsi.

"I'm waiting, asshole!" she barked.

"No, ma'am," he stuttered.

"Apologize," she growled, "to them."

He stared at her like she was an alien sent to destroy him, but turned to the class and managed, "Sorry, ladies."

The Life Skills girls were too shocked to smile, except for Talia, who grinned for the first time that Mike had seen.

"Thank you," Mike said, in a more reasonable tone. She began to usher the class away. Several of the other men began to chuckle at their unfortunate colleague. Mike stared them into silence. "Have a good day, gentlemen," she said calmly and moved on.

"Don't take shit from anyone," she said over her shoulder as she led the girls farther down Broadway. Ideas were clicking in her head. Everywhere she looked there was something useful to tell them about surviving in the city. To a lesson she began to refer to as "The Street," Mike added discussions of tourists ("Go around them. They will never move."), homeless people ("If someone asks you for money, answer them. Your money is your business, but no one deserves to be treated like they don't exist."), and subway protocols ("So help me if I ever catch any of you blocking the doors.").

An hour and a half elapsed in fifteen minutes, and suddenly they had to hustle to return in time for their next period. Mike was thoroughly proud of her inventiveness, and extremely gratified when Kinara told a derelict to have a nice day on the way back to school. She could fill a week with this sort of material, hell, she could fill a month. You don't always have to make lemonade, after all. Sometimes you can just throw your lemons against a wall and enjoy the sound they make when they explode.

By the time they returned to the classroom, Mike was

walking backward, lecturing as she moved, on the impor-
tance of watching the cars and not just the walk sign. She
didn't see a frantic Grace quivering outside her classroom
door.

"Where the hell have you been?" Grace snapped and
Mike almost bumped into her.

"Hi," she said inadequately.

Mike sensed the students scurrying into the classroom
to snatch up bags and notebooks as quickly as possible.

"Freeze!" Grace bellowed at them, and eleven girls did as
they were told. She raised a finger and counted them. "Fine,"
she acknowledged, "move on to your next classes. Move!"

They fled the classroom as if it were aflame.

"Tell me why I'm going to kill you," Grace hissed fiercely
at Mike.

"Because you're in a mood?"

Grace smashed her palm onto a desktop and Mike
jumped.

"Because I took them outside?"

"These children need permission slips to breathe funny,
and you thought you could take them on a field trip?"

"We just went for a walk," Mike protested. "They didn't
eat anything or touch anything or breathe on anything as
far as I know."

"Let me straighten something out for you." Grace took
two huge steps and landed very close to Mike. She stared
piercingly up into Mike's face, so that despite her enormous height advantage, Mike felt herself shrinking. "I
don't care what kind of hotshot you were before you came
here," Grace began. "I don't care who you scared the shit
out of and I don't care who wanted to bed you. You may
have gotten this far being some hot, nasty monster nobody
could control, but you are in my house now and these are

my children. Now, you may think it's a silly business that happens in this classroom, but if you want to make a change you come to me to do it. Or, so help me, I will grind you into a fine powder and sweep you right onto the side-walk. Do you get me?"

Until this point, Mike had been, without a doubt, the toughest woman Mike had ever met.

"I get you," she said quietly.

"Good," Grace said, and stared up for another moment before moving toward the door. She stopped in the door-way, sighed, and turned back. "What's your damned prob-lem with the curriculum?"

"I get to talk now?" Mike ventured, but Grace raised her eyebrows and Mike quickly backed down.

"This class is called Life Skills."

"I'm familiar," Grace said.

"None of the skills in this curriculum are necessary for the lives these kids lead. They live in New York City. They don't need to make their own clothes and dry potpourri. I just think it's a waste."

"Okay, first of all," Grace said, "these children come to school every day from a mixed bag of homes so different you wouldn't believe it if I showed you. Dalwhynnie lives in a loft on Duane Street. Her parents are famous archi-tects. Jahia is the daughter of a single mother in the Bronx, a poet. Talia hasn't seen her mother since last summer. So you don't know which of these children needs to make her own dinner tonight. Second of all, you are a substitute teacher. Just this morning you were ready to gnaw your arm off to get out of here, so I'm a little curious as to why you now think that you need to reinvent the wheel."

Mike had forgotten how little she liked being repri-manded by her employer.

"But if you think you know what would benefit these children . . . write a new curriculum. Have it on my desk by noon next Friday and I'll consider it."

Grace turned to go.

"Next Friday will be my last day," Mike said, just to re-affirm the fact. "You're looking to hire somebody."

"I am," Grace said, "I am." She left before any argument could be made.

In a cab heading toward Gotham Comedy Club later that evening, Mike told herself that it didn't matter if everything was out of joint. Her working life, her personal life. She told herself there was nothing wrong with what she was doing, as she pulled a baseball cap down over her forehead to hide her face. She repeated over and over in her head that she wasn't keeping a dirty secret, that it just wasn't anybody's business. She tried not to be ashamed that she needed a fix.

"I completely understood that she needed to talk about the fact that I wasn't satisfying her in bed," Jay said to a crowded house. "I just wish she could have talked about it with me instead of my friends."

While the audience laughed, Mike sank farther down in her booth and tried to tell herself there was nothing strange about any of it.

A DIAMOND IS FOREVER

*G*unther was wasting himself.

On a job he wouldn't leave because it meant leaving a woman upon whom he was also wasting himself. He didn't want to be the zookeeper any more than she wanted to be the rhino, but he didn't want to be nothing either. So he told himself he didn't mind that sometimes she gave herself to other men for no reason and acted like it didn't matter. He told his friends he wasn't looking for anything more and one by one they got tired of hearing it and weren't around so much. They'd all taken Jay's side anyway.

He decided that being lonely made him more like her, and he hoped that someday their world would shrink small enough that she'd notice it was just the two of them and she'd like it that way. And even while he hoped he didn't believe it.

Because Gunther knew far better than Mike how to treasure a human being, he felt the growing distance between them more quickly than she did. He had sensed a change in her over the passing months, watched her suffering from a total lack of equilibrium, and he knew that an unbalanced Mike was an unpredictable Mike. He knew there was another man somewhere in the background, and he said as little about it as possible. He knew she wouldn't listen if he told her that everything about Brian Bentley was poisonous. He just had to hope that she'd come to her senses. Quietly, privately, he hoped and kept silent. Until the night he caught her in a lie. Lying from a woman who didn't care enough what other people thought to bother was alarming.

He was leaving a press dinner in Chelsea, Australian higher-ups in for the week, as Mike was fleeing from another clandestine comedy flagellation along 23rd Street. He pinched himself for thinking he'd caught her silhouette under a streetlight. But no, on second look, that was the familiar hurried strut, the lowered head facing into the wind, the long hair flying. When he was certain it was Mike, with some shame he followed her. She kept her hands shoved in her pockets and her chin buried in the collar of her jacket to protect against the chill. He'd walked half a block behind her, from Seventh Avenue all the way to Madison Square Park. But she was too far ahead for him to catch up, and suddenly he felt like a stalker. So he'd picked up the phone to call and tell her he was there.

Mike saw Gunther's name on the caller ID and found herself in the midst of an unexpected panic. She had told him she was exhausted and heading home and couldn't meet him after dinner. She'd promised to be there all night, watching Discovery HD and sleeping off her child-induced exhaustion. If he found out, if he ever found out that she'd been going to see Jay . . . Jay who they never ever talked about. Jay who they'd both lost for different reasons.

Holding the phone to his ear, anticipating the way the sound of her voice would make the corners of his mouth curl up, Gunther watched Mike pull her cell phone from her pocket. He stopped walking when she did, hanging back as she looked at her ringing phone. He watched her stare at the display that said his name.

And then he watched her silence the phone and shove it back inside her jacket. From half a block away, it didn't look like she'd deliberated much.

When Mike started walking again, Gunther didn't follow. He didn't leave a message. He stood and watched until she disappeared into the subway.

He tried to tell himself it didn't matter, but that didn't sound true. He was beginning to lose faith.

Mike didn't think about Gunther, she felt him. She felt his huge, strong presence like a net stretched beneath all her mistakes. She felt him like the needle on a compass. But she thought about herself.

She was thinking, as she stayed late at school the following afternoon, that she had gone an entire day without thinking about advertising. She had been so focused on putting together a new curriculum for Grace, and on the odd sort of pride she'd begun to feel, knowing that for at least eleven miniature people, she was still impressive and intimidating. She knew that if Grace accepted her proposal, it meant signing on for several more weeks of teaching, but all of a sudden it sounded better than pounding the pavement, which had pounded back.

She walked all the way from Tribeca to the Meatpacking District turning her new lessons over in her head, planning to spill all of it in Gunther's lap, knowing it would make him smile and make him proud.

Life Skills didn't have to be a useless period for tatting

and darning. What if instead she could teach them all those vital tidbits that no one had ever taught her? The things she'd had to learn the hard way. She could genuinely equip them for life, spare them some of the knocks she'd taken, and perhaps fit the world with eleven more sensible, palatable women that she herself wouldn't mind being in a room with. This could be a good thing.

She would teach them basic self-defense, and maybe even Krav Maga, the Israeli art of unarmed combat. (Grace would never go for this, but she could try.) She would create a lesson on popular scams—how to spot them and how not to fall prey. She'd show them the basic principles of debate so they could learn to make points without being petulant and manipulative. She'd teach them about body image and eating disorders and why they should never base anything on the way that they looked. She'd show them, as a concession to Derek Luce, who was in traction, how to sustain themselves on food items purchased only at bodegas. She would assign them to do one thing that scared them so they could learn never to be afraid of anything.

In a million ways that surprised her, Mike found that she cared.

Gunther was waiting for her at the Drunk, hunched over his Guinness with his chin in one hand. He was a manly man from the manliest country in the world and now he was angry. He was angry with himself for giving her so much and demanding nothing in return.

She hopped onto the adjacent barstool. "Hey, sugar, you lookin' for a date?" she teased.

Keeping a secret from your best friend is easy, but it'll cost you. The pink elephant in the room always eats and drinks a lot more than you expected, not to mention the dry-cleaning bills.

Gunther looked up slowly and smiled ruefully. Jimmy placed a Jameson in front of Mike without being asked, and instinctively moved away. Jimmy did small talk, and this already felt like big talk.

"Thanks," Mike said to Jimmy's receding back. Turning to Gunther, she said, "That's not a happy face, mate. What groundbreaking journalistic pup did they kill today?"

He shook his head. "Nothing much today. Slow one."

She got nervous when he was quiet. Even his frustration was usually articulate.

"You need to quit," she said, and he sighed. "I'm serious," she pressed on, "this is bullshit!"

"Look—" he started, but hyped up on her own ideas, Mike didn't give him a chance to continue.

"You have two choices, buddy, you can be their errand boy and spend your days doing meaningless work you can't be proud of, or you can get off your ass and find another job."

"I know that," he said quietly, and Mike regretted pushing so hard.

More gently, she insisted, "You just have to choose." She was surprised that she'd made him angry, and he was very definitely angry. Mike suddenly felt as if she should apologize for something. "So...as the bartender said to the horse..."

Gunther frowned. "I saw you last night," he said simply.

Mike's stomach rose into her throat. "What?" She attempted to sound unconcerned.

"You were on 23rd Street." He felt a very great fear that she might not tolerate this, and he resented the voice inside him that was already preparing to take it all back.

"Oh," she said. "Yeah, I was." Immediately, Mike was

spinning. If he knew, if he had seen her coming out of Gotham . . . she couldn't face him knowing this.

They said nothing. Gunther promised himself that Mike would be the first to speak, but he weakened in the silence. "I don't know what to do with the lying, Mikey."

She bristled. "It was just a change of plans, big guy."

He tried, desperately tried, not to say what he was about to say. "If you're seeing Bentley, just tell me."

"What?" Mike asked, leaping at the possibility that this might have nothing to do with Gotham.

"You're a grown-up. You don't have to lie to me about it." He let her feel the edge in his voice.

"I wouldn't," she said. "I'm not." Because she knew that he meant "seeing" Bentley in the adulterous, shameful, humiliating sense, and not "seeing" in the perfectly aboveboard, nonsexual yet still subversive way in which she was actually doing it.

Gunther looked at her hard, searching her face for something, knowing he wasn't likely to find anything comforting there. "Okay," he finally said, and returned to his beer.

"Oh, Jesus." Mike sighed. Sometimes it was just too much, being responsible to someone like this. That he could know things from just looking at her that she would so much rather have kept in the dark made her want to wriggle underground. That he knew so much and was still there, that she couldn't comprehend.

"It's not what you think."

Gunther didn't look up.

"Yes, I've seen him. I've seen him a few times." As she spoke it dawned on her that fessing up to one crime was the perfect cover for the other, more odious, and frankly creepy sin she'd been committing.

Gunther nodded, still without looking at her.

"I met him for a drink last night. Sometimes he calls me and he tells me he has a lead and I go and sit and listen and it's always bullshit. And that's all that happens."

Which was true. Mostly. And now he looked at her again and Mike was unable to sort the relief at her secret being safe from the relief of earning this look.

Had he not already been living for so long with the feeling that she would never truly belong to him, that he was hanging on for a privileged period that would end as soon as she found someone strong enough to overpower her intense resistance, Gunther might have found the courage to tell her everything. He'd seen her choosing to shove him out of sight and now he couldn't even say it out loud. After a certain point he would just be prostrating himself before her, laying his huge body on the ground at her feet and he knew she would only step over him and keep walking. He wanted to scream and still he said nothing.

"I didn't tell you because I didn't want you to think there was something going on," she said, "because I knew you would. And look, you do."

"Yeah, wonder why that is."

Mike paused, surprised to find she had less rope than usual.

"Hey," she said. "I'm managing, okay? I'm not curled up in the fetal position in a cardboard box somewhere."

He could have laid it all out for her then, told her she was a disaster, reminded her of where she'd be if it wasn't for him . . . but he hated himself for even thinking it.

"So why don't you give me just an ounce of credit for being able to take care of myself?" she snapped.

Gunther began to laugh quietly. Sometimes there was nothing else to do with her.

"What?" Mike asked, relieved again.

"I'm picturing you in a cardboard box." He laughed harder.

Mike was shocked at the immensity of the relief she felt that for some reason he was no longer angry. "Well, since you're already in hysterics, here's another one for ya. I'm designing a new curriculum for the sixth-grade Life Skills class at March Academy."

Gunther wiped his eyes and pulled it together. "*You* are?"

"Why does everyone find it so hard to believe that I might actually not suck at this?"

"I don't find it hard to believe," he assured her. "I'm not nearly surprised. I'm just surprised you like it."

"I didn't say I like it. But if I can come up with a solid month of lesson plans, whatever I want, and the principal likes them, I can keep Gerry off my back and bring in some cash until something comes up. I can walk away whenever I want."

Gunther wanted to say he was proud of her, but he just smiled instead.

"This is great, right?" She didn't want to need his approval, but somehow she did.

"This is more than great," he agreed. "At least one of us has found a satisfying new career."

"Don't ever call it a career," she said. "And you don't need one, you've got a job, remember?"

"Is that what I've got? Seems more like a life sentence."

Mike said, "Tell me."

"Ah, one of my pals just e-mailed me. He filed a story back home on this Afghani bloke who's written four books but never been able to publish any under the Taliban. Now he's having his first novel out in Australia. And you know what I filed today? Celebrities without underwear. That's the news I report. I feel like I'm gonna be struck by lightning just for calling it news."

"It's the machine. It's not you."

"But I'm part of it! I'm just this useless cog. Four years ago this seemed like a great opportunity, live in New York, etcetera. Now I'm an old man at thirty-two."

"So why stay?"

He winced. No job, no New York. Back to Australia with its sunshine and coastlines and no Mike.

Mike didn't know what to say, so she raised her glass. "Sometimes the dingoes eat your baby," she said.

"Sometimes an air conditioner falls on your mother," he said. They drank.

"Do something for me," she said.

"What's that?"

"I want to do a unit with the girls on the news. How to watch it, how to know what you're watching, how to look at the source, see the bias, understand the business of it. Will you come and talk to my class?"

"About celebrities' underwear?"

"About the important stuff. The good, the bad, the ugly."

"Celebrities' underwear." He smiled.

"I'm serious," she said. "Will you?"

"For you, Mikey," he said and drained his glass, "anything."

Again, Mike felt something that made her squirm, because she understood that he meant it.

Two hours later, she arrived home expecting to find a darkened apartment. Her father spent more and more evenings packing up Deja's place these days, which was just fine with Mike. She liked to change into boxers and a

T-shirt and wander around the apartment in the evenings, picking through the vegetarian leftovers of Gerry's latest culinary experiment and watching his enormous television. Caroline grinned at her spiritedly from the mantel, but Mike never looked back. Her mother had long been another piece of furniture.

But as she turned the key in the lock this evening, Mike heard a woman's laughter and strains of Miles Davis coming from the living room. So they were at home tonight. It was strange enough that her father had a girlfriend, that he had gone from being a sullen, frustrated bachelor to someone who buys flowers just for the hell of it. That he had sleepovers, that they cuddled on the couch in front of the fireplace and drank pinot grigio and completed Sudoku puzzles together made Mike feel as if she were the stranger here, not Deja.

She tiptoed to the front hall closet and turned the handle slowly. She took special care to hang her jacket without making the hangers clang together. She slipped her boots off and carried them down the hall to her bedroom, carefully avoiding the creaking floorboard outside the kitchen, and had almost gained her bedroom door when they heard her.

"Mike?" her father called.

"So close," she muttered to herself. "Hey," she answered.

"Hey, come in here a sec," he hollered.

She thought, rightly enough, as she made her way to the living room, that no one should have to put on a happy face in their own home after eleven PM.

"Hey," she said again, leaning in the living room doorway.

"How's it going, kiddo?" her father asked.

"Just peachy." Mike tried to dial down the sarcasm, with little result.

She took in the blazing fire and the open champagne bottle on the table. Her father seemed tipsy, standing with a poker in his hand and grinning. Deja had swiveled to face Mike over the back of the couch, clutching a champagne glass.

"Hi, Mike!" Deja said brightly.

"Hi, Deja." Mike offered a half wave. Would it ever stop being strange that this woman was here?

"I hear things are going well at school!" Deja said, still smiling.

"Um, yeah. They're . . . going," Mike said.

"That's wonderful. Grace is really pleased."

Her father stared at each woman as she talked, as if he were making hand puppets play tennis.

"Great," Mike said, nodding, a smile plastered to her face. "Excellent." She was less than thrilled to know that Grace had been reporting in, though not terribly surprised. She wondered if Deja knew about the illegal field trip.

Mike looked at her father standing by the fireplace, in hopes that he would dismiss her for the evening and return to whatever ripe canoodling he had just put on pause.

"Okay, well," he said, as if suddenly getting down to business, "I—we," he corrected himself, "we have news."

Caroline smiled over Gerry's shoulder at her daughter, and for some reason Mike noticed her mother in this moment, noticed her grinning from her silver frame as if to say, "You can't be all that surprised."

"Mike . . ." Her father was puffed with pride and resembled a barrel-chested game bird, a quail perhaps. "I have asked Deja to be my wife and she has accepted." He laughed from sheer exuberance.

Mike knew enough to raise her eyebrows and part her lips in something she figured would approximate delighted surprise. Deja's eyes sparkled as she rose from the sofa.

"We're engaged! Touchdown, huh?" Her father grinned.

Mike knew she had to make sounds, but for some reason nothing came out. Her father's face began to twitch from holding the grin for so long.

Deja saw that Mike was frozen and said, "We probably seem too old for a word like 'engaged.'"

Mike formed words. "Congratulations," she said, with very little voice. She cleared her throat. "Congratulations," she tried again. She felt as if she were standing in someone else's home, which she realized she was. This was no longer her father's place. It was *theirs* now. The less than dutiful daughter was supposed to participate in this scene to earn her keep.

"I'm surprised too!" Deja said, and Mike understood that her father's fiancée was trying to rescue her.

"I am surprised," Mike said. Her father still looked as if he expected more. "And . . . it's great! It's so surprising and just . . . great! Terrific! It's great."

Her father laughed a great big two-syllable football coach laugh and crossed the room to give his daughter a hug.

"We're just gonna do this thing," he said. "No long engagement. No pomp and circumstance."

"Great," Mike said again.

"And save the twenty-second, that's Sunday night," Deja requested. "We're going to throw a little something together at my daughter-in-law's restaurant," Deja said.

"To celebrate!" Gerry barked. "You gotta see this rock."

On command, Deja sheepishly held up her left hand and from several feet away Mike was met with the majesty of a very large diamond.

"It's yellow," she observed.

"It's synthetic," Deja said.

"We're very much opposed to the politics and practices of the natural diamond industry," Gerry said, parroting his wife-to-be. And then her father pulled Mike by the hand toward Deja and Mike understood that she was supposed to embrace the woman who was to be her new stepmother.

But Deja reached out her ringless right hand to Mike, who took it gratefully. They shook warmly, as if agreeing to disagree, and Deja placed her left hand over Mike's right. But she didn't try for a hug.

Over Deja's shoulder, Caroline smiled and said, "How 'bout that?"

As soon as she possibly could, Mike slipped back to her room. She pulled out her phone and threw herself on the bed. Please answer, she thought. Please, please, please.

"You missed me already?" Gunther said when he picked up.

"Help, they're getting married," she whispered.

"Already?"

"Already."

"What do you need?" he asked. "You want me to have her taken out? Say the word, it's done. I know people."

Mike smiled up at the ceiling. "No, *you* like her."

"Not that much."

"Kill me," she groaned.

"Anything for you," he said.

BECAUSE I'M WORTH IT

On the Friday afternoon that marked the close of her second week at March, Mike wrapped up an improvised lesson on subway etiquette. She had made it all up as she went along this week, taking care to make sure that all classes took place in the classroom. Now she arranged the plastic chairs and taped off an area on the floor to approximate a New York City subway car, and led a game called, "What's Wrong With This Asshole?" At first, the students questioned her vocabulary.

"I don't think you're supposed to curse," Fenice said gently.

"Asshole is not a curse. It's an accurately descriptive term for half the people who live in this town," Mike assured her.

Each of the girls would take a turn as the "asshole," entering the subway car and engaging in an offensive behavior. The first to guess the offense got one point, and the "asshole" got two for coming up with something nobody guessed. Some were more obvious—the bag on the seat, hugging the pole (Mike had to be the pole), eating a chicken wing—and others were more subtle. Mike was impressed with Talia's quiet, insidious humming, which earned her two points.

After class, Mike took a determined stroll to Grace's office with her new curriculum in a folder under her arm. Grace's door was closed and Mike heard shouting inside.

She could just make out a male voice that quietly answered each of Grace's accusatory shouts. Figuring that the purchasing department must have stepped out of line again, Mike slid the folder under Grace's door. Before she could exit the outer office, the inner door flew open.

"Interesting delivery method," Grace said, waving the folder at Mike.

"You sounded busy."

"I'm always busy," Grace reminded her.

"Are we done?" A worn-looking man stepped from behind the door.

"For the moment. Next week, Peter. I need something fresh and I need it next week. Or you and I are going to have a serious problem."

"Don't talk to me like I'm one of your kids," Peter whined sharply as he pushed past Mike. "Excuse me," he said and left without another word.

"If you're here to collect for the bridal shower, I haven't gotten that far," Grace said wearily.

"What? No," Mike said in horror, "I don't . . . I haven't . . . are we supposed to do that?"

"Deja is my best friend in the world," Grace said. "I am supposed to do that. You are supposed to sit on the sidelines and look sour like a good evil stepchild. You can study my friend Peter there for pointers."

"Who is that guy? The gym teacher?" Mike asked.

"I wish," Grace said, tossing Mike's proposal on her desk and running her hands wearily through her hair. "That was my marketing director. I swear, these people couldn't sell a raft to a drowning millionaire."

"I'm confused," Mike said. "What is it they're supposed to be selling?"

"Schools," Grace said. "They're supposed to be selling schools." She sat heavily in her desk chair and put her head in her hands. "Why didn't I go to law school like my daddy told me to?"

"I don't get it," Mike said.

"March Schools is a not-for-profit corporation," Grace said. "We partner with municipal school boards and we're funded by the state, by tax monies, and by private and institutional donors."

"With you so far."

"But we're a private company, meaning we're not bound by all the same rules and regulations that public schools face."

"Which is why you can hire a teacher who hasn't seen the inside of a classroom in a decade."

"I prefer to think of it as exposing the minds of curious young women to a strong, competent professional who has a great deal to offer them." She fingered the proposal sitting on the desk. "And I trust that is exactly what I'm gonna get."

"Sure," Mike said, sounding unconvincing even to herself. "So you're having trouble marketing to city school boards?"

"Privately governed education scares people. There were enough excited, forward-thinking parents in Lower

Manhattan to get us off the ground here, no problem, but it's not so easy everywhere."

"Hmm, guess not. So tell me something, what sells it for you?"

Grace sighed. "Damned if I know."

"No, seriously," Mike pressed. "Why do you care? You could have a much easier job somewhere else, being a lawyer, right? So what is it for you?"

"For me?" Grace pursed her lips and took a long look around the mess that surrounded her desk. "You probably went to private school."

"Horace Mann," Mike affirmed.

"I didn't. I didn't have a school full of teachers trying to get me into college. What I did have was a family that valued education, even if they couldn't afford to send me to the best schools. Our girls don't pay to be here, even the ones whose parents could afford private school. We test them in, but once they're here they can learn as individuals, they're not segregated by class, they can grow to be women without limits. They can have the education every parent would provide if they could."

"Wow. Maybe you should make that speech to your marketing staff."

"You think I haven't tried?"

Mike laughed.

"What's funny?" Grace asked.

"I was just thinking about my last job. Making a roll of toilet paper seem inspiring should be harder than selling superior education."

Grace sighed again. "Maybe you should make *that* speech to my marketing department. Or maybe I should just become the world's oldest law student."

"Good to have a backup." Mike smiled.

"You miss it?" Grace asked.

"Mm." Mike nodded reflexively, and then paused. "I miss being the best," she said sheepishly.

"Hmph." Grace nodded.

Mike shook her head. "Have a good weekend." She turned to go, but paused in the doorway. "You won't be disappointed," she said, nodding toward the folder.

"You better hope not." Grace grinned and leaned back in her chair.

As Mike made her way down the hallway toward the front door, Cheryl-of-the-scarves floated out of a classroom, with a long cylinder of cloth slung over her shoulder. Spare scarves, Mike assumed.

"Hey, there's our newest teacher!" Cheryl crowed.

"And there's the human tapestry!" Mike returned, before she could stop herself.

"Hmm?" Cheryl questioned, still smiling.

"Nothing, sorry," Mike said.

They pushed through the front doors of March Academy and out onto the Tribeca street.

"So tell me," Cheryl asked excitedly, "how was your second week?"

"Ah . . . interesting," Mike said. "It was interesting."

"It gets easier," Cheryl said. "I used to be a classroom teacher. I've never been so exhausted in my life."

"Well, it's only temporary for me, so . . ."

"You know, if you need any pointers, just ask me," Cheryl offered. "Derek Luce is a really good friend of mine so I know tons about his curriculum."

Mike didn't mention that Derek Luce's curriculum was breathing its last even as they spoke.

"Great, thanks," she said.

"You know, I'd be more than happy to come in and do a little guest spot for you. I always come in a couple times a semester for Derek. I do makeup and skin care lessons, it's so much fun and the girls just love it! Don't tell anyone, but the students voted my eyebrow-tweezing class the best of the year."

Mike looked at her. "When did they vote?"

Cheryl just stared back. "Well, I don't know but that's what they told me." She smiled.

"Okay, well, I'll keep it in mind," Mike said.

"Terrific." Cheryl smiled some more.

"Well, anyway..."

"So our Deja is marrying your dad, huh?"

Mike had less than no desire to discuss any aspect of her personal life with Cheryl. "Um, yeah."

"Deja's great. She's like my second mom."

Of course, Mike thought, someone like Cheryl would require two.

"Yeah, so, have a great weekend." Mike attempted to move away.

"Hey, wait a sec, what are you doing now?" Cheryl asked.

Mike scrolled through a list of answers in her head that might spare her whatever Cheryl was about to suggest, but she didn't get the chance to answer.

"Because I'm heading to yoga if you want to come."

Well, this was an easy one to refuse. "I'm not a yoga person," Mike explained.

"Oh, you've done it? I didn't think you'd tried and I can usually tell with people. You don't seem like you'd have done it."

"Well, no..." Mike said. "I just know I'm not."

"Well, silly, how do you know unless you've tried?" Cheryl asked brightly.

"Because there's no winner in yoga," Mike said, certain that this would end the conversation and send Cheryl flying off to contort with more like-minded folk.

"Ohhh..." Cheryl drew out the sound and nodded sagely. "I get it. Okay. Have a good weekend." She gave Mike a pat on the back and turned to walk in the other direction.

Aware that she was being baited, but stunned by the pluck of this airy-fairy sprite, Mike couldn't help but take up the gauntlet. "Wait, wait a minute, what do you get?"

"Hmm?" Cheryl turned, innocent as a kitten.

"You said you 'get it,' so what do you get?" Mike demanded.

"Well, usually when people don't want to try yoga it's because they're afraid they won't be any good at it and they don't want to humiliate themselves."

"What are you, some kind of yoga missionary?" Mike asked, still shocked at being spoken to in this manner.

"I've just been doing it for a while and this isn't the first time I've had this conversation," Cheryl answered sweetly. "It's okay, tough guy! Yoga's really hard. I completely understand."

"Let me get this straight." Mike took a step closer. "You're *daring* me to take a yoga class with you?"

"Open level"—Cheryl stepped in too—"so you won't be the only beginner."

Mike looked down at Cheryl, who was several inches shorter, and contemplated why exactly she was allowing herself to be taken in this manner.

"You're on," Mike said. "I'll go home and change. What time is the class?"

"It's in half an hour," Cheryl answered. "You can wear some of my stuff. The studio's only a few stops away."

So it was that Mike entered her first yoga class wearing a

purple tank top and a pair of flowered bike shorts. As soon as she'd seen the bike shorts she was aware of having miscalculated badly. She was in Cheryl's world now, a foreign universe centered around patchouli and compassion.

As instructed, she left her clothing in the women's locker room. She followed Cheryl into a spacious room with wood floors and an orange ceiling from which colorful paper lanterns dangled. Late afternoon sunlight streamed in through a wall of enormous windows.

"I rented you a mat," Cheryl announced, unfurling a blue rubber rectangle for Mike and one for herself. The room began to fill with "yogis and yoginis" as Cheryl called them, only one or two of whom resembled the uptight, manicured fashionistas Mike was expecting. They stretched and flexed and warmed themselves while Mike sat on her mat with her arms crossed and wished to be elsewhere. She used to run, she remembered, right after college she'd been obsessed for a time with long runs around Central Park that left her muscles screaming and her brain empty. She liked the feeling of losing herself in motion, of the blurring scenery and the sheer force she could create. But running had been left by the wayside along with most everything else when work had picked up. She hadn't run since she'd begun working with Brian, who was exercise enough.

"Are you nervous?" Cheryl smiled in anticipation.

"I'm nervous about these shorts," Mike muttered. She wasn't nervous. She just wanted it to be over.

"I think you'll be surprised," Cheryl said.

Fair guess, Mike thought. Lately she'd been nothing but surprised. She was surprised every morning when she woke up in her father's house and heard a woman's voice in the kitchen. She was surprised to confront eleven preadolescents each afternoon. She was surprised to find herself skulking around comedy clubs and lying to Gunther and stunned at how ashamed it made her feel.

She began to have a thought about Gunther and, rather than allow it to take shape in her brain, focused on a middle-aged man across the room who she thought she recognized from a series of Molly Ringwald movies in the '80s. Apparently everyone really did do yoga.

Mike had expected a twittering Barbie doll to instruct the class, but the teacher who appeared was easily six feet tall and reminded Mike of the beautiful spear-carrying Amazons who always greeted Wonder Woman when she returned to Paradise Island. Certain she wouldn't break a sweat, Mike was heaving and dripping within twenty minutes. Cheryl glided through each series of poses with her forehead smooth and her features serene. Mike kept leading with the wrong leg and had to be reminded twice that her eyes and lips wouldn't help her to hold a pose. She felt dizzy in Downward Dog and thought her hip would dislocate in Pigeon. Her Tree looked like it was caught in a storm.

"Falling out of the pose is a wonderful opportunity to watch where our minds go when things don't go as we'd planned," the teacher offered. "Do you immediately begin to judge yourself? Do you get frustrated and wish you weren't here?"

All the time, Mike thought. Her balancing abilities were virtually nil; she seemed to topple every time she lifted one foot. But the strength poses pleased her. Her Chaturanga was "gorgeous" according to the teacher and even Cheryl seemed impressed.

"It was years before I could do that," she whispered, as Mike seemed to hang effortlessly halfway down a push-up.

Mike moved into Upward Dog and pretended not to hear.

Her limbs felt like taffy as she lay in Shavasana. Corpse Pose. Mike was pleased at the thought that somebody in India several thousand years ago had a strong sense of irony.

"Will you ever come back?" Cheryl asked, as Mike returned her sweaty gear in the locker room.

She was expected to say no, she understood that.

"Absolutely," she answered defiantly. She was going to have to defeat this yoga thing.

AUSTRALIAN FOR BEER

The sun was down when Mike and Cheryl emerged onto the crowded Friday night sidewalks below Union Square.

"So...thanks," Mike said grudgingly.

"You're welcome!" Cheryl ran a gloved hand through her blonde curls. "I'm glad you liked it!"

Even after two muscle-shredding hours she was still perky.

"I guess I'll see you Monday," Mike said.

"Big plans tonight?" Cheryl, Mike was noticing, had an interesting knack for thwarting a speedy exit.

"Um...just meeting a friend."

"I hate going out on Fridays. Too crowded, too much craziness."

"Okay," Mike said, relieved, "well, I've gotta get across town, so I'll see you Monday."

"Yeah, and actually my cat gets really antsy if I'm gone for too long."

"Sure," Mike said and tried to step away.

"Don't worry about washing these, it's no trouble," Cheryl said and waved the plastic bag of Mike's sweaty borrowed yoga clothes in the air.

Mike sighed. "Do you want to come out for a drink, Cheryl?"

"Oh, really? Well, sure, I guess I could! It's just a cat, right?"

Mike just nodded and began to walk. Cheryl followed and struggled to keep up. By the time they reached the Drunk, Gunther was fighting for Mike's seat at the bar. Throngs of exhausted TGIFers clogged the front room, attempting to make one-night conquests and sloshing beer onto the floor in the enthusiastic retelling of workplace exploits. Gunther raised his glass when he saw Mike push through the crowd by the front door. She left Cheryl to fend for herself and shoved through the herd to claim the whiskey waiting for her on the bar top.

"D'you just go for a run?" Gunther asked, noticing her sweaty hair.

"No," she said, "and I've got company. In advance, I'm sorry."

Cheryl reached the bar just in time to miss this last. "Oh, gosh," she panted, "is it crazy in here or what? Have you ever been here before?"

Mike took a deep breath. "Nope, first time," she said. "Cheryl, Gunther Stuart. Cheryl teaches at March."

"Ace! Pleased to meet you, Cheryl." Gunther extended a huge paw and Mike reluctantly noticed, as Cheryl accepted it, that her usually animated expression had grown impossibly more so.

"Get you a drink?" Gunther offered.

"Chardonnay?" Cheryl asked hopefully.

"Think you'll do better with a beer here," Gunther recommended.

Cheryl giggled. "Whatever you think!"

Mike knocked back a significant gulp of her whiskey. Gunther ordered Cheryl's drink.

"He's your boyfriend?" Cheryl whispered.

"What?" Mike snarled. "No." She thought she heard a tiny "good" escape Cheryl's lips, but as Gunther turned to hand her the beer, a slick twentysomething jockeying for bar position jostled Cheryl, causing her to pitch forward. Mike threw out a stiff-arm to keep her from barreling into the beverage.

"Hey, watch it, mate!" Gunther advised the kid, who muttered an insincere apology. "Here." Gunther offered Cheryl his more sheltered stool at the bar. "I've been sitting all day."

Cheryl eagerly hoisted herself up next to him. Mike ordered another drink.

"So, what've you two ladies been doing to amuse yourselves today?"

"We just went to yoga!" Cheryl chirped brightly, sipping her beer and staring reverently up at Gunther, who nearly sprayed her with a mouthful of Guinness.

"Sorry," he choked, "you?" He looked at Mike, terribly amused. "You did yoga?"

"Hard to believe," Mike admitted.

"Well, I'll be stuffed," he said, grinning. "D'you give her cash?" he asked.

Cheryl giggled. "She was good," she said, "really good for someone who's so stiff."

Mike glared at Cheryl but said nothing.

"Do you practice?" Cheryl turned to Gunther.

"Me?" He laughed and Mike snorted. "No, if I throw my leg behind my head I'll never see it again."

Cheryl giggled again and Mike regretted more vehemently having brought her along.

"So what do you do?" Cheryl asked Gunther and mooned up into his face while he explained.

Mike wanted to share with Cheryl the fact that Gunther was just this nice to everyone, that she shouldn't read anything into it. The accent always did it. She'd seen the dreamy look before from strange women who ended up standing next to him in a bar and suddenly thought they might win a chance to live out all their Outback fantasies. Gunther never bit.

It was getting painfully crowded and the three-wheeled conversation was evolving into a shouting match. Mike was getting antsy. With Cheryl monopolizing Gunther there was no one to deflect all the drunken male attention from her. They kept brushing up against her as they ordered their drinks, and more than one attempt was made to engage her in conversation. "Go away," she said more than once, to ambitious suitors who were so surprised that they obeyed.

"Hey," she finally called out to Gunther, "you wanna throw some darts? I can't take much more of this."

"Sure," he shouted back. "I'll go find Jimmy," he volunteered and disengaged himself from Cheryl to go rent the darts.

Cheryl whirled on her stool to face Mike.

"Tell me that he's single," Cheryl demanded.

"What?" She stalled rather than answer.

"You said there's nothing between you, right? Because obviously if you're going for it, I would never try to get in your way. I would never do that to a friend."

I'm not your friend, Mike wanted to say.

"But it doesn't seem like there's anything between you," Cheryl continued.

"He's my best friend," Mike said, which was the only true thing she could think of.

"Excellent," Cheryl said. "Every time he talks it's like Mel Gibson!!"

Gunther waved a handful of darts over the heads of the crowd and beckoned Mike toward the back of the bar.

"Come on," Mike muttered, and perhaps she shoved Cheryl off her barstool a little harder than was necessary.

Mike's game was off. Her scoring was slow and somehow Gunther was managing to keep up a constant stream of conversation with Cheryl while tossing rings around Mike. She tried to throw a 16 and nearly brained a schnockered law associate in the head. She couldn't seem to hit a bull's-eye and Gunther already had two.

"You're rubbish tonight," he teased Mike, poking her in the ribs as he handed off the darts.

"Apparently," Mike said.

"So how long have you been in New York?" Cheryl pressed. Mike had barely said a word since Cheryl had begun her romantic assault, edged out of every silent moment by the persistent third-degree seduction act.

Mike made a 17. Gunther made his second 15. Mike missed again.

She was relieved to be distracted when her cell began to vibrate in the back pocket of her jeans. She flicked it open to read a text message that said, "Where r u?" This was Brian's routine initial sally. It meant he was in the city for the night.

"The mongrel?" Gunther read over her shoulder as he stood at the line for another throw.

"You are so good at that!" Cheryl squawked as he soundly hit 19.

"Tell him to rack off," Gunther muttered as he scored

his winning point. "Tab's on you tonight." He grinned at Mike and gathered the darts to return to Jimmy.

Cheryl began to clap.

Mike punched "Heading home. Call you tomorrow," into the phone. As she hit SEND, she overheard Cheryl asking Gunther, "Do you want to maybe get out of here and go somewhere quieter?"

Mike pretended not to hear. That blonde pretzel had some nerve. She was like a heat-seeking missile, not wasting a moment since she'd come through the door. Mike was sure Cheryl was aware that she was taking advantage of Gunther's good manners. This was why Mike herself never bothered to greet unwelcome advances with kindness.

She pretended not to notice Gunther looking to her for an answer. She pretended to care about the little cartoon envelope soaring in loop-de-loops on the screen of her phone.

"Mikey?" Gunther asked. "What d'you say? Hit another spot?"

She looked at him. Though she took secret satisfaction in the fact that he was refusing to catch Cheryl's pass, Mike was annoyed that he'd let it get so far. She looked at Cheryl biting her bottom lip behind him. He could dig himself out of this one. If he was going to shoot Cheryl down he could do it without Mike's help. And if he wasn't . . . she didn't want to know. She lied.

"Brian's in the neighborhood," Mike said. "I told him to come meet me."

Gunther swallowed and looked her in the face for a moment that Cheryl mercifully couldn't see. All she had to say was "don't go." Just that. And she would rather throw a bone to that aging prig than to him.

"He's coming here?" he asked. "Here," in this case meaning, "our place."

"That's okay, we can go. Just us." Cheryl pinched Gunther's sleeve and didn't wait for Mike to answer.

He looked at Mike once more. "I don't want to leave you here," he said.

"Go," she told him. "Really, go."

She couldn't, he thought, have been plainer.

Mike felt as if she were standing behind herself while she watched him helping Cheryl on with her coat. Gunther turned to look at her again, and she knew this was her last chance to stop what was about to happen from happening.

"We've got your dad's thing Sunday, yeah?" he asked.

"Mmm-hmm," Mike answered, because suddenly she couldn't speak.

"See you Monday!" Cheryl smiled broadly, though Mike knew she couldn't get out the door fast enough.

"Mikey—" he began.

"Have fun." She looked him directly in the eyes, aborting any further discussion. Gunther opened his mouth to say something that never came out.

"You too," he said instead, but it sounded strange, like a snippet from someone else's conversation.

Something cold and heavy that had been swirling around her for weeks was now settling into the pit of Mike's stomach, something she knew she was feeding. Some very small but insistent part of her wanted to fly after them, to grab Gunther's arm and keep him from leaving, because in some way she knew this was an important exit, but she willed her feet to stay firmly planted. She stood by the dart board without moving and deserved every minute of watching them walk out.

GOOD TO
THE LAST DROP

Saturday was purgatory. Three times she went back to sleep, finally giving the digital clock on the nightstand an angry shove so the red LED faced the wall. She wanted to sleep the day away. She wanted to sleep until she could wake up and not remember last night. This was why she used to drink heavily. There was no point in remembering so much in the morning.

She lay in bed staring at the ceiling, knowing it was after noon. She wasn't tired anymore. She listened to the sounds of car horns and screeching brakes floating up from 86th Street. She imagined Cheryl, blonde curls bobbling along, crossing Fifth Avenue and catching an extraneous scarf on a loose manhole cover as a careening taxi approached. Cheryl, her helpless pink mouth forming the desperate words "Who will feed my cat?!"

Mike never claimed to be a nice person.

Besides, knowing Cheryl she'd be rescued by one of the

five remaining mounted police in New York City. Wasn't that what always happened to damsels? Someone showed up to get them out of a jam because they damned well weren't capable of doing it themselves.

Mike wondered if Cheryl's cat found her irritating. She probably mistook its natural stretching for kitty yoga.

She turned over and growled into her pillow. She tried to stop imagining Cheryl's stupid cat playing with one of Gunther's enormous shoes. It would just be the perfect capper to a thus far perfect year for those two to start dating. For her one sanctuary, the one place she could be completely herself to disintegrate into utter shit. They wouldn't be able to meet at the Drunk anymore, no, because she already knew that Cheryl thought it was dirty and too crowded, and Cheryl was exactly the kind of woman who would want to be around all the time.

Mike was never like that. Jay could have gone off and done whatever the hell he wanted. They had had their own lives. Of course, according to Jay, she had had her own life and he had been locked away like Cinderella to languish from lack of attention. Mike rubbed her eyes and tried to come up with a single thought, any thought, that didn't make her feel worse.

Her stomach rumbling, she finally rolled out of bed. The apartment was quiet, she noted with gratitude. The last thing she needed was to walk in on another of her father's romantic living dioramas.

Still in her boxers and T-shirt, Mike heard the clink of teacup against saucer too late to turn and walk out of the kitchen. Deja sat at the breakfast table with the *New York Times* strewn in front of her, sipping a cup of peppermint tea, her glasses halfway down her nose.

"Mike!" She smiled brightly. "I didn't know you were home."

"I didn't know you were . . . here . . . either."

Deja laid the "Arts & Leisure" section on the table. "I guess we've never really put an official date on my moving in here. It's been sort of gradual. I hope that doesn't make you uncomfortable."

Even if it did, Mike thought, there was absolutely nothing to be done about it.

"Is there coffee?" Mike asked.

"Oh, you know, I think your dad left some. He's at the hospital. You could probably just heat it up."

Mike flipped the switch on the coffeemaker. She opened the refrigerator door and relished the brief opportunity to stay out of view. She surveyed the constantly evolving contents of her father's fridge. *Their* fridge. She held up a package of suspicious-looking brown paste.

"What the hell is Natto?" she asked.

"Oh, it's Japanese fermented soy beans." Deja smiled. "It's an acquired taste that most people never acquire. I'm one of the few."

Mike shoved the Natto into the back of the refrigerator. She pretended not to realize she was being sullen as she silently defrosted a bagel in the toaster oven.

"So," Deja tried again, as Mike had known she would, "do something fun last night?"

"Not really." Mike stared through the little glass door at the dissolving ice crystals on her bagel. "Do you know a Cheryl Hershey from March?"

"Sure, yeah. She's a reading specialist. I mentored her a little when she first started."

Terrific, Mike thought, so Dr. and Mrs. Edwards could double-date with Mr. and Mrs. Crocodile Dundee.

"I'm looking forward to having you meet my girls tomorrow night. Kristen and Kimmy. Kristen's the older. And her little boy, Zachary. He's three."

"Mmm," Mike said.

"Kristen's partner, Emily, will be there. She manages the restaurant. And Kimmy's fiancé. His name is David."

"Great," Mike said.

"And my brother and his wife. Remy and Sara. And—" She stopped and Mike turned to look at her.

"God, listen to me," Deja said. "Just rattling off the catalog as if these names will mean anything to you. People you've never met." She paused. "I'm sorry, Mike. I get a little nervous around you."

Mike didn't know what to say. "Sorry," she tried. "Do I—"

"No! No, it's nothing that you do." Deja made an awkward flapping gesture with a hand that landed over her heart in a kind of apology. "You know, it's just...you're Gerry's only child, and here I am showing up so late in the game. Ready-set-stepmom." Deja saw Mike's expression and quickly corrected herself. "Not that I think of myself as your stepmother. You're much too old for that. You know, your dad didn't want us to meet for the longest time. And at first I was afraid that it was me." She paused again. "Well, there are so many things about your dad that I'm only beginning to understand—"

Good thing you're marrying him then, Mike wanted to say and then felt guilty. The bell on the toaster oven pinged and she hastily turned to retrieve her bagel.

"There's apricot jelly from Greenmarket in the door," Deja said.

"Thanks." Mike didn't like apricot especially. She used it

anyway. She poured a cup of the reheated coffee into a mug.

"Here." Deja began to sweep sections of the paper into one corner of the table. "Sit."

Mike had planned to let the plasma TV be her breakfast company, but she didn't know how to say so without being rude, which was a much harder thing to commit to one-on-one. She sat.

"You're right between my girls. Kimmy is twenty-nine and Kristen is thirty-four."

"You met my father online," Mike said, having intended it to be a question and realizing it hadn't come out that way.

"Oh, isn't that the most embarrassing?" Deja said, smiling. She had a way of seeming so at home in her own skin, even as she said she was mortified. "Kimmy pushed me into it. *She* would never have done it, mind you, but I guess Charlie's been doing it. That's my ex-husband. I didn't date much before your dad."

"Why not?"

"Well, I don't know about you, but...have you seen what's out there? I just...why bother? It's not as if I was miserable. I'd been married for twenty-three years and that was nice until it wasn't. I wasn't up nights worrying about being alone."

Mike crunched at her bagel. The apricot wasn't so bad.

"Did he ever show you his personal ad?" Deja asked.

Mike took a swallow of coffee. "I didn't even know he was doing it."

"Do you know what got me? His ad was all about how he'd just read Joan Didion's *The Year of Magical Thinking*. Isn't it silly, that's why I responded."

"I haven't read it." She didn't know her father read Joan Didion.

"Oh, you should," Deja said. "You should, it's wonderful."

"Mm," Mike said. She didn't want to talk about Joan Didion, really, or her father falling in love with this woman with whom she would now have to share a kitchen table for as long as she stayed here. There was nothing wrong with Deja. Nothing wrong to a degree that was irritating at best.

Mike casually picked up the "Sports" section, hoping to call a brief moratorium on getting-acquainted chatter. The corner of a large, flat book appeared and something about that corner looked familiar. Mike shoved "Dining Out" aside to uncover the rest of the book.

It was *Edwina the Mongoose*. Book Four. *Adventure at Dinosaur Canyon,* in which Edwina gets lost on a class trip and uses dinosaur bones to mark her path and find her way to safety. Mike couldn't remember the last time she'd seen Edwina the Mongoose.

"Where did you get this?" she asked quietly.

"Aren't they just wonderful?" Deja smiled and passed a hand reverently over the cover. "I found a stack in the living room, in the cabinet with your dad's old records."

Mike stared at the book, which seemed so odd, just sitting there on the table, drenched in early afternoon sunlight.

"Do you know, I used to read them to my girls? Gosh, they loved these books. But we never had this one, I don't know why."

Adventure at Dinosaur Canyon. Based on the true story of a little girl who wandered away from her parents at Sesame Place during the two seconds they turned around to find small bills to buy her an ice cream. Mike was too little then to remember. They had split up immediately to find her, Caroline searching the cargo nets and the ball pits while Gerry frantically begged the park attendants to make an announcement. Michaela had turned up right where she'd disappeared, crabby because she'd had to wait so long for her ice cream. And her parents had tearfully sworn never to turn their backs again for a second. Mike had never heard this story.

"They were such wonderful books," Deja said again. "The picture on the back, it's the same one in the living room."

"What?" Mike asked, suddenly feeling dazed.

"It's the picture of your mother that's on the mantel."

"Okay," Mike said.

"It's the only one I've seen," Deja said. "Where are the others?"

"I don't know," Mike said.

Deja frowned. Mike was afraid there would be another question, but there wasn't.

"He still has trouble talking about her," she said.

"She was a long time ago," Mike said.

Deja moved to put her hand over Mike's, but stopped, even before Mike moved it to pick up her mug.

"I just want you to know," Deja said quietly, "that I know you had a mother. And I've never quite bought into the idea that people who are thrust into a family together are 'friends.' But whatever it is we're going to be…"

Deja saw the look of horror on Mike's face that involuntarily appeared during too intimate moments. She almost laughed.

"I'm trying to say that whatever we're going to be will be just fine with me," she finished.

Mike's face began to relax. "Okay," she said. Still feeling

as though she were caught in the headlights, she paused and tried to think of something else to say. "I don't know what you want," came out.

Surprised, Deja moved to speak, but Mike cut her off.

"For an engagement present. I don't know what to get you."

"Oh," Deja said, and the corners of her mouth turned up slightly. "It doesn't matter. We just want you to be there."

"People never really mean it when they say that," Mike said. She certainly wasn't going to make that mistake again.

"Okay," Deja said. "Then how about a vase?"

"I hope you're not offended that I haven't bought it yet," Mike said, still clutching her mug.

"Honestly," Deja said, "it's the least of my worries."

CELEBRATE THE
MOMENTS OF YOUR LIFE

On Sunday, Mike combed her hair and put on a dress. She trotted downtown in uncomfortable heels to meet Gunther in the housewares department at Bloomingdale's. They had confirmed this meeting by text message. Just the perfunctory details. They hadn't spoken since Friday night.

She was perusing a case of French porcelain candle-holders when he found her.

"'Scuse me, miss," he said, "I'm looking for my friend. Tall, butch, tough as nails. Have you seen her around?"

So he was uncomfortable too. Good, she thought.

"She's tied up, screaming somewhere. You'll have to make do with me," she replied. "Nice suit."

"Thank you. You're even taller," he said, acknowledging the punishing heels.

"You're still gargantuan," she said.

"Fair enough. What exactly are we buying for the happy couple?"

"She wants a vase." Mike picked up a heavy glass

cylinder and put it down when she saw that it cost nearly $300. "Jesus, for that?" she said.

A plucky sales associate approached them. "Are you two looking to register?" she asked, smiling as though her face had been split from ear to ear.

"For what?" Mike asked. Gunther laughed.

"I see," the woman said, without moving her forehead. "Can I help you with anything?"

"I doubt it," Mike said, staring her down.

The woman looked reasonably unnerved. "I'll just be over here..." She pointed vaguely in a direction that amounted to "far away" and scuttled off.

Gunther chuckled again and Mike couldn't help but join him.

"A vase, you say?" he asked.

"That's what she said."

"What kind of vase?"

"How the hell do I know what kind of vase? There are kinds of vases?"

He smiled as they wandered through the china section. "Don't bother," he said kindly, as another sales associate approached. "You're shit at this, aren't you?" he said. "Porcelain, glass, metal?"

"Why do you know so much about vases?" she asked.

"Everyone I know's been married in the last three years. You pick up a few things."

"Explain to me why so many people want to get married."

"To you? Not sure I could. You of the 'love is for suckers' camp."

"Oh, it's not? My father's wife went out for groceries and never came back. If I were him I wouldn't want to risk it again."

"Sometimes to love is to risk losing someone, in the most grotesque and unimaginable way possible, and to know that it's worth it."

She looked at him. He looked at a vase.

"Well, wasn't that just a bowl of soup for my soul," she said. "Please find a vase."

They talked about vases, or rather, Gunther talked Mike through a series of vases until she could be convinced enough of their various distinctions to choose one in blue glass. They had it wrapped and Gunther carried it out into the street. Mike began to fill out the card in the taxi on the way to the restaurant.

"Leave room for me," he said.

"For you to what?" she asked.

"Well, it's from both of us. I'd like to fit a word or two in there."

"On this card?" Mike bristled.

"We only got one," he said.

She handed it over grudgingly. They still hadn't talked about Cheryl. Mike looked out at the traffic on Lexington Avenue and listened to the sound of Gunther's pen scratching out a message that would probably make her look cold and uncreative.

"Don't write anything too nice," she said.

He snorted in amusement.

"How strange is this?" he asked, slipping the finished card underneath the white ribbon on the package. "Dr. E's engagement party."

"It continues to sound weird, no matter how many times you say it," Mike said.

"You lucked out though. Could've been some hideous hag. Deja's good folk, no?"

"She's fine," Mike said.

They rode in silence. Mike refused to be the one to bring it up. And if he wasn't telling her anything…there had to be a lousy reason for that.

"Late night, Friday?" he asked, shifting slightly in the seat. He couldn't help himself.

"Not terribly," she said. "You?"

There. She hadn't brought it up.

"Your friend got rotten after another drink. So I took her home."

The cold lump in Mike's gut seemed to inhale.

"Cheap date," she said.

"I s'pose," he said. "Mongrel take you out on the town?"

She'd almost forgotten her little fib, and had, in fact, forgotten to call Brian on Saturday as she'd promised. She didn't answer.

"Where did you guys go?" she asked instead.

"I didn't catch the name," he said. "Some place with purple drinks. So dark you couldn't see your own feet."

He wasn't volunteering anything, then neither would she. Except sitting there and saying nothing gave the lump in her stomach room to grow. She tried to think of something to say about the stupid vase.

"Grace is supposed to approve my curriculum tomorrow. If she says yes, will you still come in to talk to the kids next Wednesday?" she asked.

"Yep," he said, still looking out the window.

By the time the cab pulled up in front of the restaurant, it seemed like there was hardly any air inside.

They followed a hostess, who was wearing nearly the same black dress as Mike, across a crowded dining room. They were pointed down a steep set of stairs to the private party room and told to enjoy themselves. Mike could think of few things less likely than that.

As they started down, still saying nothing, a small tow-headed boy appeared below them and attempted a furious scramble up the steps. He made it about halfway. Gunther, walking in front of Mike and still holding the present, crouched and put up a protective hand.

"Whoa there, little fella. You sure you're supposed to be leaving so soon?"

"No," a voice called from the bottom of the stairs. A thin, athletic-looking woman in her early thirties appeared after it. She had Deja's pert bob, only in brown instead of gray. "He's supposed to be sitting quietly with a piece of cake," the woman said, "and his devoted aunt is supposed to be watching him." The woman advanced up the first few steps until she could pluck the little boy from his perch, where he stared up at Gunther as if he were a theme park ride.

"I'd say you have to be Gunther," the woman said, shifting the little boy onto one hip and extending her other hand. "My mother has lots of nice things to say about you."

Gunther reached down and shook it. "Kristen, I'm guessing," he said.

Terrific, Mike thought. He'd already learned their names.

They all made their way down the stairs to more even ground.

"This little monster is Zachary. And you must be Mike." Kristen deposited Zachary on the tile floor and he immediately disappeared under a tablecloth. "Proud descendant of Edwina the Mongoose."

"I . . . hi," Mike said and shook Kristen's hand.

"Sorry, that makes you kind of a celebrity in our family. We loved those books."

"So I hear," Mike managed.

"There's a present table over there in the corner, if you want to deposit the vase. I'm assuming it's a vase. What the hell else do you get for two people in their late sixties? They'll probably be able to open a flower shop by the end of the night."

Gunther shot Mike a triumphant glance over his shoulder as he ferried the vase to the table.

"Oh, my God, I don't know where Zach is!" a petite brunette cried as she came skidding across the room toward Kristen and Mike.

"He's under the table," Kristen said casually. "My sister, Kimmy."

"Holy shit, that scared me," Kimmy said. "Hi, sorry. I shouldn't drink and babysit at the same time."

"Or at all," Kristen drawled, raising her own glass to her lips.

"Shut up," Kimmy said. "It's so nice to meet you. You have to be Mike."

"Then I guess I will be." Mike smiled at her new family, who seemed far too comfortable to care whether Mike was smiling or not.

The room buzzed with people Mike had never seen before. She couldn't even see her father or Deja.

"We've got a huge family," Kimmy warned, catching Mike taking inventory. "Mostly on my dad's side. He's the one in the corner with the blue and pink tie." She pointed.

"Your dad came to your mother's engagement party?" Mike asked.

"They're like two peas in a pod," Kristen said, refilling her champagne glass from a bottle on the table that hid Zachary. "Although I don't think Dad likes my mom nearly as much as he likes *your* dad. They're playing golf again next weekend. How bizarro-world is that? Zach, we don't eat shoelaces."

At Kristen's feet, Zach gingerly removed a man's shoestring from his mouth.

"I don't know if you have any experience with three-year-olds," Kristen said, hoisting him onto her hip again, "but my advice is, don't. Not if you like sanity."

"Oh, but he's so worth it, aren't you, you widdle, biddle, kiddle-pie, aren't you?" Kimmy dissolved into some form of pidgin baby talk.

"Kimberly, if I have to tell you one more time about the cutespeak—" Kristen chided her.

"Okay, I need a second opinion on this." Kimmy turned to Mike. "Do you think that a child will necessarily turn out brain damaged if people speak in baby talk to him?"

"Welcome to the family." Kristen offered Mike a wry smile behind her sister's back and raised her eyebrows.

"Ah...I don't know about brain damaged," Mike answered carefully, "but maybe...annoying?"

"Oh, crap, she's already on your side," Kimmy joked with Kristen.

"Look at us, Kims, we've got her in the middle of a family argument and she doesn't even have a drink yet. We usually drink before we fight," Kristen explained to Mike, putting an arm around her and steering her toward the bar. "What do you drink? Wine? Beer?"

"Whiskey?" Mike tried.

"Oh, you are on my side." Kristen gave Mike a sly look. "Thank God. You could have been a twit. You never know, you know what I mean?"

"Yeah." Mike smiled.

"There she is!" Mike's father suddenly appeared behind them. "That's a dress! I haven't seen you in a dress since the junior prom! You look"—he coughed—"lovely."

Mike peered into her father's face looking for signs of someone she recognized. She couldn't remember him ever using the word "lovely" before.

"Deja's training me," he explained. "But you do. And this handsome guy—" He indicated Gunther, who had resurfaced, free of the notorious vase.

"Congratulations, Dr. E!" Gunther beamed and shook his hand heartily.

"Tell me, son," Gerry asked, leaning in happily, "what do you think of my *sheila*? Enh?"

"Pretty spiffy, I'd say," Gunther answered.

"This guy," Gerry said to the gathered girls, "I love this guy!" Gerry mimed punching Gunther hard in the stomach and Gunther mimed having the wind knocked out of him.

"I gotta go mingle, kids! What a great night, huh?" He disappeared happily into the crowd.

"Does he always do that to you?" Kimmy asked Gunther when Mike's father had gone.

"On a pretty regular basis," Gunther said.

"Then you get the next drink."

Trays of hors d'oeuvres circulated and Mike tried to eat while she shook the hands of thirty or forty of Deja's friends and relatives. Kristen and Kimmy stuck close by, and Mike was grateful to find that they protected her from the endless talkers who asked too many prying questions. Maybe it wouldn't be so bad to have stepsisters who could manage to keep her drink refilled at all times. Her father was already a member of a whole new family, and he didn't seem the least bit anxious about any of it. Mike was just pleased she could tolerate them. They could have been an army of Cheryls.

Deja found the three girls next to the dessert buffet late in the evening.

"Well." She smiled. "If I hadn't burdened you two with being so short I could almost say you all look like sisters."

It was true, Mike towered over them.

"Can I just say," Kimmy began, "thank God you're not marrying somebody with a shitty daughter."

Kristen and Mike burst out laughing.

"Kimberly!" Deja scolded. "She gets the mouth from her father. Could we try to project some semblance of decency?" But she was smiling.

"A little fuckin' late for that," Kristen added and burst into laughter all over again.

"Okay." Kristen's partner, Emily, picked Zachary up. "Let's give Mommy and Aunt Kimmy some time to be silly by themselves!" She smiled and carried him away to a corner where there was, ostensibly, less cursing.

"Mike," Deja said, and put her hands on Mike's shoulders. "Come here." She beckoned with one finger.

Slightly uncomfortable, Mike bent toward Deja, who planted a kiss on her forehead. "I know," Deja told a stunned Mike, "that it's totally inappropriate, but I've had a lot of champagne."

Kristen and Kimmy disintegrated into another fit of laughter.

"It's okay," Mike said. Drunkenness she could almost always forgive.

"Good. Because I want to ask you girls something." Deja turned and called to Mike's father. "Gerry! Gerry, come here. They're all together."

Gerry hightailed it across the room, which looked

strange as Mike had always thought of him as someone who gave orders rather than obey them.

"Now?" he asked Deja.

"Now." She nodded.

"Girls," Deja began, and Mike realized that she had been inducted into an elite group. She was now, inescapably, one of "the girls." "We've been talking, and we know that joining two families together at this point in our lives is a bit of a tricky proposition, but we'd really like to do something to demonstrate to everyone just how much our kids mean to us."

"Cut to it, Mother," Kristen said.

"Well, there's been some debate," Gerry cut in.

"But we've settled on something," Deja prompted him.

They were speaking as a unit, Mike noticed. Practically finishing each other's sentences.

"We're getting old standing here," Kristen reminded them.

"We'd like you three to be our wedding party," Deja said.

Mike felt the hors d'oeuvres rising in her throat. Wedding party? Wedding party meant peach dresses and penis cake pans and getting the bride drunk at a strip club. It meant manicures and luncheons and eighteen other things that made her shake. It meant that Gerry and Deja's wedding was no longer something nice that they were doing for themselves, but something inconvenient and uncomfortable that they were doing to their loved ones. Wedding party was bad news.

"There's a catch though," Gerry said. "Kid," he addressed Mike, "I want you to be my best man."

"Oh, this is too cute!" Kimmy cried before Mike had a chance to respond.

"We thought you girls could stand up for me and Mike for her dad," Deja explained. "But you can wear a dress," she assured Mike.

"I pushed for a tux," Gerry added. "I lost."

"Ger." Deja poked him in the ribs and subtly nodded in Mike's direction.

"Yeah." Gerry coughed. "Ah, what I'm trying to say is..." He was sweating. Mike dreaded whatever embarrassing confidence was about to be rolled out in front of these strangers she was now supposed to call family. "I'm trying to say that you're my best friend, kid, and there's nobody I would rather have stand up for me than you. There." He coughed again. Deja beamed at him proudly and Mike knew that her father had been coached.

She was supposed to say something. Something moving and gracious. She looked around for Gunther who could feed her lines Cyrano-style and make it all easier for everyone. But he was all the way across the room trading tips with her father's fantasy football league.

What was a daughter supposed to do as best man? Weren't best men supposed to take you to Vegas and get you drunk and possibly arrested? Mike and her father didn't do this sort of thing. Mostly they just went to a deli and ate knockwurst. What kind of best man was she supposed to be?

Kristen and Kimmy had put their drinks down and already fallen into a group hug with their mother. Mike and her father were just standing there, looking at each other. There are certain things a person can't say no to, and Mike knew that this was one of those.

If this were a commercial for long-distance phone service, she thought, what would the daughter say? "Dad, I'd be honored," or "Oh, Dad..." with a single tear.

Mike said, "Okay. Sure."

Her father reached out to shake her hand, and suddenly Mike wished they could be just a little more like a regular family.

Gunther watched this from across the room. Mike hadn't sought him out all evening, not since they'd walked in together. For the first time, he wondered why he was there.

I'M LOVIN' IT

Mike was formulating a theory that said the difference between "finding yourself" and being a fuckup was about five years. The twenty-six-year-old who lost his job and moved to Costa Rica was destined to be a surfer. The thirty-one-year-old who fell off the corporate ladder was destined to be a serf. It was wildly unfair of her and probably unrealistic, but being at sea in your twenties can feel so much more forgivable.

Every day that she awoke to stare at the ceiling of an apartment she didn't pay for, and took the subway to a job she didn't want, Mike felt a little less like the self she recognized and a little more like her own worst nightmare. Gone were the days when she would greet catcalls with thoughts of "You wish." Now it was more like, "Who, me?"

She wondered if she looked any different from the outside. It didn't seem to matter at school, where no one cared how she looked. A week after the party, a note from Grace was waiting for Mike in her mailbox in the teachers' lounge. "My office. ASAP."

Though she was slowly acclimating to being summoned to the principal's office, Mike still felt the ghost of an adrenaline surge each time she entered the waiting room. She almost wished she were being hauled in for "unnecessary roughness" on the lacrosse field again. Those were the days.

Grace, who would someday require surgery to have the phone removed from her ear, was barking once again. "I am looking at an e-mail suggesting that my science teachers should be, and I quote, 'perfectly comfortable working without visual materials' for the month it will take to get a case of biology textbooks and wall diagrams. Does that sound reasonable to you? Our children are supposed to be learning human anatomy right now. What are these teachers supposed to do, slice themselves open and point?"

There was a moment of silence during which Grace motioned impatiently for Mike to sit down across from her desk.

"I want you to listen to me carefully, and I will speak slowly to make sure you comprehend. By Friday morning, there will be a human nervous system on display in my eighth-grade biology classroom, and either it will be in a book, or it will be yours. Are we clear?"

She slammed the phone down. "I swear to God, the Dairy Queen fires these people and we hire them."

Mike laughed.

"And you, you damned crazy person—" Grace slapped the folder Mike had submitted down on the desk. "You want to teach little girls what to do in case of an alligator attack."

"Just as a bonus lesson."

"No alligators."

"Fair enough."

"Where the hell did you come from?" Grace stared down at Mike as if she had just washed ashore.

"Advertising," Mike explained.

"I still don't know why I like you," Grace said.

"You may not be the only one."

"Give me one good reason, right now, why the mad ravings in this folder are gonna be more useful to these girls than cooking and cleaning and whatever the hell else Derek Luce was teaching them."

"One?" Mike sputtered. "How about a hundred—"

"*One.*"

"Okay," Mike said, raising her chin defiantly as she spoke. "Because I would rather live in a world where eleven more women knew how to take care of themselves, than have a thousand more who knew how to make pies and knit scarves. There's a reason they used to call that class Home Economics, and I don't care how many self-interested Tribeca parents think it's cute to have a twelve-year-old doing decoupage."

"You don't know what decoupage is."

"And yet I'm thirty-one and still standing," Mike insisted. "More or less."

Grace pursed her lips in a way that Mike found slightly intimidating and knew was probably terrifying if you were a twelve-year-old who had cut Social Studies.

"Two and a half months," Grace said.

"Sorry?"

"You want to teach them your way, I need a two-and-a-half-month commitment. That's how long Derek Luce is going to spend recovering from his fifteen-foot fall into a pile of fruit."

"That's a long time," Mike said.

"You sit here hemming and hawing and it's gonna be all over."

"I'm looking for other work."

"Not for two and a half months, you're not. Not if you want to work for me. Not if you want to teach eleven little women to take care of themselves."

"Can I think about it?" Mike asked and even as she said it she knew there was nothing to think about. There were no more excuses to make. She had stopped trying and she wasn't sorry.

"If you need to think about it I don't want you here." Grace picked up Mike's folder and held it above the trash can beside her desk. "Going once—"

"Fine," Mike said.

"Fine?"

"I'll do it. Two and a half months. I teach what I want," she said quickly.

Grace looked suspicious for a moment, then she leaned toward Mike across the desk, her fingers tented beneath her. "You get a week's worth of lesson plans to me every Wednesday. I have them back to you by Friday with my notes. *You don't argue with my notes.*"

Mike paused and squinted up at Grace, though sitting in a chair she was nearly as tall as Grace was standing. "You're a little scary," she said.

"Why the hell do you think it says 'Principal' on that door?" Grace smiled, and it was still kind of scary.

Mike was officially employed. And it frightened her to realize she didn't mind.

At least the time she spent preparing her lesson plans was time she couldn't spend wondering why Gunther was suddenly so far away. If she had intended to put some distance between them with the Bentley charade, she had succeeded. He'd been mysteriously busy since the night of the engagement party. Too busy to see her for drinks or a movie. Too busy to watch Discovery HD and eat her father's vegan fajitas. Gunther was never too busy for her.

"I'm working on something," he said.

"A hangover?"

"Just . . . something," he repeated. She wished she hadn't made a joke when she'd finally gotten him to pick up the phone.

"Will you still have time to talk to my kids?" She expected him to point out that she was referring to them in the possessive. She knew he wouldn't back out of a commitment. He was far superior to her in that regard.

"I'll be there," he told her.

"I've made a tape for them. Five different news programs covering the same story. I got Fox, CNN, MSNBC, BBC, and ABC. And I'm making a handout that explains who owns each organization. I wish I could get some Al Jazeera footage, but Grace vetoed that as too controversial."

Gunther chuckled softly, but it sounded as if he were busy doing something else while he talked to her.

"So I was thinking you could walk them through it," she continued. "Explain how you investigate a story, how TV news is produced. Where they can go for a different take."

"Sounds good," he murmured, distracted.

"Hey, you doing a crossword over there?"

"Look, I've gotta go. See you next Wednesday at eleven?" He was trying to get away from her again. And she was only half-sure that she knew why.

"Wednesday," she said.

For the next week and a half, Wednesday was all Mike

thought about. Wednesday, and avoiding Cheryl. She fled every time she saw the blonde curls bouncing around a corner. She declined further invitations to yoga and made sure to be out of earshot by the time Cheryl could get out the words, "your Australian friend." She didn't want to know. Didn't want to hear that the reason he didn't have time for her all of a sudden was because the thing he was working on was Cheryl.

She didn't want to wonder how a person who liked her could simultaneously enjoy Cheryl. Maybe she just wasn't amusing him anymore. Maybe he was outgrowing her, as the rest of her life seemed to be doing. Maybe she was going to be left with Brian Bentley and eleven preteens who only bought her act about half the time. Maybe that was all she'd really earned.

When the infamous Wednesday finally arrived, Mike was too jittery to eat breakfast. Half an hour before her class would file in, she caught herself looking in the ladies' room mirror on her way to meet Gunther in front of the school. She had washed her jeans and bothered to brush her teeth after coffee. She felt as if she were preparing for a job interview. And this was Gunther! Silly, ridiculous Gunther, who barely fit through doorways and said "mate" instead of "buddy." Gunther. Her best mate.

As she rounded the corner to head down the front steps toward the security station, she stopped as if she'd hit a wall. Standing below her, waving happily as the huge oak door swung shut behind Gunther, was Cheryl. Her superfluous scarves fluttered in the breeze from the open door and Mike thought of many-armed Shiva, Hindu god of destruction. Blonde, perky Shiva, who was intent on bulldozing her way through Mike's only solid bond with another human being. Sly, manipulative, backstabbing, self-interested, not nearly good enough for him, Shiva. Cherva. Shivyl.

She was too far away to hear what they were saying, but she saw Cheryl throw herself into Gunther's arms for a hug that was immediately returned, if less enthusiastically. So he'd been too busy to talk to her, but he'd had time to let Cheryl know he was coming to school.

This, Mike reminded herself, was why school was a bad place. You could be thirty-one years old and school could still make you feel like a powerless twelve-year-old who was now being suspended for punching Pete Garces, even if you had only done it because you sort of liked him. School sucked. And now she was trapped here for two and a half months. Fucking school.

As he pulled away, Gunther glanced up the stairs and saw her. He looked almost embarrassed that she had seen the hug, which only made her more certain that he had everything to hide. He waved. Mike raised her hand for just a second to acknowledge him.

Cheryl turned and beamed a saccharin smile up the stairs. Mike returned the smile with her mouth closed. If they were expecting her to trot down and wait while Gunther's ID was checked through security, they could shove it. She stood where she was and watched him duck his head as he filed through the metal detector. She waited until the two of them made their way up to where she stood and hoped that Cheryl would trip on one of her many strands of beads and fall down the stairs. She didn't care anymore about being a nice person.

"Look who I found!" Cheryl chirped as they neared Mike.

"Like a haystack in a haystack," Mike said.

"Mikey," Gunther said, because he had trouble breathing while he was looking at her. All Mike noticed was that she only got a one-word greeting.

"I hear somebody is doing a guest lecture today!" Cheryl seemed oblivious to the tension so thick it should have flattened her curls.

"Yup," Mike said. She looked at Gunther and he looked back, but neither of them said anything more.

"Don't be nervous," Cheryl admonished him. "They're pussycats once you win them over."

"Of course, until you win them over, they're piranhas," Mike said, raising her eyebrows in challenge.

"You'll be fine," Cheryl went on. "I bet kids love you."

"Of course they do," Mike agreed wryly. "Everybody loves Gunther."

She wanted to stop. She wanted to stop being such a schmuck and just ask him why he'd been keeping his distance. She wanted to go back in time so she could tell Cheryl to go home to her stupid cat instead of coming out to the Drunk. She wanted everything to be different.

They stood in silence for a second too long, Cheryl looking back and forth between the two of them, having finally picked up that perhaps something was going on here to which she was not privy. "Well, I'm sure it'll be great," she said to no effect whatsoever.

"Shall we get to it then?" Gunther asked.

"Yeah," Mike said and she turned, expecting him to follow her.

"Kiss for good luck," she heard Cheryl say, and looked back just in time to see her clawing her way up Gunther's arm to plant one on his cheek. "See you," she told him.

Not if I see you first, Mike thought.

THE BEST A MAN
CAN GET

So this is your new stomping ground," Gunther said, suddenly aware of how long it had been since he'd been alone with her. Mike trotted quickly ahead of him through the maze of corridors that led to her classroom, trying to keep two steps ahead. It was an old tactic that came from having legs twice as long as everyone else's. Everyone except Gunther.

"Are they really piranhas?" he asked, as they arrived outside the classroom door. She turned to look up into his face and was surprised to see a nervy smile. They were just a bunch of little girls after all, and he was four times their size. The man had reported from Beirut, from Sudan, once upon a time. Surely he wasn't intimidated by a cadre of miniature people who owned Bratz dolls. Then she remembered her own first day and a sudden urge to protect him overtook her.

"Baby piranhas," she said. "You can outswim them."

"I'm sorry I haven't been around," he said.

She felt the same relief that came from that first sip of whiskey washing down her throat. A tiny warmth seemed to fan out through her bones, diminishing for a moment the cold thing that seemed to swell in her stomach every time she felt him moving farther away.

"You've been busy," she said.

"I've got a good excuse," he promised.

She didn't want to think about his excuse right now. His excuse was probably off reading *Where the Red Fern Grows* with a frustrated fifth-grader.

"Come on in," she said. She opened the door to the classroom in time to see the rapid cessation of frantic girly activity. Twenty-two arms and legs quickly returned themselves to the undersides of eleven desks. Headbands and ponytails were adjusted and tightened. Tapping fingers were silenced in a hurry. They were on their best behavior.

"Ladies." Mike signaled to the class.

"Good morning, Mr. Stuart," they chanted in unison. "Thank you for joining us. We hope to make your stay a pleasant one."

"Their idea," Mike assured him. "Sadie's father manages a hotel chain."

"Good morning, ladies." Gunther grinned broadly at their upturned faces. "That was quite something."

They stared at him as if he were a Madame Tussaud's exhibit come to life.

"Call me Gunther," he instructed them.

They gaped on, too much in awe of his sheer size and dialect to call him anything at all.

"Gunther is the New York bureau chief for an Australian wire service," Mike explained. "You wanna tell them what that means?"

"Not as grand as it sounds," he said. "We gather and

distribute news to numerous media outfits in Australia, just as your Associated Press does here. My job is to live in New York City and send back information about stories in this country that might be of interest to Australians back home."

"Excuse me." Dalwhynnie spoke up from the back of the room.

"Ah, yes," Gunther called on her hesitantly.

"Do you play basketball?" Dalwhynnie asked.

Mike stepped forward immediately. "Does that seem like an appropriate question?"

"He's really tall," Dalwhynnie said. "I don't think it's rude. It's not a bad thing."

"If you were asking me to help you with a math problem, and I answered you by talking about ice cream, would you feel like I was listening to you?" Mike challenged her.

"No," Dalwhynnie admitted.

"So it's rude," Sassafrass admonished from the adjacent desk. "Inappropriate."

"Sorry," Dalwhynnie told Gunther sheepishly.

"This goes back to our job interview seminar from Monday, right?" Mike reminded them. "It's important to respond to what the other person is giving you and to hold your own ideas for a more appropriate time. You're showing a prospective employer that you can stay on task."

Gunther looked at her in utter wonder.

"They're learning how to interview," Mike explained.

He nodded, mute.

"Sorry for the interruption," Mike said. "Carry on."

"Right," he said. "So I phone stories in to Sydney. I dictate them over the phone and someone called a copy-taker writes them down in Sydney and sends them out over the wire so they can be printed in various newspapers."

Mike watched carefully as Fenice, Talia, and Jahia all stirred as if to ask a question. She looked on proudly as they stared cautiously at each other before somehow tacitly deciding that Jahia would speak first.

"Excuse me," Jahia began.

"They've learned to speak up in a group without hand-raising," Mike whispered to Gunther. Again he looked at her in quiet shock.

"So what kinds of stories do you cover? Did you write about 9/11?" Jahia asked.

"Ah, no," Gunther said, "I wasn't living here then. If it happened today I would cover it. But mostly it's not . . . big stories. It's mostly smaller, special interest pieces."

"Like the Kyoto Protocols?" Fenice asked.

"Or secret Taliban training camps?" Talia added.

"Well, no . . ." Gunther hesitated. "You see, we have reporters all over the world. So I only cover what happens in the States."

"Like welfare reform and the Social Security crisis," Fenice offered. "My mom works for Primetime."

Gunther hesitated.

"Well, you see, those are important domestic issues in America, but they don't really affect Australians. Any more than Australian tax structures would be of interest to you."

They looked at him blankly.

"Why don't you give us a couple of examples of the stories you filed this week?" Mike encouraged.

"Sure, yeah," he said. "Well, there was a woman from Canberra, that's the capital of Australia, who was arrested in North Dakota."

"For what?" Talia prompted.

"For, ah . . . well, she wasn't wearing enough . . . clothing. In a restaurant."

A rustle of excitement swept across the room.

"And then there was the ongoing Justin Timberlake dating saga."

The rustle continued.

"And Russell Crowe was on the Martha Stewart show making biscotti."

"Oh!" Sadie spoke up. "You're an entertainment correspondent! Like Maria Menounos!"

Mike could see Gunther losing more ground with every question.

"No, no..." he said. "I know it sounds like that. It's just...well, you see, I'm supposed to send back stories of universal interest. And unfortunately those don't tend to be the most...vital...bits of journalism..."

"Puff pieces?" Fenice suggested.

"They're not supposed to be. I mean, I...as a reporter you have to go where the work is. We'd all like to be breaking huge, important stories every day, but that isn't really how things happen. It's not like you see on TV—"

"News is too commercial," Brooklyn said.

"Exactly!" Gunther agreed. His face was red and he looked like he might break a sweat. Mike remembered that first-day feeling, how it seemed as if they were looking right through her. Like their little X-ray eyes could bore through the convincing adult artifice, right down to what was basic and true and wickedly private.

"Maybe we should look at the video," Mike suggested, "and you can talk a little bit about media ownership and how to watch the news."

In all the years she'd been buying him drinks, Gunther had never looked so grateful.

He lectured beautifully on the differences among various news outfits in covering the development of electronic voting machines in the U.S. He explained with precision and insight the influence of forces like Rupert Murdoch in determining reporting angles in various markets. He encouraged them to look into the power structures in news reporting, to take into account the way advertisers' interests were reflected in the finer points of broadcast news language. He fielded every question with ease. It was like watching him come to life again.

Mike suddenly remembered their very first conversation. The same night she'd met Jay. She had gone out drinking to celebrate her latest success at Logan, and Jay had picked her out from across the room, marched over and ordered her a drink. She'd shot him down repeatedly but he wouldn't leave her alone. And Gunther had stood by and watched his friend growing more foolish with more liquor.

"Why do you hang out with this guy?" she'd finally asked him. And Gunther had laughed and said, "I don't, I just can't seem to get rid of him." And Mike had laughed. And while Jay passed in and out of the conversation trying to get Mike's attention, she had watched the Abu Ghraib scandal break on the barroom TV with Gunther. He had just arrived in New York.

"I'm covering the whole country," he'd said.

"Just you?" she'd asked.

"Just me." And he'd grinned with pride and excitement and told her he couldn't wait to get started.

Watching him now, Mike, who didn't like to think about loss, remembered what it would mean for him to quit this job that was draining his energy and his spirit. It would mean thousands of miles.

By the time the class wrapped up, the girls were completely in Gunther's thrall. Mike watched each little girl file past him and shake his hand on the way out of the room, as she'd instructed them ahead of time to do.

When they were alone again, she smiled at him.

"My hero," she said.

But he put his chin in his hand and said, "I don't know how much more of this I can take."

Mike paused, afraid of what was coming next.

"This job is killing me, Mikey."

She swallowed hard, a map of the distance between Sydney and New York etching itself across her brain. "Believe me," she said, "they make everything I do feel tiny. They're just too young to be shattered and disillusioned. Don't let it get to you."

"It's not them," he said. "They're right! My father always used to say, 'If it doesn't make sense to a child, it probably doesn't make sense.' What I do sounds like bullshit when I try to explain it to them, because it is bullshit!"

"Your father also told you stories of a mythological man-eating bush creature," she reasoned.

"Don't joke about the Bunyip."

"I rest my case," she said.

He sighed. "I don't do anything anymore, Mikey. I wake up and sit in front of the TV in my underwear looking for stories. I honestly can't remember the last bit of hard news I filed. There are wars going on all over the world and the only one I report on is among the hosts of *The View*. Apparently that's what people want to read."

"You can't change the game," she said.

"Yeah, but I can quit playing it."

"Tell you what, give me a few hours to wrap up here and I'll meet you and we'll talk about it. There has to be some way to make it better."

He looked sheepish then. "Oh, I, ah ... I can't tonight."

The lump in her stomach woke up.

"It's just I've promised Cheryl I'd join her for sushi."

"You don't like sushi," Mike said.

"I could tell her I'm not feeling up to it."

They stood for a moment and cataloged silently the things they couldn't say.

"No," she finally said. "I should have gotten in line earlier."

This wrongness between them seemed so much bigger in the sudden absence of eleven little girls.

"I figured you probably had plans," he said. "How about tomorrow night?"

She could have been free. She didn't really have to go to the UCB Theatre to watch Jay ripping her to shreds, though that had been the plan. But she wasn't prepared to just fill in the spaces in Gunther's social calendar if he had better things to do. Mike smiled at him, a lying smile that said, "I don't care what you do. Move back to Australia for all I care."

"Tomorrow night's no good. I've got a friend in town."

He knew exactly which friend she meant. His face darkened. He had gotten the message and he'd been right to start cutting his losses.

"Catch up with you later then," he said. "I'll give you a buzz."

Now, Mike thought, they were both lying.

YOUR FLEXIBLE FRIEND

Mike wasn't sleeping well. She felt as if her skin were tightening around her. She began to watch herself in the mirror as she brushed her teeth and she noticed dark circles under her eyes. She stayed up later and later each night, hoping to be so tired that she could fall asleep as her head hit the pillow. It never seemed to work.

Talk in the apartment had lately focused solely on the upcoming wedding. Where they should do it. When they should do it. How and who with. Gerry had sent Mike an e-mail to say she should await bridal shower instructions from Grace. Mike wanted nothing to do with any of it. It had nothing to do with her.

She found her father and Deja sitting at the kitchen table one evening, picking at Thai takeout and making plans.

"We don't want to wait," Gerry said.

"Or we'll be a hundred," Deja added.

"Something soon. Maybe next month. Very small and casual," he said.

"Intimate," Deja clarified.

"Great," Mike said, even though she couldn't remember the last time anything had been great. She sipped a Diet Coke and watched them at the kitchen table. So this is what two parents would have looked like, she thought, and then immediately regretted it.

"About the bachelor party, Mike..." her father said.

"Oh, yeah, listen, I've definitely been thinking about it," she lied. "I just haven't nailed down the details yet."

"Actually, I was sort of thinking you'd let me plan it."

"You want to plan your own bachelor party?" she asked.

"Well, maybe less of a bachelor party and more of a..." He looked to Deja, who smiled her encouragement. "A father-daughter experience."

"You want to go to a game or something?"

"No, I was thinking more...Just let me take care of it, okay? It'll be a surprise."

Though she felt a little guilty, Mike was grateful to say that yes, that would be just fine with her.

"We're having lasagna tomorrow, if you want to invite Gunther over for dinner," Deja suggested.

Mike let loose a small, bitter laugh. "If I could nail him down..." she said.

"What's that mean?" her father asked.

"Gunther's a busy guy," she said. "Got a new girlfriend and all."

"Gunther's seeing someone?" Deja asked.

"Apparently," Mike said. She stared at some invisible crud on the rim of her soda can to avoid seeing the way they were looking at her.

"Is it serious?" her father asked. He looked concerned.

"You're already engaged," she reminded him.

"Yeah, but you're not—"

"Ger," Deja hissed, "ssh." She shook her head in disapproval.

"Oh, Jesus, you have to be kidding," Mike whined.

"Would it be the worst thing in the world?" her father asked.

"Gerry," Deja tried again.

"I'm serious!" He blundered on. "He's sure as hell better than that putz you used to live with!"

"We're not really having this conversation, are we?" Mike said more to herself than to her father.

"That Aussie is good people!" Mike's father barked.

"Mike, did you see our engagement announcement?" Deja waved a newspaper between them, authoritatively diverting them from the minefield.

"Nice," Mike said.

Her father began to speak and Deja mimed a closing mouth with her hand. They sat in silence for a moment and Mike concentrated on the small item that concluded "a second marriage for each."

"At least I don't look like a deer in headlights in this one," Deja said. "My first engagement picture was a disaster. A disaster in the *New York Times*. And of course your mother and father looked just gorgeous in theirs."

Mike stood still while her father shifted uncomfortably in his chair.

"I wouldn't know," Mike said.

"Oh, come on, you never showed it to her?" Deja poked Gerry playfully in the ribs.

No one spoke. Still smiling, Deja looked from Mike to her father and back again.

"Maybe you should go get it," she said gently to Gerry.

"I gotta go see about the grocery delivery," he said brusquely and rose quickly from the table. A guest list

fluttered to the floor in his wake. Mike picked it up and replaced it in front of Deja.

"We don't do pictures much," she said.

"I see," Deja said quietly. "That's a shame."

Mike made as much noise as possible tossing her Coke
can into the recycling bin. "Lesson plans," she said, beating
a hasty exit. She headed for her room and chose not to
think about Deja sitting alone in the kitchen.

Caroline winked from the mantel as Mike passed.

As she lay in bed hours later, with sleep only a distant
possibility, Mike wondered if maybe she'd just grown too
accustomed to living alone. Maybe it was too hard to sleep
with other people around.

The next morning, Mike faced the inquisition. She'd
come to school half an hour later than usual to lower the
odds of running into Cheryl in the hallway. What the hell
was she supposed to say? Hope you're enjoying my best
friend? Don't worry, I'm sure I'll eventually find another
human being I can put up with for more than fifteen minutes at a time? Take care of him for me? This wasn't a Molly
Ringwald movie. It was her stinking failure of a life.

And she was about to discover that twelve-year-old
girls, newly acquainted with the endless fascination of
other people's business, were what would happen if you
combined Barbara Walters with a pit bull. They were
barely in their seats before the questions began.

"Is he your boyfriend?" Sadie asked.

"Who?" Mike stalled.

"Crocodile Hunky," Fenice quipped.

"Don't be someone who says things like that," Mike said.
"Seriously. Never say that again."

"He is sooooo cute," Jahia crooned. "Really, really you
have to tell us if he's your boyfriend."

"He's not," Mike said. "Really, really."

"Why not?" Dalwhynnie asked in wonder. "Does he have stinky breath?"

"No."

"I kissed a boy with stinky breath last summer," she explained.

"That's too bad," Mike said. "But he's just my friend."

"Men and women can't be friends," Fenice announced, rather grandly for someone under five feet tall.

"Where did you hear that?" Mike asked.

"I watched an old movie with my mom called *When Harry Met Sally*. It was on AMC."

"*When Harry Met Sally* was on AMC?"

"Yup."

"God, I'm old," Mike muttered.

"So you're not really friends," Fenice pressed.

"Well, that's crap," Mike said. "Men and women can absolutely be friends. In fact, I'm gonna go ahead and say that men make better friends than women."

They looked mystified.

"It's true," she said. "Do you want to know why?"

"Is he ... you know ... bad at it?" Sassafrass bravely ventured.

"Bad at what?"

"You know ..." Sassafrass looked to Sadie for affirmation. "*It.*"

"Okay, that's enough. Totally inappropriate! Way, way, way out of line, all of you! You don't ask other people about their personal lives when you know absolutely nothing about any of it, okay? You don't make assumptions based on patterns of social behavior that may very well not apply to everyone, and you sure as hell don't try to push two people together just because neither of them has anyone else, because you just end up making them feel miserable and humiliated! Sometimes, people just like to spend time with each other and there's absolutely no attraction involved. And it doesn't matter how well they understand each other or how great the companionship is. Sometimes, a man and a woman can have more fun together than they have with anyone else and it doesn't mean they need to jump into bed and fall in love! Sometimes—"

They stared at her, stupefied, and she knew she'd lost them after "inappropriate."

"Oh, forget it!" Mike snapped. "I'm reinstituting hand-raising."

They groaned as a unit.

"No! Until you show me that you're mature enough not to stick your noses into other people's business, you can raise your hands like little babies."

Shockingly, they showed her very little respect during the lesson on preventive medicine that followed.

When Mike finally escaped the alligator pit that was her classroom that afternoon, she was too discombobulated to remember to avoid the teachers' lounge. She stopped in to pick up her mail and spotted Cheryl, angrily dumping about a cup of sugar into her coffee. It was too late to slip back into the hallway.

"Hi," Cheryl said, but in a tone of voice that suggested, "I hate everything."

"Oh, hey," Mike answered, determined not to stop moving between her trip to the mailbox and her flight back out the door. "I am running so late today. Late, late, late! Well, see ya!"

"Oh," Cheryl said, "where are you rushing off to?"

Trying to produce a destination Cheryl couldn't argue

against, Mike said, "Yoga! Gotta use that second class I paid for! Can't wait to get really . . . contorted."

"Oh, you know they're closed today, sweetie. They're re-painting."

No, come on, Mike thought, how was that freaking possible?

"Oh," she said. "Oh, well . . . shit." She was forced to pause at the door.

"You know your friend Gunther's a really interesting guy," Cheryl said, throwing her spoon into the sink as if it were a dagger.

"Maybe I'll just go for a run," Mike said. From you.

"Reeeally," Cheryl drew the word out, "interesting." She threw her head back and took a giant swig of her coffee as if it were a shot of whiskey in a Western saloon. Unable to maintain her cool as the hot caffeine scalded her throat, Cheryl began to cough and sputter.

"So I'll see you later!" Mike tried to make a break for it.

"I mean, just what the hell is his problem?" Cheryl spat angrily.

"Did you, by any chance, have a drink at lunch?" Mike asked.

"So I had a glass of wine and an antihistamine!" Cheryl squealed. "So sue me! I don't have any kids this afternoon. I'm an adult! I'm a grown-up, lonely, sex-starved woman in the prime of her life!"

Mike knew few things in the world, but she knew drunk when she saw it and this was most certainly it.

"Cheryl," Mike reasoned, "if Grace catches you sloshed on school grounds you're gonna be out of a job."

"So what!" Cheryl moaned. "I'm already alone and miserable. What difference is unemployed going to make?"

"I know you say that now…"

"I say it now and I'll say it then!" Cheryl laughed somewhat crazily to herself.

Mike wished again that she had never entered the room. She knew that if she walked out now, Cheryl wouldn't be able to fend for herself, she would certainly get herself fired.

"Go home, Cheryl. Seriously. You're about to be in a lot of trouble."

"You wanna talk about trouble? Trouble is being thirty-six and knowing that nobody but your cat would care if you disappeared. Trouble is watching yourself develop jowls. Like a bulldog! That's trouble!"

Mike sighed deeply. Cheryl might have irritated her to her very core, but somewhere Mike knew that Cheryl was good. Cheryl was…kind. She helped children to read. She did yoga and was tender with animals. She was…oh, fuck it, she was a person. Mike wanted to walk away, but she couldn't. "Get your coat," she said.

"Where are we going?"

"Just get your coat before I change my mind."

Mike got Cheryl packed up and out onto the sidewalk in three minutes flat.

"Where are we going?" Cheryl asked again.

"We're walking away from school so no one sees you falling into a cab." Mike looked back to make sure no one from March was out on the sidewalk. "And you're going home."

"No!" Cheryl whined. "I don't want to go home. Let's go somewhere. Let's go to that terrible bar you like."

"You don't need another drink, Cheryl."

"I need fun! I need company!"

"Where are all the freaking cabs in this town?" Mike said to no one in particular.

"Oh, hey, let's go get a cookie! There's a coffee shop that has the best black and white cookies!"

"I don't want a cookie," Mike said. She tried to flag down a taxi with its off-duty lights on.

"He turned me down flat," Cheryl said.

Mike lowered her arm. She turned to look at Cheryl, who looked pitiful with her scarves flapping impotently in the breeze.

"Where is this coffee shop?" Mike asked.

"I think he has erectile dysfunction," Cheryl said loudly when they were seated at a table.

"Oh, Jesus," Mike said. "I don't even want to know what you're talking about."

"You're blushing…" Cheryl giggled. "'Cause he's like your brother, right? So you don't wanna think about his hoo-hoo."

Mike was blushing. She felt as if her face would burst into flames. Perhaps she had overestimated how much she actually wanted to know about Cheryl's failure to ensnare Gunther.

"Never say 'hoo-hoo' to me again," Mike told her sternly.

"I don't get it," Cheryl moaned into her own hand.

"You have to move your hand," Mike said. "I have no idea what you're saying."

"I'm attractive, right? Do you think I'm attractive? I mean, I know I'm not *foxy* or *smokin' hot*, but… I'm okay, right? Would you sleep with me?"

"No," Mike said.

"Really?" Cheryl pleaded.

"I think we're getting off track. What happened?" She almost felt guilty for asking.

"Well, we went to dinner. And he paid! And I thought that was a really good sign."

Mike didn't tell her that Gunther always tried to pay.

"And he can have a conversation!" Cheryl continued. "Not so many men can do that, you know? There were no awkward silences. And he asked me about me! No one ever seems to want to know about me."

Mike smiled at the thought of Gunther asking Cheryl about yoga and scarf shopping. Gunther, who could be kind to absolutely anyone.

"We talked for three hours! *Three hours!* Do you know how long it's been since a man wanted to talk to me for three hours?"

Mike could well imagine but pretended she couldn't.

"And then he insisted, I mean insisted, on taking me home. He said it was late and dark and not safe for me to walk alone. I mean, come on. If that's not an invitation into someone's pants, I don't know what is! Not safe? I mean, this is New York!"

Mike hoped the coffee would sober Cheryl up soon, as the other patrons were starting to stare.

"So we get to my door, the door to my apartment, not just the building, and I say, 'Why don't you come in and meet Count Chocula?' That's my cat. And you know what he says?"

"Tell me," Mike said.

"He says he has to be up early. He says he's 'working on something' and he can't afford to be a 'zombie' in the morning."

Mike didn't even try not to be glad that Gunther had used the same excuse with Cheryl that he had with her.

"And he kissed me on the cheek and *thanked me* for a great evening. And then he left! He just left!"

Mike willed her facial muscles out of a smile. "That's terrible," she said.

"I know!" Cheryl cried. "I've gotta tell you, it's been a very long time since I've gotten any. I mean a *very* long time. I just want to sleep with someone. Anyone."

"So sleep with someone," Mike said.

"But it's complicated!"

"No, it's simple. Pick someone out and do it." Someone other than Gunther.

"You can do that? I can't do that. I have to like them. And he's so tall, you know? I was sure he would be—"

"More coffee?" Mike interrupted her and sprang from the table.

"No, I'm good," Cheryl said.

"I'm gonna get more coffee." Mike practically ran back to the counter. She didn't need the details of Cheryl's speculations on Gunther's ... anything. She had heard enough. And what she heard had done something to the cold lump in her gut. She felt as if it were melting.

Though a small part of her felt something resembling guilt, she slipped into the bathroom and sent Gunther a text message.

"Meet me at the Drunk at 7? Plans cancelled. Need to talk to you."

He agreed. The hours between four and seven seemed to drag on forever. Mike was early getting to the Drunk. She walked around the block twice before going inside and claiming her usual seat. She drummed her fingers on the bar and kept looking toward the door.

"You meeting a date?" Jimmy asked as he poured her drink.

"What? No, just Gunther."

"You seem jumpy."

"Long day," she said. Long month. Long year. She looked at herself in the mirror behind the bar. She never used to look in mirrors. These days she had to check in, just to make sure she still recognized whoever was looking back. She did look nervous.

"Mirror, mirror, on the wall," Gunther said behind her. Mike jumped in her seat. She hadn't even seen him come in.

"Jesus, don't sneak up on me like that."

"I didn't know I was capable of sneaking up on anyone." Gunther hopped up next to her and tapped the bar with a wink at Jimmy. "So what's the news?"

"I think that's your department," she said. Her heart was beating too fast. He smiled and tipped his glass back and didn't look at her.

"Nothing fit to print today," he said.

Mike looked at him but he stared down at the bar.

"So tell me why I have to hear from Cheryl that you're not seeing Cheryl?"

She had caught him off guard. He peered at her quizzically. "Who said I *was* seeing Cheryl?"

"Come on, buddy, I don't need a road map," she said. "I can barely get a hold of you all of a sudden. What am I supposed to think?"

"You're not supposed to think anything. You're supposed to know that if there were anything going on, anything worth telling you, I'd be telling you."

"You don't tell me much of anything lately," she said.

He looked into the bottom of his glass and said nothing.

"Where have you been, Gunther?"

He snorted.

"What?" she pressed.

"Where have *I* been?" He was angry again.

"Okay, what exactly did I do?" she asked. "Because this is definitely something worth telling me."

He pursed his lips and shook his head and didn't speak for a long while. "Things are changing, Mikey."

"What things?"

Gunther didn't know how to say to her what he needed to say, that he couldn't go on like this, that he was willing himself to decide that enough was enough. That lately he was loneliest when he was in the same room with her.

Gunther's drink was empty and his glass thunked loudly on the bar when he replaced it, but Jimmy wisely kept his distance.

"I don't know," he said finally. "Just...everything. Everything's different. We don't even see each other anymore."

"Well, *I'm* not the one who's always busy," she said and she could hear her own desperation. It was like they were rolling down a hill and she didn't know how to make it stop. Suddenly she realized she would do anything to make it stop. They sat in silence and Jimmy quietly refilled Gunther's beer and moved away.

"I'm not the only one," she said. "I'm not the only one keeping secrets."

"I told you there was nothing going on with Cheryl. You've known everything, all along."

"Then it isn't Cheryl," she said. "But it's something. You have no time anymore. You won't tell me where you're going, you won't tell me why you can't see me. And I'm the one keeping a secret?"

"Fine!" He turned on her with a ferocity that shocked her. "You want to know where I've been? I've been working! I've been doing an investigative piece on Rupert bloody Murdoch's media holdings. Something I can pitch and sell. Something that might get me the bloody hell out of my sinkhole of a job! Because I'm rotting here! I wake up in the morning and I don't even know why I'm bothering, and I can't take it anymore. I have to do *something*! Anything."

He looked haggard, exhausted. She wanted to reach for his hand, to hold him up somehow, but she didn't know how.

"Why didn't you tell me?"

"Because I was going to surprise you if I sold it. And if I didn't, you didn't need to know." He sank against the barstool next to her.

"If it's important to you, I need to know."

"You don't get to have it both ways, Mikey."

She wished he could just understand without her telling him, because she couldn't imagine saying it out loud. "I don't owe you anything," she said, instinctively trying to push off to a safer distance.

He looked at her in disgust and Mike felt as if a huge rubber band inside her were being stretched to its limit. Maybe the distance wasn't so safe.

"That's right," he said. "You don't owe anything to anyone. Next time Bentley cancels on you, you find a way to amuse yourself." He pushed his glass away and stood up.

"Where are you going?"

"G'night," he said. And just like that, the rubber band snapped. She had to pull him back. She had to do something to keep him from walking away.

"Wait," she said. "Please, just wait a second—"

"I'm done waiting, Mikey," he said.

"It's Jay!"

He stopped and stared at her.

"I haven't been sneaking around to see Brian. It's Jay. And I'm not *seeing* him the way you're thinking. I've been . . . I've been going to see his standup. I've been going to the clubs, sitting in the back, just listening."

"Cripes," he said. "Why?"

"Because I am trying to figure out what the hell he's talking about! I am trying to decipher why my fucking life is falling down around my ears and I don't seem to be able to do anything to stop it! I'm fucking it all up. Everything."

He knew it was all the same, that reaching for him was just her way to keep from falling, but he didn't care.

"Not everything," he said.

"Everything that matters. I'm supposed to be on Madison Avenue. I'm supposed to be living in my own apartment. I am a fucking disaster! Everything I touch turns to shit and I don't know what I'm supposed to fix."

"And you think Jay knows?"

"I think he's making a career out of knowing," she said.

"He doesn't know anything. Have you talked to him?"

"He doesn't even know I've been there," she said. "Please don't disappear on me." She didn't want to talk about Jay. She just wanted to keep him from walking away. She was afraid that there was begging in her face.

"Jay," he repeated, and it sounded strange to Mike to hear Gunther say it. "Okay, I'm here," he said at last, and he sat.

Though she didn't have a great deal of practice, Mike was grateful with all her heart.

"We're a pair, yeah?" he said.

The sudden and burdensome knowledge that she could lose Gunther had unmoored Mike all over again. This sensation of utter vulnerability was so unfamiliar and so unnerving, she felt slightly dizzy.

What happened next happened so fast and was so surreal that Jimmy would be the only one who could say for certain that he'd seen it. As he turned to check on his two best customers, Jimmy nearly dropped a bottle of Midori.

Mike had stood and moved closer to Gunther, and though he made no move to stop her, she was the one who kissed him.

It took a minute for Gunther to register what was happening, and the very shock of it made him pull away, his hand on her shoulder.

"What are you doing?" he asked.

"Do you want me to stop?"

He hesitated. "No."

She kissed him again, because this was real, this was concrete, this was something he couldn't walk away from and she knew it. It felt better than anything she'd done in longer than she could remember, and she didn't want to stop and think about what it meant.

"Let's not do this here," he whispered into the side of her neck.

"My father's on call overnight," she said.

"We'll get a cab," he said, and threw a couple of bills from his wallet onto the bar without looking at them.

Jimmy watched them leave, and thought, as he always did, that any guy going home with Mike must be in for one great night and a world of hurt.

They made it nearly sixteen blocks. Mike wasn't sure when she began to panic, but suddenly in the cab she couldn't concentrate on pawing at the buttons of Gunther's shirt. Everything was so familiar and so foreign at the same time. This scene she'd played so many times, but never with him. Never with anything at stake.

"What's wrong?" he said, taking her two hands in his and backing off.

"Nothing," she said.

The driver stole a glance at them in the rearview mirror.

She kissed him again. She'd started it, she couldn't stop now.

Again, he pulled away. He looked into her face and Mike wanted to cover her eyes like a child. "You don't want to do this," he said, and despite all his kindness it was an accusation.

She swallowed hard. There was no good answer now. She watched him wrestling with the urge to tell her it was alright, but it wasn't alright. And there was no way to go back.

"It's nothing," he said, and his voice was husky and strange. He took his hands from hers and she slid back toward the window on her side.

"There's a subway," he said, "I'll just pop out. Have you got the fare?"

"You don't have to," she said, but of course he did. Of course he did. He asked the driver to stop at the next corner and as the cab pulled up to the sidewalk he turned to her.

"It's fine. It wasn't anything, it doesn't . . ."

She knew what he was trying to tell her—that they hadn't and it didn't, because he wanted to pretend as much as she did that they hadn't just dug up something that couldn't be undiscovered again. But they had. And it did. It was there with them now, and it would stay between them.

"Ring you tomorrow," he said and she nodded. He slipped out and disappeared around the corner.

Mike closed her eyes and let her head fall back against the seat.

"You still want the same place?" the driver asked.

"Same place," she said.

She could feel the vacuum closing in.

WE'RE NUMBER TWO;
WE TRY HARDER

Things were disintegrating. Big things, little things, things Mike used to recognize and rely upon. She wanted to use the few hundred dollars in her bank account to buy a plane ticket to someplace far away. She could wash dishes at a beachfront restaurant on some island. She could be a waitress in Berlin. She could find a place to hide from the avalanche of changes that were threatening to crush her.

She had violated the only inviolable rule and now she would be punished. She couldn't even speak to him.

Discontented and demanding children provide an excellent place to hide. All was not well in the Life Skills class and Mike relished the opportunity to be a teacher instead of a person. A flyer had been distributed school-wide the previous week that announced the approach of that most provocative of academic events: parents' night.

Mike noticed a general sullenness within the class in the days that followed the distribution of the fluorescent pink invitation to trouble.

As she neared the end of class on a Wednesday afternoon shortly after the horrible evening with Gunther, Mike noticed several of the girls looking at each other slyly.

"So, don't forget to bring in your magazines for tomorrow, ladies, when we will continue our discussion of unhealthy standards of beauty in Hollywood. Extra credit if you can find photos of starlets eating."

Stealing a last glance at Fenice for affirmation, Brooklyn spoke up. "Mike?"

"Brooklyn, what's up?" Mike asked.

"Um, well, we were just wondering about something…"

"Spit it out," Mike said.

"Um, okay, so next week…um, so, we just wanna know, like…"

"Brooklyn, you got an A on your public speaking assignment and you didn't lose points for a single 'like.' Let's not backslide. What's your question?"

"What are we gonna do for parents' night?" Brooklyn asked bravely.

"What do you mean?"

"Well, my sister was in Mr. Luce's class last year, and they made sugar-free brownies and crocheted iPod cozies."

"I see," Mike said. "Well, we've changed our approach to Life Skills."

"Right." Fenice picked up where Brooklyn left off. "But what are we gonna have to show them? My mom's gonna want to see something concrete."

"Fenice, we have been learning incredibly valuable information in this class," Mike said, aware that she sounded slightly defensive. "You yourself have switched seven families in your building to green power. Your mother has already seen a lot."

"They're gonna want brownies," Asia piped up. "Or something."

Mike wasn't precisely thrilled herself at the prospect of entertaining as many as twenty-two suspicious, questioning parents who were expecting to see healthy granola and hand-sewn pillows, and would be met instead with... what? The Life Skills class was no longer producing the sort of happy homemaker artifacts that would have appeased concerned mothers and fathers. In fact, for all that Mike knew they were learning, the girls weren't producing much of anything. She could put their nutrition logs on the wall, or show photos of their self-defense training or their trip to visit the admissions office at New York University. But that wasn't going to be enough to get her through what Grace had announced would be a ten-minute presentation with question-and-answer session to follow. On the spot, Mike resorted to one of her fail-safe client appeasement techniques.

"Okay, everybody write down three suggestions for parents' night presentations and bring them in tomorrow. I will take your ideas into consideration and we will come up with something. But I really think they're going to see the logic in everything we've done. I think they'll be pleased."

"No," Dalwhynnie said, shaking her head. "We should definitely at least make them crudités."

They began to pack up their books, chattering amongst themselves about oatmeal cookies and computer-generated art projects and other potential parents' night show-offerings. Mike noticed that Talia was lagging behind the rest, quietly but forcefully shoving her books into the bottom of her bag.

"Talia," Mike said. "Hang back a sec."

Talia shrugged and watched the other girls file out.

"What's going on with you?" Mike asked, sitting on the edge of Derek Luce's desk and crossing her arms.

"What do you mean?" Talia stonewalled.

"Well, you haven't opened your mouth all week, you're in kind of a bad mood, I just want to make sure you're okay."

"I'm fine," Talia snorted. "I just don't need any more stupid homework," she added.

"I asked you to bring in one celebrity magazine, which I know you happen to have in that bag already—yeah, I can see you reading *US Weekly* behind your textbook during class, and by the way, I practically invented that trick."

"Whatever." Talia rolled her eyes.

"Whatever?"

"Yeah, *whatever*."

"If you have a problem with this class, I wish you would tell me about it."

"I just don't need any more work," Talia muttered.

"Talia, you're reading the magazine anyway. You should be glad that it's homework."

"The other thing."

"The other thing...the suggestions for parents' night? Talia, that's gonna take you three seconds! Are you kidding me?"

"I have a lot of homework for other classes!" Talia was growing more agitated.

"Welcome to life," Mike said sternly.

"Why do I have to write up stupid suggestions for stupid parents' night when my parents aren't even gonna be there?!" Talia exploded.

Mike could feel the moment turning into one of those precarious situations that might require a real teacher, someone who was actually good with children.

"Wait a second, why wouldn't they come?" she asked carefully.

"My dad works at night," Talia said.

"Okay, well that sucks." Mike tried to be understanding, as Cheryl was forever suggesting. "But it's one of those sucky things that he probably can't do anything about, right?"

"Whatever," Talia said quietly. "Can I go?"

"Wait a minute, what about your mom?" As soon as she said the words, she regretted them. Grace had said something about Talia's mother. What about your mom? As if she hadn't been asked the same hideous question a million times when she was Talia's age. And there was never a good answer. Sometimes, Mike remembered, she would avoid the topic altogether, change the subject, leave the room, make it someone else's responsibility to explain. "I don't have a mom," she would occasionally offer, as a get-out-of-jail-free card. But sometimes she told the truth and these were the worst times, these were the times when she ended up making somebody else feel better about her own dead mother.

"Never mind, it's none of my business," she said quickly.

"My mom's in Afghanistan," Talia said, and she stared Mike defiantly in the face. "She's in the Army Corps of Engineers."

"Holy shit," Mike said, though she was relatively sure this wasn't the right answer.

"Exactly," Talia said.

Mike stared down at the small face that was capable of expressions it should have been too young to muster. She searched for words that meant she understood, about being abandoned and being afraid and angry, but calm too, because at a very young age you could learn to survive. She wanted to explain about Caroline and Gerry and Deja and Edwina the Mongoose. She wanted to say she was sorry that things were unfair.

But "you must miss her a lot" was what she said.

"You think?" Talia snapped.

Mike was suddenly overcome with wishing that she didn't have to be the adult in this conversation. It was so much less exhausting to feel things out loud the way Talia did.

"Engineers are cool," Mike said.

"I know."

Mike told Talia she didn't have to do the extra homework. But it didn't feel like enough.

She headed home in an odd mood. As she emerged from the 86th Street subway station, her phone began to ring. Bentley. She picked it up anyway.

"Long time no speak," he said.

"What's up?" she asked, making little effort to sound interested.

"I'll be around tonight."

Good for you, she wanted to tell him. He had never seemed less important. "Okay," she said.

"I thought maybe you'd come by for a drink."

"I can't tonight," she said. "I've got too much prep for school."

Silence on the other end. "That's among the worst excuses I've heard," he said finally.

She wondered why he kept trying.

"I've got news," he pressed on in a brighter tone that sounded false. "I'm meeting next week with BPK and they sound awfully interested."

"You're kidding," she stopped walking. Barron, Petrie & Klein. "Who?"

"Dana Petrie. Straight to the top."

Mike closed her eyes and smiled to herself. She laughed quietly.

"Dana always liked you," he said.

"Say hi to her assistant for me."

"Sorry?"

"Lauren. Dana Petrie's assistant. She's a nice girl."

"You'll forgive me if I forget that the moment I hang up," he deadpanned.

"You'll forget it whether I forgive you or not," she said.

"I need to know that you're on board if they make an offer."

"Of course," she said, "I could start in May."

"May is a month and a half away, darling. If they say jump I can't tell them you'll do it in May."

"I made a commitment." She surprised herself, but hearing the words she knew it was right.

"I'm going to pretend you didn't say that," he said. "Why don't you come up here tonight and we'll talk game plan?"

"You don't need a game plan," she said. "Let me know how it goes."

"I'm only in tonight," he said, and there was something of a beg in his tone.

"Enjoy the view," she said and snapped the phone shut.

When she reached the apartment, her father was in the kitchen, stirring a large pot on the stove.

"How was school?" he asked, chuckling. It might have been funnier if their old times had been like this, if he had been home to cook dinner back then or to ask about her day. If he had been there to talk to her then the way he was always trying to do now.

"What's for dinner?"

"Autumn harvest stew with root vegetables. Deja's recipe," he said, and Mike silently mouthed the last two words with him, now a familiar refrain.

"I have to put something together for parents' night." She sighed, dropping her coat over the back of a kitchen chair and pulling a beer from the fridge.

"Parents' night," her father breathed. "I used to love that."

Mike tossed the bottlecap toward the trash can and missed.

"You loved it?" she asked, reaching for the errant cap.

"Sure!" he said. "Seeing what you'd been up to all year. Meeting your teachers, hearing 'em say nice things about you."

"Nice things, huh?"

"Occasionally." He grinned over his shoulder. "Michaela has a very strong personality."

"Ha," she said. "I bet."

"Not like I was surprised," he said.

"They want me to make some kind of presentation."

"Sure," he said. "Show 'em their class projects, let 'em see what the kids have been working on. Parents love that."

Mike regarded her father in his scrubs-cum-apron and wondered what he used to say when people asked where her mother was.

"I've got this one little girl," she said, "her mom's a soldier. Overseas. And like a moron I asked if she missed her."

Her father shrugged. "I'm sure she does," he said.

"Yeah, well she didn't exactly need me to say it."

"You used to miss your mother."

"No, I didn't," Mike scoffed.

Her father turned to look at her, the wooden spoon in one hand suspended over the other.

"Of course you did," he said, and his voice was odd and hoarse.

"Dad, how would I have missed her? I didn't even know her."

He stared at her silently and Mike wasn't remotely sure what she was supposed to say.

"You missed her," he said, finally, turning back to his soup.

Mike wasn't sure why she couldn't let it lie, but something moved her to say, "Maybe I missed having a mother, but I never had anyone to miss."

She saw the way her father's shoulders tensed. "Why would you say that?" he asked and it sounded pinched.

"Ah...gee, I don't know. Because this is the first time we've discussed her that I can remember?"

Her father said nothing. Mike felt strangely calm. She tried to recall the last time Caroline had come up and she couldn't. She wanted to laugh, because all she could think of were conversations that Tony Micelli had had with Samantha on *Who's the Boss?* Her father wouldn't know who Tony Micelli was.

"I'm right," she said. "You didn't talk about her."

"You didn't ask about her," he said quickly.

Talia would have asked, Mike thought. Talia would have gotten right to the point.

"Yeah, I knew better than that," Mike said. Gerry looked wounded and that wasn't what she wanted. But they were discussing it now, they had already started and she didn't want to turn tail and run. "Don't get upset. I'm not accusing you of anything. It's just true. Once she was gone, she was gone." She wasn't sure if she was being cruel, though she suspected maybe she was.

Her father didn't seem to have anything to say, and rather than push any further, Mike threw her coat over her shoulder and took a long sip of her beer before heading for the door. "Soup smells good," she said, so he would know she didn't hate him for any of it.

She landed heavily on the long sofa in front of the flat-screen TV. Teaching just one class a day was exhausting; children who needed you to say the right things when there were no right things were even more so. She conjured pictures in her head of the succession of nannies who had tried in vain to say the right things to her as a child. There was never one who lasted. She wondered who was home every night when Talia got there. Maybe no one. Maybe an aunt or a cousin who only served to remind Talia that her mother was far away. It was probably much easier to have a mother you didn't miss than one you did. Mike had never had to worry, at least, about something terrible happening. The terrible thing had happened long before she could have begun. It was probably harder when you had to send letters and videos and hope and pray that she'd come back.

Her father appeared in the doorway still holding the wooden spoon. His face was ashen.

"I was supposed to ask you if Kimmy can borrow your video camera. She wants to tape Deja's shower."

"Okay," she said. She hadn't meant for everything to be so awkward.

"Okay," he said. He paused for a long time and Mike debated telling him that the spoon was dripping squash puree on the hardwood floor.

"When you were in the first grade," he said, "on parents'

night, they had put up all the drawings you did. And the teacher, she takes me aside. She says, 'Dr. Edwards, the children were assigned to draw their family, and I'm afraid I didn't understand Michaela's drawing.' So she points to it and I go over to look—it's up on the wall with all the others. She points to this big goofy-looking guy in a white coat, and she says, 'I'm assuming that's you, but I'm wondering what this is. Do you have a pet at home?' You know what you drew?"

Mike shook her head no.

"Edwina the Mongoose."

"I don't remember," Mike said.

"I must have it somewhere," he said.

Neither of them looked at Caroline smiling from her pedestal.

"Thanks for loaning the camera to Kimmy," Mike's father said.

"No problem," she told him. When he'd gone back to the kitchen, Mike used a tissue to wipe up the floor.

NO BOTTLES TO BREAK—
JUST HEARTS

Mike often wondered why a perfectly good word like "shower" had ever been applied to a gaggle of women drinking champagne cocktails and constructing ribbon hats. Had it all arisen from some long-antiquated ritual in which the village women gathered to give the bride her annual bath? And if so, why had some intrepid pioneer woman not eventually pointed out that she could damn well wash her own ass and told them all she'd see them at the church? Certainly if there was no actual cleansing at modern-day bridal showers, they could give the word back. A shower was the humid sanctuary into which you escaped to forget that you'd alienated a colleague or to scour off memories of the guy you wished you hadn't gone home with. It was the cool tile retreat in which you hid to postpone an argument while your boyfriend slammed pots and pans around in the kitchen. Mike was willing to share the term with a light rain, but not with the ladies who luncheon. Couldn't they content themselves with a word that wouldn't feel so compromised? Perhaps "rhino-plasty": a reconstruction of the proboscis or celebration of impending nuptials. What about "gulag"? As in, "Don't forget to pick up the wine coolers for Sharon's gulag."

The idea of Deja's gulag was, for Mike, as appealing as being set on fire and thrown into a pit of hungry tigers. But she knew the invitation was coming.

Since their frank and intimate coffee klatch, Cheryl seemed to see Mike as a dear friend and confidante. Knowing what she knew and Cheryl didn't, however, a re-morseful Mike had been treating the school corridors as one big game of Ms. Pac-Man. Cheryl was the pink cartoon ghost who would eat up one of Mike's lives with sheer guilt, so Mike peeked around corners and looked both ways before exiting her classroom. She was prepar-ing to leave the girls' room and had just cracked the door, only to find Grace standing directly in front of her. Mike jumped, slammed the door shut, and promptly opened it again.

"Is someone after you, Michaela?"

"Sorry?"

"You've been skulking around my school like a crazy person for a week now. You're scaring the children and you're making me jumpy."

"Sorry," Mike said and smiled ruefully.

"Do I want to know?" Grace asked.

"Definitely not," Mike said.

"That's what I thought." Grace thrust a powder blue en-velope with a gold bee embossed on the flap toward Mike.

"What's this?"

"This is the invitation to your stepmother's shower," Grace said. Mike winced at the use of "stepmother." She slipped a finger under the flap of the envelope and drew out the blue and gold card. Her stomach did a cannonball toward her knees.

"No," she couldn't help saying as she scanned the invitation.

"Yes," Grace said. "And I want you to listen to me, Michaela Edwards, because I'm not going to repeat myself. Deja spends her whole life taking care of other people and for one day, *one day,* the rest of us are going to take care of her. She would never do this for herself and she would never do it by herself, so you and I and Kristen and Kimberly and Cheryl are going to do it with her."

"Cheryl?" Mike asked sharply. "Why would Cheryl be coming?"

"Because Deja was her mentor here and she wants to be there. You have a problem with Cheryl?"

"No," Mike lied. She had about eighteen problems with Cheryl, none of which would be particularly appropriate to address at this time.

"So," Grace continued, "one week from Saturday, you will show up, you will smile, and you will show some appreciation for all that this woman has brought to your life. Do you get me, Michaela?"

"I do," Mike said.

"Good. I swear, it's like talking to one of my children sometimes. That must be why I like you."

"You have children?" Mike asked. Somehow it was hard to picture Grace with kids she wasn't being paid to govern.

"Four. Three girls and a boy."

"Wow," Mike said.

"You have no idea," Grace said.

Suddenly, Mike had no idea about a lot of things, and at

the top of the list was how she was going to get through Deja's "Day of Beauty" bridal shower. They were going to a spa. For an entire day. What, Mike wondered, could you do at a spa for an entire day? *An entire day with Cheryl.* In fact, it was probably going to be like spending an entire day in Cheryl's head. No doubt there would be color consultations and skin rejuvenating and all kinds of other girl torture that Cheryl would have come up with if she'd only had the chance. A spa. A spa was just a big bathroom you had to pay for. It was going to be the ladies' room at A. S. Logan all over again, but for eight hours. And Grace would be watching to make sure she was smiling.

The following Saturday, Mike dragged her reluctant non-girly ass to a red door on Fifth Avenue, marked "Ardor Day Spa." Already it was sickening. She was running late, which she swore to herself was unintentional and as she was buzzed in through the front door, she took one last deep breath of freedom.

The door swung shut behind her and the last stripe of daylight was squeezed into nothing. Mike realized she couldn't see anything. She was in a cave. She could hear running water and as her eyes adjusted to the dim light she could make out walls of actual rock. The air smelled like peaches and invisible harps were playing. From a high perch above a glass reception desk, a willowy redhead whispered, "Welcome to Ardor." Cheryl had to have picked this place.

Mike asked for the Fuchs bridal party and was asked to check her shoes at the front desk. The redhead seemed quietly scandalized by Mike's cowboy boots, which she gingerly lifted with two fingers and placed behind the desk.

"Don't lose those," Mike told her.

The redhead said nothing as she handed Mike a check and led her down a low-ceilinged stone corridor festooned with jewel-toned sconces. The redhead seemed to glide along without touching the ground, which only made Mike more aware of her own heavy steps. She hoped the redhead hadn't seen the prominent hole in her sock. The invitation should have mentioned the shoe thing.

The redhead paused outside a frosted glass door after what felt like miles of curving stone corridor. "Your party is inside," she said.

Mike hesitated. She couldn't have found her way out again if she'd tried.

"Your party is inside," the redhead repeated with barely discernible irritation. Mike was the redhead's worst nightmare, she could tell.

"Thanks," Mike said. "That's great." The redhead waited, but Mike wasn't moving. She didn't want her entrance to be evaluated. She raised her eyebrows to see what the redhead was waiting for, and with disdain, the redhead moved away. "It's been your pleasure, I'm sure," Mike called after her. She was probably drowned out by the harps.

Behind the glass door, Kristen and Kimmy were reclining on velvet sofas in red terry-cloth robes, reading *US Weekly* and *Glamour,* respectively.

"Oh, thank God you're here!" Kristen sprang up from her sofa. "Is this not the kitchiest place since Mohegan Sun?"

"I've never been," Mike said.

"It's this, but with robot wolves," Kristen confided.

"Mike," Kimmy chimed in, "we each have to pick a spa service and then we're all getting our makeup done together."

Mike looked to Kristen. "Mom's idea," she said. "Sorry."

"Cheryl's in with Mom and Grace; they're getting pomegranate pedicures right now," Kimmy said. "And I'm definitely doing a hot stone massage." She thrust the spa services menu toward Mike.

"Where's Emily?"

"Watching Zack. Honestly, she hates this kind of thing. You can leave your clothes in one of those glass cubes over there," Kristen said helpfully, indicating a wall of transparent cubbies.

Mike didn't want to leave her clothes, any more than she'd wanted to surrender her boots. She didn't want to see Cheryl when they were dressed alike.

"There's a little dressing room behind that wall." Kimmy pointed. Mike got it over with, ducking behind the glass cubbies to slip out of her jeans and sweater and into the lush red robe. She felt like some strange refugee from the Liberace museum. The harps faded and were replaced with Enya's plaintive wails.

"Great," Mike heard Kristen mutter, "now it's an Irish Indian casino."

"Native American," Kimmy corrected her.

Safely out of view, Mike combed the spa menu for options that didn't sound terrifying. There was a honey pumpkin pedicure, a strawberry shortcake pedicure, and a chocolate raspberry one. Mike shrank from the idea of strangers covering her feet with fruit. The manicures were no less appealing, as she couldn't see her raggedy, bitten fingernails being painted red or pink. She would look ridiculous. She would look like Cheryl.

"A massage, I guess," she said when she emerged.

"Excellent choice," Kimmy offered.

"Did somebody say massage?!" Like a puffy red phantom, a robe-clad Cheryl seemed to have appeared from out of nowhere. "That's perfect! I'm getting one too—we can go at the same time!"

"Great," Mike said. She wondered if it was too late to sign up for the fruit salad foot facial.

Another ethereal spa attendant arrived shortly to escort Mike and Cheryl into a massage room with two tables.

"Oh, we don't need to be in the same room," Mike tried to explain.

"It's the only way we can get everyone through at the same time," the attendant whispered.

Cheryl paid no attention to Mike's obvious reluctance. She removed her robe and laid facedown on one of the tables, taking no care whatsoever to minimize nudity. Mike, on the other hand, somehow managed to climb underneath the sheet fully clothed, removing her robe only once she was completely covered.

"I'm really surprised that you're shy about your body," Cheryl said.

"Excuse me?"

"I just think it's surprising. I mean, look at you. You don't even have to work at it, do you?"

Mike couldn't think of a single thing to say that didn't end in "Please go away." She buried her face in the uncomfortable donut head support and willed Cheryl to disappear.

"You are so lucky," Cheryl said. "It's a compliment, you know," she continued when Mike didn't respond.

"Thanks," Mike answered from the face donut. She could hear Cheryl drumming her fingers on the table across the room.

"Deja's nails look amazing. Wait 'til you see them."

Mike grunted and prayed that one of the long-haired

whispering spa banshees would appear soon so Cheryl would be forced to stop talking.

"So Gunther called me last night," Cheryl said, just as two large, Nordic men entered in white pants and T-shirts. They reminded Mike of the sort of faceless bare-chested slave-boys who always appeared in sitcom dream sequences. Without a word, each took his position beside his victim and began to oil up his hands.

"Hey, can you put on whale songs?" Cheryl requested, before returning to her favorite subject. Mike tried to push her face farther into the donut. "Actually," Cheryl went on, "I called him and he called me back. We talked for like, almost ten minutes. Mike, did you hear me?"

"I heard you." Mike was torn between the appeal of Cheryl's chatter blocking out the whale songs and vice versa.

"I think we're going to be friends. I didn't want things to be awkward."

"Stupendous," Mike said. As long as things weren't awkward! Her face was burning and she tried to blame it on the headrest.

"Am I hurting you?" the blond with the "Ivan" name tag leaned down to ask Mike. "You're tensing."

"Oh, she carries a ton of tension," Cheryl pointed out. "You might want to focus on her neck and shoulders. I can see the muscles tightening from across the room sometimes. It's amazing you have a neck, Mike."

Mike thought that it was amazing Cheryl had a neck, considering how much she herself wanted to wring it.

"Can I ask you something personal?" Cheryl asked in a high tone.

You were just prancing around naked, Mike thought, how much more personal do we need to get?

"No," Mike said.

"Did you say no?" Cheryl laughed. "That's funny! Nobody ever says that!"

Mike made a mental note to say no to her students more often, to prevent them from growing up to be chatty and invasive.

"Are you sure there's nothing between you and Gunther?"

"What? Ow!" Mike lifted her head too quickly and felt a shooting pain emanating from the nerve Ivan was working in her shoulder.

"Try not to move," Ivan suggested.

Mike replaced her head in the donut. "I already told you, Cheryl. We're friends."

"He talks about you a lot."

"Well, I talk about Jeremy Shockey a lot, but we're not dating," Mike snapped.

"Who's that?"

"Never mind," Mike muttered.

"I just think it's interesting that you look like you look and he's a guy and he's straight and you spend all this time drinking together and ... nothing's ever happened?"

"Try to relax," Ivan whispered.

Mike took a deep breath. "You know, I'm having trouble hearing the whale songs," she said.

"Ooh, sorry!" Cheryl said hurriedly. "They're so soothing!"

They weren't soothing. They were like nature's version of power tools whirring in the next apartment. They were unnerving and disturbing, but they weren't Cheryl.

"There you go," Ivan hissed.

From the next table, Mike heard Cheryl complaining that her butt was tense.

The makeup lesson was no improvement. Though Deja

hugged her and said she was so glad Mike was there, she knew from the moment they gathered in the makeup room that the torrent of awkwardness had only just begun. They each sat in a high chair facing a lighted mirror.

"You were late," Grace leaned over to say to Mike.

"I'm here," Mike muttered in response. She thought perhaps she caught Grace smiling out of the side of her mouth.

"Nice feet," Mike said, attempting to give the pomegranate pedicure its due.

"Thank you," Grace said.

The exuberant makeup artist who joined them introduced herself as Joliet.

"Juliet?" Kristen asked.

"JOH-liet. With an O."

Mike bit her lip.

"Well, since you ladies are celebrating Dina's upcoming wedding—"

"Deja," Grace corrected her.

"Sorry?" Joliet asked innocently.

"Her name is Deja."

"Like déjà vu? Seriously?" Joliet grinned in astonishment.

"Seriously," Deja said.

"What a weird name!" Joliet exclaimed. Her utter absence of tact was so shocking that for a moment no one said a word. The urge to defend Deja occurred to Mike so suddenly that she didn't even stop to analyze it. Grace moved to stand and face Joliet, but before her cotton-festooned feet could reach the floor, Mike said, "Yeah, give a kid a name like that...it's pretty much a *life sentence*, Joliet."

Kristen sputtered and Deja suppressed a smile.

"I mean, you're stuck with it. Trapped. One might even say *imprisoned*," Mike went on.

Joliet smiled blankly and Mike understood that she had no idea she shared a name with a state penitentiary. "It just must feel so *solitary*," Mike said directly to Joliet, "wouldn't you think?"

They all erupted into laughter then, even Cheryl, and Mike caught Deja and Grace exchanging proud looks.

"So, makeup. Let's get to it," Mike suggested.

"Okay, sure." Joliet tried to recover from the sense that some colossal joke had just been had around her and without her knowledge. "Well, like I was saying, since *Deja* is getting married and you'll all be there, today I'm going to train you to do each other's makeup! 'Kay?"

"Seriously?" Kristen asked.

"Mm-hmm!" Joliet said, with utterly no irony.

"We had sort of a bad experience with that as kids," Kimmy warned. Joliet ignored her.

"Brides always need help on that special day, and you're all going to be in the pictures, so you'll want to learn to cover those dark circles."

"Oh, my gosh," Cheryl chimed in, "I have the biggest zit in my sister's wedding photos. It's awful!"

"I get it, we're supposed to be scared pretty," Grace muttered.

"So let's pair up," Joliet suggested. "How about the two older ladies—"

"Ooh, not nice," Cheryl whispered.

"And you two—" Joliet pointed toward Kristen and Kimmy. "And that leaves our curly friend and the model-y one!"

Cheryl and Mike looked at each other. There was no polite way to say, "I don't want her anywhere near my face," though Mike was sure she wasn't the only one thinking it.

"Ladies," Joliet told them, "start your brushes!"

She walked them through each step. Mike applied Cheryl's makeup first, at Joliet's insistence, since neither of them would volunteer. It felt uncomfortably intimate to be painting Cheryl's face when Mike had spent so much time actively avoiding it. And she wasn't exactly dexterous when it came to applying the maquillage. She had to use a Q-tip to clean up the jagged eyeliner and she nearly drew blood trying to curl Cheryl's lashes.

"Sorry," Mike said, as she brushed on the last coat of gloss. "It's probably not supposed to hurt."

"That's okay," Cheryl said. "You have no idea what you're doing. You couldn't help it."

She looked at herself in the mirror over Mike's shoulder. "It actually looks pretty good," she said. "What do you think?"

Mike looked at Cheryl's caked and coated face and tried to say the right thing.

"You look . . . very pretty," she said.

"Well, that is a really nice compliment," Cheryl said, genuinely touched. "Have you been back to yoga? You seem much more compassionate." No one missed the sarcasm.

It was Cheryl's turn to work on Mike, who tried to lean back and fall asleep the way she usually did at the dentist. She tried not to think about Cheryl's conversation with Gunther. He wouldn't have told her anything. He couldn't have.

"Ooh, I need you to keep those eyes open!" Cheryl said. "Unless I tell you to close them."

So much for sleeping through it. What had seemed strange when she was the active party seemed even stranger now that she had to sit there and allow Cheryl to be in control.

"You don't take care of your skin," Cheryl said, sponging on a thick layer of foundation.

"Okay," Mike said.

"I think that's silly at your age."

"Why, what do you do?" Mike asked.

"Oh, well, facials and I moisturize morning and night. I want to be well preserved. You have small pores though, so you get away with it."

"I don't really give it a lot of thought," Mike said.

Cheryl let out a mirthless laugh. "Sure you don't."

"What does that mean?"

Cheryl stopped and held a blush brush above Mike's nose. "Well, it's not like you need to." She resumed her task and worked in silence for a moment before asking, "What must it be like to look like you look?"

Mike squirmed uncomfortably.

"Hold still," Cheryl told her. "I mean honestly, the way men look at you. I couldn't believe Gunther wanted to go out with me when he spends all his time staring at you."

Mike felt like she was stuck on an elevator riding up and down through various levels of discomfort. Cheryl knew something. She had to. "He doesn't stare at me," Mike said.

"Oh, of course he does. We all do. It must be so much easier."

"What? What do you think is easy?"

"Come on." Cheryl put the mascara tube down on the counter, leaned back, and crossed her arms. "Don't even pretend that you don't have a huge advantage over the rest of us. The world rewards beautiful people, Mike. They've done studies on this. Like you said, you can sleep with any-one you like. You know they say tall people actually get paid more than short people? It just makes it easier to get along in the world when you look like you just walked off a magazine cover."

Mike stared at her, dumbfounded.

"What, has no one ever said this to you?"

"Not in so many words."

"It's completely true though, you have to admit."

"Gee, that must be why I'm doing so well in life."

"Oh, don't get all pissy," Cheryl said good-naturedly. "Enjoy it! I know I would. I think we'll do a dramatic eye on you." She reached for the shadow palette. "Honestly, I think it's strange you don't make more of yourself. God, if you pulled yourself together a little bit, you'd be unstop-pable."

"At what?" Mike snapped. "I have never understood this."

"Understood what?" Cheryl selected yet another eye shadow.

"This fixation women have with other women's looks. The way other women dress, the way they wear their hair, what lipstick they wear. I don't give a shit!"

"Well, you don't have a lot to improve on. That's why we care so much. We're just trying to fix what we have." She dusted powder over Mike's nose and nearly made her sneeze. "Be grateful."

Mike was suddenly furious. This, she knew, was the dis-cussion that women in ladies' rooms had been tacitly hav-ing with her forever. "Explain to me why the way that I look has any impact on you! Why is this a competition?"

"Um, hello? Because it's the world!"

"It's not like I fucking traffic in it!" Mike snarled.

"Sure you do," Cheryl said calmly.

"No, I don't!"

"It's the currency of our culture, Mike. You can say rich people aren't any happier than poor people, but they sure have a good reason to be."

There was nothing Mike could say and she knew it. She wasn't about to share it all with Cheryl, all her messes, all she lacked. There was no winning. She closed her eyes and tried to take deep breaths.

Cheryl ignored Mike's growing irritation. "You know who you are?" she said. "You're the tomboy who's covered in motor oil until the last scene of the movie when she puts on a dress and gets the guy. You probably could be a model, actually, or an actress."

"Why in the hell would I want to do that?" Mike asked.

Cheryl looked at her as if she had a second nose. "Because you could," she said. "There! Take a look!"

Cheryl stepped aside so Mike could see herself in the mirror, or rather, so she could see the strange otherworldly character from *Blade Runner* who stared back.

"Jesus Christ," she said.

"Great, right?" Cheryl asked.

Mike's eyes peered out from what appeared to be two huge tar pits. Her cheekbones looked dangerously sharp and pointy, and her lips glistened with a dramatic, plummy red sheen.

"It's going-out makeup!" Cheryl said.

It was carnival makeup. It was hideous and suddenly she realized they were all staring at her. Grace, Deja, Kristen, and Kimmy were all looking on in stunned silence.

"Wow," Joliet said. "Much more feminine."

"Such a waste she doesn't do more the rest of the time, right?" Cheryl proposed to the group.

Mike vaulted down from her chair and out of the room. She found the bathroom and tried to crane her whole face under the tap, only succeeding in smearing dark kohl all over it. The tomboy covered in motor oil. Such a waste.

Kristen and Kimmy entered quietly as Mike was using paper towels to scrape the foundation off.

"Are you okay?" Kimmy asked.

"No," she said.

"We overheard," Kristen said.

"Lucky you," Mike said.

"Way out of line," Kimmy offered. "Way, *way* out of line."

"There was nothing you could say to that," Kristen said.

"She makes me want to rip my face off," Mike said, vigorously hurling a ball of crumpled towels into the trash. She leaned against the sink, shaking.

"You're not alone," Kristen said. "Too bad Emily and the boys had to miss this, huh?"

"Lucky them," Mike said.

"Oh, don't worry." Kimmy smiled. "I've got it all on tape." She lifted the video camera. Mike stared at it and her jaw dropped slightly.

"Don't worry," Kristen rushed to say, "we can totally edit out those last few minutes."

"Of course we will," Kimmy said, but Mike kept staring.

The video camera. She was such an idiot for not thinking of it before.

IT DOES A BODY GOOD

There would be no brownies, Mike resolved. No cute pictures to hang on the wall, no embroidered pillow oracles of homekeeping futures. The Life Skills class didn't have Martha Stewart, but they had Mike Edwards and that had to count for something.

Monday's class convened with grumbles and whines as eleven little girls extracted loose-leaf suggestions to impress their parents.

"Forget them," Mike said.

The grumble and whine seemed to surge in a wave.

"Flip those pages over—Talia, you need paper too—and write down your favorite thing that we've learned in this class."

They seemed to hesitate, slowly turning to look at each other to confirm that the teaching train had jumped the track again.

"Now!" Mike barked, and they scrambled to comply. As soon as their scratching pens were stilled, Mike collected their papers. One by one, she read them to herself and wrote their names and their answers on the board.

"What are we doing?" Jahia whispered to Kinara.

"Don't get your Hello Kitty backpack in a bunch," Mike said over her shoulder. Her gears were starting to turn. If she could make this work, she would be paying homage to (or ripping off, depending on your perspective) one of the seminal advertising campaigns of her youth.

Mike finished writing and stepped back to look at the board. Daisy and Jahia had both chosen self-defense. Talia loved journalism. Fenice enjoyed the job interview unit most. Asia, Sadie, and Sassafrass had all picked debate. Brooklyn was nostalgic for their early unit on stain removal, which Mike attributed to her fondness for making a mess. Dalwhynnie liked the first aid lessons. Makenzee voted for city etiquette and Kinara, shockingly, for nutrition.

There it was, and the final product began to take shape in Mike's head already. This feeling was familiar, the idea factory was open for business. She could feel the dust falling away from the gray matter of her brain.

"Okay," she said, gaining momentum, "When I call your name, tell me what you want to be when you grow up." She added their answers next to their names and surveyed the collective data.

"Mike?" Fenice spoke up.

"Yeah."

"What are we doing?"

"We're documenting this class. We're going to show your parents exactly what it is you've been doing and why."

She smiled at them triumphantly and something in the rush of her confidence and enthusiasm was infectious. They brightened, even Talia, who wanted to be a news producer when she grew up.

"Tomorrow," Mike told them, "during our double period, we're shooting a commercial."

She pressed the drama teacher and procured a significant loan from the school's costume collection. She stayed
in her classroom until almost seven-thirty playing with
lighting possibilities. She left school and went straight to
Kimmy's to pick up the video camera.

Kimmy and David lived in a spacious one-bedroom in
east Midtown. Though she had declined their invitation to
attend the weekly sibling meal over and over, Kimmy didn't
seem the least put out when Mike said she wanted to stop
by. David answered the door in an apron and the inviting
smells of garlic and honey drifted out into the hallway.

"Hey, come on in," he said, removing her coat and
hanging it in the closet before Mike could protest.

"I can't really stay," she said.

"Hey, Mike!" Kimmy called from the kitchen.

"This way." David led Mike down a long hallway that
fed into a large living room and open kitchen. Kimmy
stood behind the stove, stirring lazily at a sizable pot. Emily
sat on the floor in front of the sofa with a snoozing
Zachary in her lap. Kristen lounged behind her, massaging
Emily's shoulders.

"Mike!" they seemed to cry happily in unison.

"You came!" Kristen said. "I didn't think you were coming!"

"Actually, I just needed to pick up the camera," Mike
said ruefully, waiting for them to be offended.

"Oh, Dave, will you grab that for her?" Kimmy asked
from the kitchen.

"You're here, you should eat," Kristen said.

"Nah, you didn't plan for another mouth," Mike hedged.

"We always plan for another mouth," Kimmy assured

her. "We plan for six other mouths. Have a seat. Have a beer. Stay a while."

This wasn't how she had pictured these dinners. Mike had imagined a white tablecloth and all the women in skirts. They were so casual, so comfortable.

"Seriously, stay," Dave urged, depositing the camera bag on the coffee table. "You're family."

"Family doesn't need to RSVP, in this family," Emily explained breezily.

"Pop a squat," Kristen encouraged.

Though her instinct was to find her jacket and scoot down the long hallway, out the way she had come, something made Mike stay.

"So what's with the camera?" Emily asked.

Mike was given a beer and she sat down and explained about parents' night, Talia, and the video.

"Jesus," Kristen said when she had finished, "that is so much cooler than anything the parents ever got when we were there."

"Wait a second, you guys went to March?" Mike asked.

"Hell, yeah!" Kimmy said. "I was the goalie for the first soccer team they ever had."

"Go get the yearbook, Kims," Kristen instructed and Kimmy disappeared excitedly into the bedroom.

"Mom was so into the way they did things, she thought it was so much better than any other school around."

"So your mother was a teacher at the school you went to?"

"I know, freaky, right?" Kristen grinned. "But honestly, it was sort of great. You know, you got to run into your mom in the hallways!"

"The only downside being she knew *everything* we did, all the time. And our teachers would sometimes come over for dinner, which was odd." Kimmy reemerged and opened one of the yearbooks she had placed on the coffee table. She knelt next to Kristen and flipped through the pages.

"Oh, my God," Kimmy said, "this was the year you had the 'fro." Kristen slapped her on the arm.

"It wasn't a 'fro! That was awesome hair. That was Jersey mall chick hair and it was cool!"

"Ah, the wall of bangs." Emily laughed. "That's a classic."

Mike scooted toward the table and leaned over to see the photos as they flipped along. She recognized the hallways and the art room.

"I would have hated girls' school," she said.

"Really?" Kimmy questioned. "How come?"

"I don't know," Mike said. "Girls. I usually played with boys."

"Oh, no, it was awesome," Kimmy argued. "I mean, we didn't have to think about wearing makeup or what we wore. I showed up at school in sweatpants half the time."

"That was high school, Kims," Kristen said. "That's why you couldn't get a date."

"I like her sweatpants," David piped up.

"No, it was cool," Kimmy continued. "You could just sort of be whoever you were. You didn't have to put anything on because it was just girls. Didn't you feel that way?"

"It was pretty great," Kristen agreed.

"Of course *you* liked it," Emily teased.

"Not like *that*." Kristen elbowed her partner playfully. "You just kind of ignored the fussy girls. They found each other and the rest of us didn't bother with 'em."

Dalwhynnie and Sadie, Mike thought. The fussy girls.

"Oh, look, there's Mom." Kristen pointed.

Mike had to look twice, but there was Deja, leaning against a desk. Her hair was long and she wore a headband

and one of those amazing holiday-themed sweaters that all teachers seem to wear. Something about the view out the windows behind her looked familiar.

"Three-oh-two," Kristen said.

"You're kidding," Mike said, leaning in closer. "Her room was 302?"

"Forever," Kristen said.

It was Mike's classroom. She recognized the peeling linoleum under the radiator, the deli across the street, which was now a Pinkberry. There were no stoves then, but it was the same room. Mike had inherited Deja's territory.

She stayed longer than she had intended, but they were eating and drinking and laughing. Mike had never felt like this in the company of women. Like herself. Not edgy or defensive, but fine. At home.

When she finally slung the camera over her shoulder and began the stroll to catch the 4/5 at Grand Central it was nearly eleven-thirty. Young professionals who had stayed too long at the sake and sushi joints along 47th Street trickled onto the sidewalk to smoke their cigarettes as she passed. Though she knew she would be up late writing copy for tomorrow's shoot, Mike felt a surge of energy. She jumped slightly at the sound of a woman shouting her name, but looked around for the guy it was intended for.

"Mike!" the voice shouted again, and this time Mike spied a bobbing ponytail across the street and a waving hand. The ponytail ran carelessly across the street, cigarette wagging wildly, and arrived breathless in front of her.

"Oh, my God, it is you!"

"Hi!" Mike had no idea who this woman was and her expression must have said as much.

"Lauren!" the ponytail said, laughing. "From Dana Petrie's office!"

"Oh, my God," Mike said, remembering suddenly. Their paths had crossed at a couple of Christmas parties over the years, but mostly it was the sound of Lauren's voice that was familiar.

"I saw you walking and I was like, oh, that is so Mike Edwards! How are you?!" Lauren was incredibly enthusiastic and more than slightly soused.

"I'm fine," Mike said. "How 'bout you?"

"Great! I'm great! I'm at a birthday party. Oh, my God, where have you been? You, like, dropped off the face of the earth!"

Mike bristled. "Freelancing," she said. "I'm freelancing." No one could prove it was a lie.

"Really? Awesome! I bet you have a ton of work!"

"Yeah, well, it's great to see you, Lauren. I need to get home and get to some of that . . . work."

"Okay, well, great, great to see you." Lauren waved her cigarette as Mike started to turn away.

Dana Petrie would probably burn Mike in effigy if her name ever came up. Mike stopped. She turned back. Lauren was still standing, looking after her. She waved again, with exuberance.

"Hey, by the way, did anything come of Dana's chat with Brian Bentley?"

"Hmm?" Lauren looked happy and blank.

"The meeting. Brian said he was coming in last week."

Nothing from Lauren.

"To discuss coming over there? He said they were interested. Really interested. You don't know what I'm talking about?"

"Dana's been out of the country for two weeks. And between you and me, you couldn't pay her to sit down with Bentley. She'd rather lick a cactus."

Mike nodded, longer than was necessary, but she couldn't stop. "Thanks," she said.

"You bet!" Lauren waved again, cheerily, but Mike was already walking away.

Bentley was a liar. He had always been a liar.

Mike was too angry to get in a cab or ride the subway. She walked faster. She crossed 47th Street and began heading uptown. She pretended for the first few blocks that she wasn't beelining for Brian's pied-à-terre by Columbus Circle, but she couldn't help it. He probably wasn't even there, she told herself.

The rain came out of nowhere and within blocks she was drenched, but she walked on anyway. She grew angrier with every step. How long had he been lying to her? Had he made everything up? Every prospect, every exciting conversation that kept her stringing along, kept her thinking that maybe, just maybe, there was real possibility. That maybe he would help her to get back on her feet, because, face it, they both knew he owed it to her.

Still dripping wet when she arrived at the building on 64th and Central Park West, Mike neglected to smile at the doorman, who looked at her with a mix of admiration and disgust. The concierge remembered her face, and was announcing her before she could give him her name. Brian was there, alright. Too chickenshit to call her, this time.

Mike was ushered into the lobby and made her way up to the fourteenth floor. He was waiting in the doorway of his apartment when the elevator doors peeled open, holding a glass of whiskey.

"What the hell happened to you?" he asked through his salesman's smile.

"I drowned," she said, pushing past him and taking the

glass from his hand. She knocked back half the glass and tracked dirty wet footprints through the foyer.

"Suits you," he said. "But it's not the best time at the moment. You're dripping on the carpet."

"This won't take long," she muttered.

She heard a rustling in the bedroom. He wasn't alone. If it had been his wife, Mike wouldn't have been allowed up, she knew.

"Where'd you get this one?" she asked.

"Is that jealousy?" He smiled, but she knew he was irritated at being interrupted. (Young women could be so skittish when they were trying to overcome their better judgment.) "You're welcome to join us," he said through clenched teeth.

Mike moved past him into the living room. The carpet was getting soaked.

"Fine." He went to the bathroom and Mike heard him poke his head into the bedroom to say, "Just business, darling. Be with you in a minute." He reemerged with a plush bath towel, which he threw at her. "Sit on this, then."

Mike toweled off her hair and threw the towel over his leather sofa.

"To what do I owe the pleasure?" he asked her.

She was so angry she hardly knew where to begin.

"Hardly seems fair to make me sit here and look at you like that." He indicated the clothes that were still sticking to her body.

"Drop it," Mike said.

Brian sighed, and in a somewhat testier voice, asked, "What exactly are you here for then?"

"You said you've got leads?"

"Oh, yeah. Yeah. New bites every day. Should hear something soon." He looked down into his glass as he said it.

"How was that meeting at BPK?"

"Excellent," he said. "Excellent. They're interested. They're discussing an offer."

"And they'd want me too, of course."

"Of course."

"Did you meet in Dana's office?"

"Where else?" he said. He refilled his own glass and stood at the bar with his back to her. He didn't offer to fix her one.

"I don't know. Paris. Brussels. She's been out of the country for two weeks."

She saw him stiffen and freeze.

"You didn't have a meeting. They were never interested. You've been lying to me for months." She was too enraged to shout. "Has anyone been interested, Brian? Has a single one of the 'bites' you're getting *every day* been real?"

He slowly turned to face her.

"I lost my apartment. I lost my *career* over you. You have a house in Westchester and a wife who for reasons that escape me still takes care of your sorry ass. And you've been sitting here in your ivory tower and bullshitting me for *months!*"

His face darkened and he glared at her for a minute. "I'm getting rid of the apartment."

"What?"

"Do you have any idea how much I pay for this shithole every month? You think my funds are endless? Ursula spends like the bloody Queen. In another month I'm not going to have a house in Westchester. I probably won't have a bloody wife for that matter!"

"Cry me a river," she said.

"You think you lost a career over me?" he spat. "I'm the

only one who would have you! You would have been nowhere without me!"

"I am the best at what I do," she seethed.

"And you're a bloody scorpion. You didn't lose it over me, sweetheart. You never had it in the first place."

"You don't have any leads, do you? It's over."

He said nothing.

"That's what I thought." She got up to go.

"You know," he said quietly, without a trace of his usual bluster, "at least my cow of a wife doesn't try to bite my balls off when I'm already down."

Mike stopped just short of the front door. He didn't deserve her pity or her compassion. She should have torn him apart, but somehow she didn't have it in her. It was too exhausting to be the scorpion. Shaking, unsure of how to navigate in such unfamiliar waters, Mike fled.

WHEN IT ABSOLUTELY, POSITIVELY HAS TO BE THERE OVERNIGHT

Mike cornered Grace in the teachers' lounge the day before parents' night. "Where are you gonna be tomorrow?" she asked.

"Everywhere, why?"

"Because you need to be in my classroom when the parents come in."

"Pardon me, I must have misheard. It sounded like you were telling me where I *needed* to be." Grace gave Mike the look that usually made her cower.

"I was." Mike was unfazed. "I did. You do."

"Unless you're planning to set the parents on fire, you don't need me there."

"No, that I could take care of myself. And it's not that I need you there, it's that you're gonna be glad you were there. And bring that marketing guy."

She turned triumphantly, leaving Grace staring after her.

"Michaela, we don't mix the parents with the corporation so you can take that silly spring out of your step."

Mike turned and bit her lower lip. "Fair enough," she said. "But I'm scheduled to present to the parents at eight forty-five. Will you be there?"

"We'll see," Grace said.

"You'll be there," Mike whispered under her breath as she walked away.

"I heard that!" she heard Grace call after her.

Mike's confidence was buoyed by the sight of Talia leaving class hours before the parents were to arrive, with a DVD in a padded envelope.

"This was a good idea," Talia said, when Mike handed her the envelope.

"I used to get paid to have good ideas," Mike said.

"Now you get paid for us to have them," Talia said, and Mike caught the hint of a dimple forming in her cheek.

"You ever think about working in advertising?" Mike asked.

"No," Talia said.

"I don't blame you," Mike said.

The parents who filed into her classroom several hours later and tried to squeeze themselves into the tiny chair-desks made Mike laugh. She knew Dalwhynnie's yuppie mother and father immediately. They each shook her hand and told her they were pleased with Dalwhynnie's "advancements." Fenice's mother was every bit as regal and elegant as her daughter. Brooklyn's father was obviously the guy in paint-spattered $300 jeans. And Asia's mother asked four questions before Mike could begin the presentation. Grace glided in at the last minute, as Mike had assumed she would. Mike smiled gratefully at her and Grace made a "get-on-with-it" face.

"It's nice to see you all," Mike said, when the parents were more or less comfortably seated. She looked around the room. "Your children look a lot like you.

"The girls were a little nervous about what I would be showing you this evening. As you all know, I'm replacing Derek Luce while he recovers from his unfortunate accident, and I've taken a slightly different approach to Life Skills. So we don't have any cookies for you, and I'm afraid I don't teach anything involving yarn. But if you'll take a look at the board behind me, you'll see a pretty good sampling of exactly what it is I do teach. Ladies and gentlemen, the young women of March Academy."

She flicked the light switch on the wall to OFF, then raised the remote control in her hand and pointed it toward her laptop.

A large static image of the Life Skills classroom appeared on the board and then faded to black—Mike had set up a projector to run the film. The words "GOT SKILLS?" appeared, and then "MARCH ACADEMY."

Asia's face materialized on-screen first. She wore a pint-sized judge's robes and stood with Sadie and Sassafrass, in business suits, in the classroom, which had been reset to resemble a makeshift courtroom. "I may not look like much now," Asia said to the camera. Sadie stepped forward to add, "But I'm a March student." "And someday, I'll rule the courtroom," Sass concluded. The film cut to footage of a classroom debate, the girls heatedly, but with precision, arguing over the school policy on cell phones in the classroom. Next came Dalwhynnie in a doctor's lab coat, who explained that "I'm just a kid now, but someday I may save your life." Dalwhynnie working on the CPR dummy flashed across the screen. The parents gasped and smiled as each of the girls appeared in sequence, illustrating the work they'd done in class and the accomplished women they might someday grow to be. Mike heard, with satisfaction, Fenice's mother whisper, "Remember those milk commercials?" to her husband.

Finally, Talia filled the frame, holding the camera bag from Mike's video camera. "I'm only in seventh grade," she said, "but I go to March Academy, and someday I'm gonna shoot the news." Mike smiled, knowing what came next. "For now, I shot this video." Talia smiled on-screen.

The parents erupted into spontaneous applause. Mike looked across the darkened room for Grace, who was beaming at the screen. She glanced toward Mike and nodded her approval. The lights came up and the parents approached Mike in ones and twos, their excited chatter and laughter filling the room.

"Kinara's making her own menus now," Kinara's father exclaimed, "we don't argue over every meal."

"That's wonderful," Mike said.

"Did you suggest a career in disaster relief?" Brooklyn's mother asked.

"She came up with it herself," Mike told her.

Mike watched them shuffle out, still twittering spiritedly, until she was left alone with Grace.

"I did good," Mike said.

Grace shook her head. "You did well," Grace corrected.

"I feel like they got what I was trying to do."

"We all got it. It took a while, but we got it."

Mike grinned herself. "I am so not a teacher," she said and laughed softly.

"You're something else, Michaela. You are something else altogether. I've gotta move on. But I want a copy of that tape on my desk in the morning."

"DVD."

"Whatever. I want it." Grace moved to leave but turned around in the doorway. "Congratulations," she said. "Job well done."

"Thank you," Mike said. "It's been a hell of a long time."

When she finally shut off the lights in the classroom and closed the door, she reached for her cell phone. She punched three on the speed dial and then stopped. Calling Gunther was a reflex. She couldn't hit SEND.

Even though he had said he would call her, he hadn't. Either he was waiting for her to do it or he just didn't want to talk to her and she preferred not to think too much about which it was. His absence gnawed at her. He was the person she called when she left school, left the house, climbed up from the subway. He was a reason to look for a cell phone signal. She had never measured the space he occupied and now it seemed much too big and empty.

She closed the phone quietly and slipped it back into her pocket. She told herself that there was something wrong if she couldn't enjoy her small triumphs without recreating them for anyone who would listen.

Deja would listen. The thought crept into her head before she could check it, and it sat there, alien and insistent. Deja would understand.

Deja was sitting in the den, reading, when Mike got home.

"How was it?" she called, before Mike even had her jacket off.

"It was good," Mike called back.

"Did you bring a copy home?"

She had. But what would they do? Sit there and watch Mike's cute video and then sip wine and do each other's hair? Mike didn't know how to do that. She didn't know how to play family just because all the pieces were now assembled.

She pulled the DVD from her bag anyway. She paused for a moment before walking it into the living room.

"Oh, great!" Deja cried when she saw it. "I'm going to watch it right now." Deja took off her glasses and let them hang from the chain around her neck. She snatched the disc from Mike and hurried to plug it into the player.

"Now if I can just figure out how to work this thing," she muttered.

Mike watched her puttering and realized that she would never be as much at home in this house as Deja was. She might never be as much at home anywhere. She was missing something, and no fairy tale stepmother could teach it to her now.

"I'm tired," Mike said.

"There! Now you should work," Deja told the TV.

"I think I'm gonna go to bed," Mike said.

Deja looked surprised. "You don't want to watch with me? Your dad's out with Charlie watching some baseball game, but...I would love to have you tell me about it..."

Mike understood that the balance she maintained with Deja was becoming every day a more dangerous place where feelings could be hurt, rifts created, and responsibilities neglected. And it was this, more than anything else, that made her want to run. She didn't need to take on another human being, and she didn't want to be taken on herself. She just wanted to be.

"It's pretty self-explanatory," she said. "I'll see you in the morning."

Deja was gone in the morning, off to tutor or shop for vegetables at the farmers' market. A note had been slipped under Mike's door.

"I'm proud of you."

Mike suppressed the urge to push it back under the door the way it had come.

REACH OUT AND
TOUCH SOMEONE

S omebody should have explained to Mike about losing, that nine times out of ten, it's not the air conditioner falling from a clear blue sky. Now she was losing again and she couldn't even hear the whistle as she approached the ground.

Gunther called, finally, when he realized she never would. Mike was on her way into school. She stopped just short of the front doors and sat heavily on one of the wide stone steps. She might have been grateful that at least one of them could see a crossroads when he came to it, but instead she behaved like a squirrel taken by surprise.

First she answered. Then she froze before saying hello.

There was an awkward moment in which Gunther, certain that he had heard the phone being answered, began to wonder where Mike was.

"Mikey?"

She tried to say hello but produced a breathy, hissing sound before getting the word out.

"You okay?" he asked.

"Fine," she said, as quickly as possible. "I'm fine, how are you?"

He paused. "Okay."

"Good."

"Yeah."

"Good," she repeated, and felt like a monkey.

There was a pause during which they both regretted everything about the conversation thus far.

"The day is almost upon us, eh?" he said.

It sounded to Mike like an unfortunate prophecy of doom and she tried to decode it. When she couldn't come up with anything that didn't make her uncomfortable, she said, "What day?"

"The wedding," he said gently, hoping she hadn't been drinking or suffering complete mental collapse.

"Oh, yeah, of course. Yes. It's coming."

"Looking forward?"

"Yup. Terrific. It will be."

She was talking like Yoda. She needed to find out what he wanted and get the hell off the phone. She shouldn't have answered in the first place, she thought. They had nothing to say to each other. God, how was it possible that they suddenly had nothing to say?

"Why are you calling?" she asked and hated the way it came out.

"Oh," he said, only slightly undone by her incredible lack of tact, "I . . . Deja called me."

"Oh, yeah?" Mike's voice cracked, and just then a pack of girls returning from morning recess bolted past her in a thundering herd.

"Are you at the zoo?" Gunther asked, concerned.

"Only figuratively," she said. "I'm at school."

He laughed too hard at her joke.

"So you were saying..."

"Right." He cleared his throat. "Deja phoned. They've lost their photographer, apparently. I, er, I could give her some names. I thought, actually it could be my gift. There's a wire service photographer who shoots weddings on the side and he's terrific. He's available. It's all but worked out."

"Great," Mike said. "That's... that's lovely." She thought that Deja would say "lovely."

"Right," he said, "glad you think so."

"I do," she said.

"Good."

There was a pause.

"I still don't—"

"Of course!" he jumped in. "I don't have her number. Deja didn't leave her number. Bit panicked, I think."

It was like he was a part of the family. He was the one they called when things fell apart.

"Oh, I... yeah. It's in my phone. I think I have to hang up to get it. I'll text it to you?"

"Sure," he said. "Great."

"Okay, then."

"Okay. Oh, and, Mikey?"

"Yeah?"

"Should I pick you up? For the rehearsal?"

She winced. "I'll just head over with my dad and Deja."

"Sure," he said again, and she listened for disappointment in his voice. She couldn't tell if she heard any.

"You have fun at the zoo then," he said. She could hear his smile and she felt a painful tug inside her chest.

"Thanks. I'll text you." She hung up. She heard a bell ring inside and knew she should get to her classroom to prep. But her limbs felt heavy. She dug her fingernails into her palm and willed herself to stand, nearly forgetting to send Deja's number. She held her thumb over the SEND button, suddenly feeling as if she was supposed to say something, offer him something more, only she wasn't sure she had it. She sent the message and went inside.

Mike didn't feel like teaching a class. She didn't want to put on a show or pretend that she was capable of leading them anywhere. She wondered how Deja had managed for thirty years, how Grace could pull herself together on the days when having four children was exhausting. She wondered how teachers acted like teachers when underneath it they were just people.

She had her laptop unpacked and networked when the girls came in. They were doing a lesson on internet predators, how to spot them, how to avoid them. It was important, but it was depressing, and more depressing she did not need.

The Life Skills girls were buzzing with excitement when they came through the door. Mike could feel it tumbling off them in tiny energetic explosions. Jahia knocked her books from her desk when she went to sit down. Brooklyn and Dalwhynnie erupted in giggles. Asia kept scratching her leg over and over.

"Serious stuff today, guys," Mike said.

Kinara and Sadie twittered.

"We're gonna talk about how to be safe on the internet. How many of you have e-mail addresses? Show of hands."

Eleven hands were thrust into the air.

"And how many of you have ever chatted with someone you didn't know online?"

Eight hands went up.

"Wow," Mike said. "And how many of you tell your parents when—"

"Excuse me, Mike?" Fenice delicately interrupted.

"Yeah?"

"We wanna talk about it."

"It what?"

"The movie!" Asia squealed. "They loved it! They loved it so much!"

"My parents talked about it all weekend!" Dalwhynnie chimed in.

"My mom said it was totally amazing and like, really high production values for such a low-budget project, and"—Fenice spun around in her seat to face Talia—"that she can totally get you an internship when we're in high school."

"Really?" Talia lit up.

"It looked so good!" Brooklyn cried. "Like a real commercial."

"Well," Mike said, "that's what I do."

"No, seriously," Kinara said, "don't you love it? What did Gunther say?"

"What?"

"Yeah, what did Gunther think?" Talia piped up. "'Cause he knows good camera work."

"He...he hasn't seen it." Caught off guard, Mike tried to appear unfazed.

"He hasn't seen it?!" Sassafrass practically shouted. "Was he away or something?"

"No. He just...I haven't shown it to him."

"But he's your best friend," Sadie said, bewildered, and looked to Sass for confirmation.

"I...he's..." Mike struggled to find words. "I know that," she said. "We just...we didn't hang out this weekend."

"Is everything okay?" Fenice asked maternally.

"Everything is fine, except that we have a really vital lesson to get to and we don't have time to talk anymore about the movie, okay?"

"But—" Makenzee attempted.

"Seriously." Mike wagged a warning finger in Makenzee's direction. "Chat rooms. The problem with chat rooms is that you think you know who you're talking to and you don't."

"Sometimes you do," Makenzee said, still chagrined at being silenced.

"Sometimes you might, but really you can't prove it. The scary people we refer to as predators are counting on the fact that you can't see them or hear them. They could pretend to be anyone, right?"

The girls weren't in the mood, but they humored her and grumbled their assent.

"You can usually tell if someone's faking," Fenice asserted.

"Sometimes you can," Mike agreed. "That's good. That means you're already aware of the possibility and you're on the lookout. But you shouldn't really have to police these people. You shouldn't be exposed to them in the first place. It's great that you talk to your friends online, but you really shouldn't ever have a reason to talk to strangers."

"My dad says I'm not allowed," Kinara said.

"Your dad's got a good idea there."

"I don't tell my dad," Sassafrass muttered.

"Because probably you know it's not the best idea, right?"

"Right," Sass grunted.

"Check this out," Mike said. She typed a web address into the browser on her laptop. "This site is all about something called parental controls."

"We have that on our TV so my brother can't watch porns," Asia said brightly.

"Same idea," Mike said. "This is a way for you and your parents to decide together what's safe for you to see and do online and what isn't. Parental controls are a tool that can block out the creepy stuff that you shouldn't be dealing with."

"Like crazy Unabombers?" Sadie suggested.

"Among other things. I'm gonna show you guys how this works, and your assignment tonight is going to be to go home and talk about it with your parents. Those of you who don't already have this stuff set up should encourage your parents to think about it."

"But I'm not looking at dirty pictures," Jahia said, "or like, reading about crack or something."

"That's not the point," Fenice said sagely.

"What's the point?" Jahia snapped back.

Fenice drew herself up as tall as she possibly could. "The point, *Jahia*," she said sharply, "is that your mom and dad are supposed to give you certain tools when you're growing up so you can go out in the world and be a good person."

"I am a good person, *Fenice*." Jahia took a step toward Fenice.

"Yes, you are a good person," Mike said. "You're both good people, and, Fenice, what you're saying is true."

"Yeah," Fenice continued, "'cause you may think you're all smart, but maybe you don't know everything, and if they don't help you and tell you stuff and teach you what you need, then maybe you'll go out in the world and mess shit up! That's why people have a mom and dad in the first place."

A collective gasp escaped the girls as they realized what

Fenice had said. *Shit.* Eleven heads snapped toward Mike, in anticipation of the worst. She would yell. She would send Fenice outside. Or worst, she would send Fenice to see Ms. Washington.

They waited.

Mike didn't move.

If they don't help you and tell you stuff and teach you what you need, then maybe you'll go out in the world and mess shit up! That's why people have a mom and dad in the first place.

The words echoed in Mike's ears like clanging bells, too loud for her to hear that Fenice had just committed a major March Academy no-no. Mike started to shake.

"Mike?" Talia asked cautiously.

"Is she okay?" Kinara whispered to Brooklyn.

"I'm sorry, Mike," Fenice offered.

When she still didn't acknowledge them, Jahia said she was sorry too.

"Maybe she's in a coma," Asia said. "I saw that on *CSI.*"

"She's not in a coma," Talia snapped. "She's upset." Talia took a step toward Mike. "Mike?" she said again. She put a hand on Mike's shoulder and Mike jumped.

They were all looking at her as if her head was going to spin around.

"Sorry," she gasped.

"What's wrong?" Makenzee asked.

"Parental controls," Mike said. She had the strange sensation that something wet was in her eyes.

"Parental controls?" Dalwhynnie repeated.

"I didn't have a mother," Mike said. She hadn't meant to say it. It just came out.

"Whoa," Sadie whispered.

"I didn't have a mother," Mike said again. "I don't have the things. What did you call them?" She turned to Fenice.

"The tools?" Fenice offered, still slightly afraid that she was in trouble.

"The tools," Mike said. "I mess everything up." She was crying. She was supposed to be their teacher, not a person, and she was messing that up too.

"No you don't," Talia said firmly.

Mike looked at her gratefully. "I do though."

"You're great!" Asia said, mystified. They all thought so. Everything they saw was exotic and strong and brave and funny. They didn't know her messes.

"I don't know how to be with people," Mike said. It was all coming out now, bubbling to the surface and flowing off her in a gurgling wave. "I'm not good. To other people. I can't...I don't bring anything to anyone. I don't know how to take care of other human beings."

They looked at each other, completely bewildered.

"You don't know me," Mike tried to explain.

"We do too," Talia argued. "We see you every day."

"You're great," Asia said again, pushing her glasses up on her nose.

Mike tried to smile at them.

"I think this is cathartic for you," Sadie said.

"Where did you learn that word?" Mike asked.

"Dr. Phil."

"Of course," Mike said.

"I didn't mean to make you upset," Fenice said.

"You didn't," Mike promised her. "It's not you."

"You'll be okay," they told her. "This is good for you. We're here."

They were miles ahead of her, Mike thought. Miles and miles.

Unexpectedly, Talia suddenly threw her arms around Mike's neck and hugged her tightly. When she pulled away she only looked slightly embarrassed.

"My mom always says," Talia told Mike, "that what you don't learn from your parents, you learn from your kids."

Mike looked at her for a long time.

"You must have a really smart mom, Talia."

"Yeah." Talia smiled. "I do."

Grace paused for just a moment, as she did every day, outside of Mike's classroom. Mike used to notice every time, in the beginning. She used to feel like she was being monitored, which she was. As time had passed she had stopped noticing. It was alright that Grace was watching; there was nothing here Mike wasn't proud of.

With the girls gathered round her, petting her, comforting her, telling her that everything would be alright, Mike didn't notice Grace stopping in the doorway. She didn't notice the door opening or Grace crossing the room. She didn't notice when the girls parted.

The first thing she knew was that Grace, standing beside her, had wrapped her arms around Mike and was holding her. Mike stiffened.

"What are you doing?" she asked.

"I'm showing up for you," Grace said. "People will show up for you when you need them. Why don't you know that?"

YOU'RE IN GOOD HANDS

It was Saturday. Bachelor Saturday, which had turned into father-daughter Saturday. Already feeling like an open wound, Mike wasn't sure how much lifelike cheer she could produce. She had been sitting in the kitchen for an hour. They were supposed to leave. Her shoes were on, her coat sat on a chair. She was ready and her father hadn't appeared all morning.

She heard him moving around in the bedroom. The muted sounds of his conversation with Deja drifted through the walls but she couldn't hear what they were saying. Mike started on her third cup of coffee.

When that was gone and another half hour had passed, she stood up to go knock on the door. She didn't want to sit and wait all day. Just as she rose, she heard the sound of the bedroom door opening. She quickly rinsed her mug and placed it in the sink. She needed to pull it together. She was a lousy best man for letting her father take her out, instead of doing it the other way around. She should have taken him golfing or something. It would have been the right thing to do.

"Mike?" Deja stood in the kitchen doorway.

"Hey, do you think you could light a fire under him?" Mike asked. "The day is kind of slipping away here."

"Your dad's not feeling well," Deja said.

"Oh. Well, is he okay?"

Deja paused. "Physically, he's fine," Deja said.

"I don't understand."

"I don't know if I do either, but if it's okay, I'm gonna take you today."

Mike swallowed, suddenly feeling as if the stakes for whatever was supposed to happen had risen about a mile. "Doesn't that kind of defeat the purpose? If he doesn't go?"

"I know," Deja said, "but I think it's better than nothing."

Mike was too uneasy to say anything at all.

"I read a book about blended families," Deja said, as they rode the subway.

Mike hadn't checked on her father before they left. He would have come out if he'd wanted to see her.

"They said you should never try too hard with step-children, because they'll only resent the intrusion. And I quote, 'Avoid forced togetherness.' So I'm just breaking all the rules."

They were riding toward Brooklyn, a borough Mike avoided with all the zeal appropriate to a born-and-bred Manhattanite. They passed Union and then 9th Street. "Doesn't Gunther live in Park Slope?" Deja asked.

"Yeah," Mike said. Deja probably thought Gunther was the best thing about her.

Mike didn't like suprises. She especially didn't take to the idea that "forced togetherness" meant spending her

Saturday afternoon so far afield. Deja was just the sort of person who would know a wonderful Moroccan restaurant hidden away among the brownstones. No wonder her father had bagged at the last minute. It was ridiculous to travel so far for a restaurant.

"I know you won't tell me where we're going," Mike said, "but do I get to know the general vicinity?"

"Well, I think technically it's Bay Ridge," Deja said. "Although I've never been very good with Brooklyn. Think of it as an adventure. It'll give us some time to get to know each other better."

No one needed to be good at Brooklyn, in Mike's estimation, but she neglected to mention this. It was only the second time they'd ever been alone together. After what seemed like an eternity, Mike followed Deja out of the subway station at 25th Street. They stood across the street from an enormous gothic gate.

"I don't get it," Mike said. "You wanted to spend time with me at a cemetery?"

"Come on," Deja said.

Mike suddenly wished they were at a Moroccan restaurant. Her pulse quickened uncomfortably. What if Deja was one of those grand-gesture people and she was about to give a speech on the shortness of life in a brazen and discomfiting attempt to make Mike more enthusiastic about the impending nuptials? This didn't seem like a Deja thing to do, but Mike reminded herself that she really didn't know this woman. She hardly knew her at all. She could just be some crazy person that her father met online after all. It's not as though they were family. Nonetheless, Mike tried to prepare a response that would convey adequate enthusiasm and cut the exercise short, if necessary.

"I'm not really a hang-out-in-graveyards kind of person," Mike called out. She trailed after Deja, who seemed to have a general idea of where she was going.

"This is an important graveyard," Deja said, never stopping or turning around. They trudged on past endless headstones and mausoleums. The place was old, full of plaques and onlookers. Mike remembered trying to find Jim Morrison's grave in Paris, the afternoon she'd slipped away from her French class. She'd been suspended for that, but she'd had her first Belgian beer and always thought it was worth it.

"I bet that book wasn't big on bringing your . . . blended children to cemeteries, huh?"

"I bet that book would burst into flames if it knew about this." Deja laughed. "But sometimes you just have to do what's right."

They walked on, Deja occasionally stopping to check the map she had printed before leaving home. "Almost there," she said. "It's pretty here, isn't it?"

Mike didn't answer. Even if it was pretty.

Finally, Deja stopped and turned to face Mike, who nearly bumped into her. "Okay," Deja said, somewhat breathless, "like I said, I know I'm crossing a line, but right is right." Mike was too surprised to pull her hand back when Deja took it, and too curious to resist when they stepped off the path.

Too late, Mike realized what she was about to see. She stopped. She let go of Deja's hand.

"This?" Mike asked, suddenly angry. "Does he know that you brought me here?"

"He knows," Deja said. "He couldn't do it, Mike. He was going to, he wanted to. He couldn't."

"This is sick—" Mike started, but Deja had stepped

aside and now she was standing two feet away from a headstone that read, "CAROLINE MORTON EDWARDS, Cherished Wife and Mother, 1948–1979."

Mike couldn't move. Her head felt light, as if she were looking out from behind herself at a set piece from a movie. There was a headstone with her mother's name on it. The ground or the air had shifted abruptly and nothing was real.

"My mother is buried in Brooklyn?" she asked softly.

"It's where she grew up," Deja told her gently. "Right near the park."

Mike had nothing to say. She felt as if her skull were expanding like a balloon, and soon it would be too light to stay attached to her shoulders. Maybe it would float off into the air over Green-Wood Cemetery. Maybe this film set headstone would be the last thing she'd see.

"He should have brought you here," Deja said, "a long, long time ago."

"I didn't know," Mike said, not completely sure to what she was referring.

"You didn't even know where she was," Deja said, as if to remove some sort of blame.

Mike stared. Her mother was an idea, a photograph on the mantel, a pile of children's books. She wasn't real. She had never been real. She had never been a presence. But you had to be real to have a headstone in Green-Wood Cemetery. You had to exist in some physical, corporeal form. You had to have existed once.

"He didn't think you'd come if he'd told you."

"Right," Mike said. She wouldn't have.

"You had a mother, Mike. And you had a right to know where she was buried and to come visit if you wanted. And to know who she was. You should have at least had photographs and stories and memories."

It had been so long since Mike had imagined photographs and stories of her mother. She didn't have her own memories and her father never offered any of his and she had learned early, so early she didn't even remember learning it, that it was better not to ask. She didn't remember anymore being hastily removed from his lap and replaced on a sofa because he had to leave the room. She didn't remember the way his face would seem to cave in on itself when she asked for her mother. She just remembered not to ask.

"He loves you, Mike, and he loved Caroline, so much that when she was gone he had to put her away. I think he almost had to pretend that she didn't exist so he could stop missing her so much. He wanted to do the right thing for you. He just didn't have the strength to keep her and himself alive at the same time."

It was all whizzing past Mike, and entering her just the same. All these years she had been without a mother and really that mother had been in Brooklyn, under a rock, waiting to be visited and brought flowers and sat by. Except Mike couldn't picture herself doing any of those things.

"He did the best he could."

Mike wondered if Deja expected her to cry or to break down. She hoped she wasn't supposed to fall in a heap at her mother's grave because she didn't have it in her. She didn't do things that way.

"He says you're a lot like her."

"I don't know what that means."

"I know," Deja said. "That's okay. Maybe you can start to find out."

Mike nodded because she thought it might make Deja stop talking.

"I'll give you some time," Deja said.

"For what?" Mike asked.

"So you can be with her." Deja walked away and Mike was left standing, not with a *her* as Deja had suggested, but with an it. A stone and some grass, and from this she was expected to construct a mother? She wondered if Gunther were home in Park Slope right now, and whether she could find his apartment if she just walked north on Fourth Avenue. It couldn't be that far. She could knock on his door and he would be so surprised and she would say, "Pour me a drink. I have had the world's strangest day." He would say the right things. It wouldn't matter that everything was alien and not right between them. He would be there because she needed him. He would make her feel like herself again.

Mike noticed that the grandparents she'd barely known had stones buried alongside her mother. There was no space for her father here, which was probably fine as there was no space for Deja either. Mike wondered where she would be buried if an air conditioner fell on her as she walked home that afternoon. She looked at the dates on her mother's headstone again.

1948–1979.

"She was my age," Mike murmured to no one in particular.

Her father was sitting in the living room when they arrived home. Mike and Deja had ridden the train in silence. Mike wasn't angry, but she wasn't grateful either. She wasn't anything. She was just trapped in someone else's movie, hoping the reel would run out soon.

Her father stood up when they came in. He didn't say anything and neither did Mike. Deja calmly walked to him, leaned up to his face and kissed him on the cheek. He looked at her and Mike saw something in that look that she didn't have a word for. Deja patted him gently on the chest and exited into the hallway without a word.

Mike stood across the room from her father and stared for a long time, silent. She thought she could hear the building moaning slightly in the wind.

"I know," he finally said. "I should have been the one to take you."

She didn't know how to answer.

"I know that," he said again. He looked different to Mike. Older. She searched for signs of the college football player but couldn't find any in his stooped shoulders and hanging head.

"The truth is," he said, and his voice shook just slightly, "that if you could only have one of us you should have had her. Caroline would have done it all so much better. She was so much better." Fat tears were sliding down his cheeks but he stood before Mike as if he were meant to take some kind of punishment.

"For months after she died I waited for her," he said. "I figured she could leave me but there was no way she could leave you. You were just a little...tiny thing. You needed her. Some days I couldn't even move. Couldn't get out of bed. There was this...thing, this weight sitting on my chest. I only kept going because of you. There were days..."

Mike had never seen her father cry. Even now she was surprised that the mechanism existed inside this big man.

"It was gonna kill me. I know that sounds silly, kid, but it was. And I couldn't fix it. I couldn't make it stop. I would smell her perfume in a coat closet and think I was having a heart attack. I couldn't show that to you. I couldn't..."

It took a long time for Mike to realize she was crying too.

"So I took all the pictures down. I put all her clothes in boxes and I sent them away. I'm sorry, Michaela. I didn't know what else to do."

Mike didn't remember the last time her father had called her by her name.

"I'm like her?" she asked. She was surprised at how much she wanted to know.

"Oh, God." He sighed. "Sometimes the way you look at me when I'm being an idiot..." He smiled. "All the writing, the creativity, you know that's all from her."

Mike's eyes were blurred with tears but she didn't try to wipe them away.

"When you smile..." he said. He looked down to the coffee table where a large leather album lay. "This was Deja's idea," he said. "But I made it myself. I owe this to you."

For the second time in one day, Mike found herself unable to move. She felt as if her boots were glued to the carpet. Her mother was underneath that leather cover. When she opened it, Caroline would no longer be just that winking photo on the mantel and a headstone in Brooklyn. Mike didn't know if she was ready to gain a mother and lose her all over again.

Whether time had slowed or her brain was deceiving her, Mike didn't realize he had moved until her father was holding her. He held her so tightly that he picked her right up off the ground, and Mike didn't try to stop sobbing into his shoulder. She shook and cried and her father held her up. And when she quieted he took her to the sofa and sat her down and opened the book that would give Michaela Edwards back a piece of her mother.

GETTING THERE
IS HALF THE FUN

Gunther was the one she wanted to tell everything to, as soon as she could find the words. She regretted kissing him, more than anything, because never before could she remember needing so much for things to be safe again. Her shell had been smashed and now she was an oozing, quivering blob who could only hope to crawl under a rock for shelter. You should never kiss your rock unless you're sure.

If the roles had been reversed, Mike might have found a reason not to attend the rehearsal dinner. She would have called in sick or pleaded subway delays to avoid showing up at the waterfront restaurant at the appointed hour. But Gunther arrived as promised, with his friend the photographer in tow.

"We can't thank you enough," Deja told him. "You're a lifesaver."

"Anything for the Edwards family," he said.

Mike flinched at the ease with which he was able to include Deja in the family he didn't even belong to. He admitted kindness as if it didn't cost him a thing.

They smiled at each other from across the room. He'd called first. She needed to take the hard walk over. She owed it to him.

She waited nearly forty-five minutes. She engaged in conversation with anyone and everyone she could think of, catching Gunther's eye occasionally, but turning back to Grace or Emily or Deja's ex-husband before actually crossing the room to talk to him. It was only when she saw him chatting with Cheryl that she felt compelled to approach.

The two of them were deep in conversation when Mike joined them, and she heard Gunther clearing his throat as she approached. Cheryl looked behind her and saw Mike, who thought she sensed an abrupt change in the tone of their patter.

"Hi," she said.

"Hey, Mikey," Gunther said and smiled, warmly if awkwardly.

"Don't you look pretty," Cheryl said stiffly.

"What's going on?" Mike asked.

"Eating and drinking," Gunther said, holding a potato puff aloft in a cocktail napkin.

"Nice place," Cheryl said, looking toward the large windows that let out on the harbor.

"Mm-hmm," Mike concurred.

"Sure is," Gunther said simultaneously.

Cheryl looked from one to the other and then drained her half-full glass of chardonnay in two swallows.

"I'm gonna get some more wine," she said, smiling broadly.

Left alone, they found a million things to look at and nothing to say.

"How's that speech?" Gunther finally asked.

Gerry and Deja had strictly decreed that their wedding reception would be free of long· toasts and pageantry. Speeches by their children-cum-attendants were to be made at the rehearsal dinner or not at all.

"I've rewritten it about three hundred times," Mike said.

"Oh, yeah?"

She fished for a way to explain to him in a sentence all that had happened during the past week. He took her silence for discomfort and tried to fill it.

"Can't be easy, giving your old dad away."

"It's not even that," she said. "There's so much…"

"Yeah," he said.

She wished fervently that they could have just talked to each other, in the shorthand they used to use. It was like they were hobbled now.

"You know I'm not good at this stuff," she said, and she hoped he understood that she meant utterly everything.

"No one's good at speeches," he said.

They stood in silence and listened to the jazz band playing "Girl from Ipanema." Kristen appeared at Mike's elbow.

"Hey," she said, "Kimmy and I are gonna give this toast as soon as the song is over. And then you can go, 'kay?"

"Okay," Mike said, but her stomach pitched nervously.

"Just so you know, we're keeping it super short and sweet. I am no good at this." Kristen grinned, patted Gunther on the arm, and disappeared to find Kimmy.

"See?" Gunther said. "Nobody's good at this." His smile only made her feel farther away.

The music began to fade, and Mike watched Kristen and Kimmy taking the microphone from the singer. Kimmy tapped it lightly.

"Already on," Kristen told her.

Kimmy ignored her sister and began. "Hi, everyone!" she said warmly. "My sister and I wanted to take a minute to say a few words about the happy couple while you're all good and liquored up enough to believe them."

The assembled guests laughed appreciatively, while Kristen took the mic.

"As you all know, our mom is one terrific lady, and we have never seen her quite so happy as she's been since she met Gerry. We knew it was serious when she told us she was thinking of trying red meat for him."

Laughs from the crowd.

"She didn't like it," Kimmy said. "Sorry, Ger."

"And Gerry is a truly great guy," Kristen went on. "He has been warm and welcoming to us from the beginning, and has given our dad someone to share his golf club membership with." She and Kimmy giggled together.

"We have an extremely cool new sister," Kimmy said, "who seems completely unfazed by the sheer craziness of our family when we're all together, and of that we are truly in awe."

"We love ya, Mike," Kristen said and Mike blushed. "And more than anything we just want to wish Gerry and Mom many, many happy, silly, vegetarian years together. We love you both!"

Gerry and Deja clapped furiously and the rest of the crowd joined in. Kimmy motioned for Mike to come up and take the microphone.

"Go get 'em," Gunther whispered, and Mike could not have been more grateful to hear his voice. She turned to smile at him and it was the first time they'd really looked at each other all evening.

Kimmy handed the microphone off as Mike stepped up and cleared her throat.

"Hi—wow this is loud," she said, surprised at how her voice filled the room. "I'm Mike, Gerry's daughter."

Her father beamed and the corners of Deja's eyes crinkled up.

"A lot of you don't know me, but...I hope that I will know you, because you're obviously very important to Deja. I was...shocked...is really the only word that fits, I was shocked when my father told me he had met someone."

Taking the joke as it was intended, the assembled friends and family chuckled.

"Not because he isn't a hideously eligible bachelor of course, but I guess because we'd gotten pretty well used to being on our own, the two of us." She looked at her father. "I think we thought we were doing okay and I guess, in our own way, we were. But since Deja's been around..."

Mike's hands were shaking. She wanted to do this right. She wanted it to be special.

"I didn't know my mother," she started again. "But from what I know of her, I know she would be grateful that you found us." Mike saw the tears in Deja's eyes. "We're not an easy family to infiltrate. We're small, but we're tough. But I think you've made us...easier. You've given something to my father, everyone can see it, something that no one else has been able to give him."

She swallowed hard.

"You've given something to me that I didn't know I needed." Mike paused. "And, Dad, I haven't been much of a best man. But you have been a great man. I want you to know that I think you're very brave. For everything a long time ago and for everything now. I don't think I've ever had the courage that you do, but I hope that someday I might. To second chances"—Mike raised her glass—"and to both of you."

The crowd toasted and cheered, but Gunther clapped the loudest. Gerry hugged her for a long time. Deja took Mike's face in both her hands, looked up and smiled and nodded. "You're a good one," she said.

Mike escaped from the crowd and the noise and the honesty as soon as she could. Gunther found her after the dancing started, standing just beyond the French doors and staring out at the water.

"The view's much prettier out here," he said. "Take a walk with me?"

They carried their drinks out onto the large terrace overlooking the harbor.

"Too cold?" he asked.

"Just cold enough," she said.

They stared at the lights of the Brooklyn Bridge.

"I feel like I haven't seen you in ages," she said finally.

"I know," he said.

"We haven't done this very well."

"No," he agreed. They looked in opposite directions for the longest time.

"God," he said, "I don't know how to be awkward with you, Mikey."

"I know!" she said, with immense relief. She set her drink down on one of the flagstones. "We can shake this off though, I mean, come on! It's not such a big deal, right? It doesn't have to be."

"It doesn't," he affirmed. "Absolutely not."

"Where have you been?" she asked. "How goes the article?"

"They bought it," he said quietly, smiling.

"The *Sydney Morning Herald*? They bought it?"

He nodded and she checked the impulse to throw her arms around him in congratulations. "That's amazing! That's incredible! They bought it!"

"There's more," he said, sheepishly.

"Hit me," she said, lifting her glass again.

"They want to talk about a job. A real reporting job. News. Investigative. Everything I've been missing."

"They what?" She could feel a punch in the gut coming. She didn't want to ask. She wanted to turn away and dodge it and never hear what he was going to say. "What does that mean?" she asked.

"It means I'm flying to Sydney next week to talk with them," he said. He paused. "I did it, Mikey. I quit."

Sydney. How, she wondered, could he have slipped so far away so fast? It had only been weeks. How could he pick up and leave her in only a few weeks?

"I don't know what to say," she said. "I'm...gob-smacked."

He laughed. "I was hoping you'd say you're happy for me."

"Of course," she said, and she almost choked on it. "I'm just...it's so fast."

"I had to make changes, Mikey. I was stuck, I was drowning."

"I know," she said. "So, when? I mean, if you—"

"Still working out the details. But it would be soon."

She couldn't imagine every day being like the past month. Every day without him. She wasn't supposed to be without him.

"Say something," he said.

"Sometimes the dingoes eat your baby," she said.

He looked into the bottom of his glass before peering into her face. "Mikey, sometimes they don't."

She looked at him. He was almost grinning at her, holding back so she could catch up. "What does that mean?" she asked.

"You ever think that that's what's been wrong with us all this time? That we decided everything would go to shit and so it did? Careers, relationships, all of it."

"You're psychobabbling," she said.

"I'm not." He laughed. "I've just been thinking lately of all the things I haven't done. Things I wish I would have tried and failed at, at least I'd know."

She said his name in hopes he'd be shamed into ending this discussion. They were dancing much too close to the edge of a real conversation and Mike felt the cold thing in her gut rearing up again.

"There are moments," he said, "where things can be . . . improved on, even if they can't be perfect. There are moments where it's better to give it a shot."

"Gunther," she said again.

"Are we ever gonna talk about it? Because I can't pretend forever that—"

She was having trouble swallowing. "I guess we're talking about it now," she interrupted him. She wondered if she was having an asthma attack. She was sure that this must be what it felt like, the inability to draw a proper breath. She wanted to stop. She wanted everything to stop before they took that last step and there was no going back. Before everything was irrevocably different.

"Mikey," he said softly.

"You never tell me that I'm beautiful," she said, and her own voice sounded harsh in her ears.

"You don't need me to tell you," he said.

"But why don't you? Everybody else does." She wondered what it was she was accusing him of.

"Because what everybody else says wouldn't be what I mean and you know it," he said.

"Why are you doing this now?" she asked. Now, when you're leaving me, she thought, now, when it doesn't even have a chance to matter.

"Because I can't wait anymore," he said.

Mike's heart was attacking her. What she knew seemed romantic to him, the water, the courageous avowals before he sailed for distant shores, seemed cruel and punishing to her. She didn't want to be the thing he would always be glad he tried. She wanted all of it, every day, or none of it. She wanted him in the bar and on the phone and in her classroom and in her bedroom or she wanted him to disappear so she could start the process of losing all over again. But halfway seemed wrong. One time seemed wrong. Just to be something he didn't have to regret not doing.

"Do you know how long I've wanted to say this to you—"

He never got the chance to finish the sentence, because before Gunther knew what hit him Mike was kissing him again. Not the way he wanted to be kissed, not like the last time, but fiercely, angrily. This was how she lashed out, this was how she took control.

"Hey, hey, slow down," he said, pulling back and taking her hands.

"I don't want to slow down," she said, which was true, she couldn't. If she slowed down the cold thing inside her would expand, it would have time to mount a real attack and she would be overtaken. She would be frozen solid with the fear and the panic and the pain of losing him. Give him what he wants, she thought, and send him away, knowing that he wasn't any different from the rest of them.

"We've waited too long to rush through this," he said and he touched her face. "So long..."

She didn't know how to digest his kindness, his warmth, when he'd just gotten through telling her that he was leaving her. For every ounce of her that wanted to hold him as tightly as she could, there were two that told her to stay far, far away. He rested his forehead against hers.

"What do you want me for?" she demanded.

"For everything," he said.

Mike could hear pieces of her insides breaking and crumbling away. She had been right all along. You couldn't do this without losing. You couldn't love without pain.

When he kissed her again she didn't fight the tiny explosions in her chest.

They didn't say goodnight to anyone. They were in a taxi and hurtling toward Brooklyn over the very bridge they'd been staring at when everything had changed, immeasurably, forever.

DOES SHE OR
DOESN'T SHE?

Waking began as warmth against her back and the sense of being a clam in a shell, safe and untroubled.

This, in itself, was the trouble.

As soon as she was alert enough to perceive the enormous arm, like a suspension cable, draped over her waist, her eyes snapped open. The sadness hit her like a wave and knocked her to the bottom of something she had thought she could float above. She was nestled against the wall of his chest and her sleep had been oddly deep and dreamless. The best sleep she'd had in too long to remember.

She didn't move. He was still dozing.

They had really done this. She remembered every instant, because she had known as she was doing it that she was storing it all away. She was packing him into boxes and moving him into the basement so she could get up every morning and live some semblance of her life when he was gone. It didn't seem fair now that she had to wait for him to actually go.

It was her father's wedding day. She was in Brooklyn. She'd had sex with Gunther. She looked toward the window, hoping to see heavy frost and perhaps an airborne pig. Gunther was going back to Australia and there wasn't a pig in sight.

In any other apartment, with any other man, she would have delicately slipped out from beneath the arm, disengaged herself from the foreign bedding, silently collected her various accoutrements, and been on the sidewalk before he was yawning awake. He wouldn't have had her phone number or her last name, in all probability, so there would have been no phone calls to dodge or e-mails to delete. No strings to cut on her way out the door.

Here in his bed, there were so many strings she could have done macramé.

He snorted and the enormous arm moved just slightly before she heard the gentle rhythm of his breathing resume. What would they do now? He had seen her naked, physically, yes, but more than that. The word "unbridled" came to mind with all its terrifying, wild horse implications. She couldn't pretend anymore. He'd seen everything. Now she would be naked all the time, except the time would be short, very short.

Her best friend, her safe place, was gone.

His hand moved on her hip. His finger traced up the side of her ribs and back down. She closed her eyes.

Everything was over.

"You're awake," he said, and it felt like an accusation. "Sleep okay?"

"Yeah," she said, still facing the wall.

He kissed the back of her neck and whispered, "Mikey." She wasn't doing that again. They were not going to do it again.

"What time is it?" she asked. She rolled toward him, forcing him to move away to make room for her, and she propped herself up on her elbows.

He grabbed the alarm clock. "Ten-thirty," he said.

"Today's the day," she said. She needed to go. She had so much to do. It wouldn't be running, she had a legitimate reason to go.

"Hey," he said, "you okay?"

"Oh, yeah." She tossed it off too quickly and knew it sounded false. Well, it was false, so screw it.

"I have to pick up the rings." She flopped down onto the pillow and pulled the covers up to her shoulders. She couldn't let him keep looking at her that way.

"We've got plenty of time."

She didn't like that "we." He was looking at her with half a smile. The other half was buried under that look he always had when he was handling her.

"You hungry?" he asked, which meant he'd registered that she wanted out of the bed and he wasn't going to try to fight her. Because he knew better. Because he knew her so well. Well, freaking good for him.

She was spinning and she wasn't sure how to stop. "Not really," she said. She wanted to get dressed, but she didn't want to be unclothed in front of him in the process.

"You're not okay," he said, and there was something so sad in his voice.

"I'm fine," she said. She tried to smile but she couldn't get her mouth to open.

"We can talk about this, you know," he said.

That was it. Better to be naked than to stay in that bed and have *that* conversation. She threw back the covers and dove for her underwear. "We don't need to talk about anything." She didn't look at him. She just slipped into her dress and wiggled her toes into shoes that hurt much more in the morning than they had the night before. Gunther sat without moving and watched her.

"What are you doing?" he asked.

"I'm getting dressed. What does it look like?"

"Mikey—"

"Nobody likes a disorganized best man!" She exited the bedroom and hurried into the kitchen to find her purse. Gunther pulled on a pair of shorts and followed her.

"Stop," he said.

"I'm like two hours from home right now, big guy. Don't have time."

"Mike, stop."

"What?" she snapped, more than she'd meant to and when she turned to face him she saw that the look she'd wanted most to avoid was already there.

"Don't do this," he pleaded.

She sighed. "I can't have this conversation right now," she said.

"Don't do this with *me*," he said and already he was angry.

"Don't do what with you?" she challenged, more at ease with his anger than his pain.

"I've been around far too long for either of us to pretend that I don't know your M.O., Mikey. I've seen you do this, with how many men? But you don't get to do it with me."

"Oh, spare me," she said.

"You wanted to be here as much as I did," he said, and she could see as he said it that he knew this was exactly the wrong move. "Come on," he said, "you and me, this is different. This is not like everybody else. It never has been."

"No, but it is now, isn't it?" she said.

"Not fair," he said.

"Admit it, it isn't different. It just took longer. Admit that you would have made a move a long time ago if you thought for a second that I would have gone for it." Though she couldn't have said it out loud, she understood suddenly that she could get rid of him. This was the moment she could finish it. She could drive the stake in just a little deeper and then he wouldn't try anymore and she wouldn't have to feel like an insect with a pin through it. She wouldn't have to make a teary trip to the airport to wish him triumph in his new life without her. "Everybody's got a strategy. And I've gotta hand it to you for having the patience. But you got what you wanted in the end."

She thought she could stare him down but she couldn't look at his face. She took her purse and her coat.

His voice stopped her at the door. "You're what I wanted," he said. He was so quiet. It wasn't a fight, it just was.

"I'm what everybody wants," she said.

"No," he said. "Not your body, not your face. You."

Open the door, she told herself. Open the door. "Right," she said.

"No, you don't have to stay," he said, and the ferocity in his voice was frightening, "but you don't get to call me a liar. I'm not the liar."

She wanted to go, but they were ending something and she needed to see it through. She said nothing.

"I know you, I know about all your missing equipment, and I want you anyway. Right now. As you are."

The air seemed to be getting thinner again. She knew she ought to move but she thought her knees might buckle. "As I am," she choked out one last gasp of sarcasm.

"And just so we're straight, the reason I've never made a

move is because what happened last night wasn't just about *me* wanting *you*. I'm not gonna make it easy for you to roll over me like you do everyone else, just because you're afraid of what might happen if you stayed."

She couldn't believe that he, of all people, had the nerve to use the word "stay." But it's almost over, she thought. She had almost survived it.

"Mikey." He softened. She could feel him gazing at her and it made her feel hot and faint, like she'd run up too many stairs. "Mikey…"

He took a step toward her and it gave her the strength to yank the door open and disappear into the hallway. She didn't look back as she raced down the stairs and out into the street. She had no idea how to get to the subway and she didn't want to throw up on a sidewalk in Brooklyn. Brooklyn. Yet again, she was being ripped apart and tortured in fucking Brooklyn.

IT'S THE REAL THING

Her father was in the kitchen drinking coffee. He put his mug down and looked up when she came in.

"Hi," he said. He looked at the dress she'd been wearing the night before. "You disappeared last night."

"Sorry," she said.

"It's okay." He smiled. He had always wanted this for her. Always wanted her to come to her senses and choose Gunther, the good guy. "Coffee?"

"Fast," she said. "Don't wanna get behind today."

"Sit with your old man," he said. He pushed out a chair for her. She poured a cup of coffee and dumped too much sugar into it.

"Where's Deja?"

"At Kristen and Emily's. Bad luck to see the bride on the wedding day, right?"

"Did you see Mom?"

"We got married in a courthouse. Nobody else there. So, yeah, I saw her."

It was the first easy reference either of them had ever made to Caroline. There was no tension, no preamble. She was just there, somewhere, within reach.

"Thank you for what you said last night," he said.

"It was nice. The dinner and everything."

"I'm getting married," he said.

"Yeah." She smiled. "You are."

He looked at her and Mike suddenly felt old, as if they were playing the wrong roles.

"I want you to know," he said, "that you can stay as long as you want. I know I didn't make it seem like that at first. But I mean it. This is your home."

"I appreciate it," she said. "But soon I'll need to go."

"When you've got something that pays enough."

"Soon, Dad."

"Okay."

They sat in silence for a long moment.

"I should get a move on." She pushed away from the table and rinsed her mug in the sink. "You need anything?"

"Nah," he said, leaning back in his chair. "I might go for a walk."

She had one foot in the hallway when he said, "Mike, just so you know—"

"Yeah?" She leaned back with one hand on the door-frame.

"I'm sorry I said Jay was a putz."

Mike laughed. "S'okay. I forgot all about it."

"It's just . . . I always thought the big guy liked you for all the right reasons."

Mike tried to keep her face from moving. "Okay," she said.

"Get going," he said. "You've gotta get me to the church on time."

Gerry and Deja were married in an intimate ceremony at the U.N. chapel. Mike was surprised to learn that it had been her father's idea. He liked the history of the place, the idea of what it represented.

Mike stood next to the groom and looked away from Gunther. She couldn't help but see him out of the corner of her eye, sitting in the third row of pews, next to Cheryl. She thought she caught them whispering as the music began. It didn't matter, he could whisper to anyone he liked.

Deja wore a pale yellow suit that Grace had said was reminiscent of Jackie O. Mike watched ten years fall away from Gerry's face when she appeared. Suddenly he was all shiny, standing straight and tall. Zachary carried the rings and managed to get almost all the way down the aisle before veering off at a distracted run. Everyone chuckled, watching Emily take his hand and lead him the rest of the way. Kristen and Kimmy walked with Deja, and Kristen rolled her eyes at Mike when Kimmy began to sob.

"Gerry and Deja chose to marry in the chapel at the United Nations for a reason," the minister began. "Because this is a place for the peaceful joining together of individuals who began at the far corners of the earth. It is a place for the melding of divergent pasts into a single vision of the future. It is a place for love and a place for hope."

Mike noticed that Gerry was holding Deja's hand. He had become a part of something, a new family, a new, bigger identity. It surprised her to realize that her father was going to be good at being married. She wished suddenly that he could have taught it to her the way he'd taught her to catch a football or make a burger. This part seemed too hard to learn on her own.

She tried to distract herself, to think of Boutros

Boutros-Ghali, of Nicole Kidman in *The Interpreter*. But Nicole Kidman is Australian.

"Seriously," Kristen whispered to Mike, as they stood in the receiving line after the ceremony, "your date is a fox."

Gunther was standing on the steps outside the chapel, chatting with one of her father's friends. Mike hoped she was smiling in response, but she could no longer tell.

The reception was held in the basement lounge of a fancy Chinese restaurant uptown, with an eel swimming through a huge aquarium. No seated dinner, thank God, so she wouldn't have to sit with him. They hadn't said a word to each other all afternoon, and his last "Mikey" still echoed in her head. Several times she'd caught him staring at her from across the room. Each time she'd turned away as quickly as she could. Just get through the day, she thought. Just get through the day.

"You look even more sour than usual, Michaela," Grace teased her as Mike picked at a pork dumpling.

"It's the shoes," Mike told her.

"Mm-hmm," Grace said, and Mike felt transparent. "I told your friend Gunther, he made quite an impression with your class. Maybe we can talk him into coming back."

"Maybe you can," Mike said, "but I doubt it."

Grace looked at her sideways. "Trouble in paradise?"

"Wouldn't know, I've never been," Mike said.

There was a general tinkling sound as several of the guests began to drum chopsticks against the sides of their wineglasses. Deja and Mike's father stood up on a step in the doorway and he very audibly cleared his throat.

"Ladies and gentlemen," Mike's father began, "if I could just interrupt your dim sum for a moment."

"We wanted to thank you all for being here," Deja said.

"Gerry and I are so blessed to have such wonderful family and friends. And we especially want to thank the very beautiful best man—"

Mike smiled sheepishly at assorted shouts from the assembled guests.

"—and my lovely attendants, my beloved daughters. We would be nowhere without our very accomplished ring-bearer—"

Emily and Kristen held Zachary in the air and he giggled.

"—and I owe a special thanks to Gunther Stuart, who saved us at the last minute from a wedding day with no photographs!"

The crowd clapped and hooted and Gunther raised his glass and said, "To you," to Deja and Gerry. Mike stared at her shoes.

"And now," Gerry said, "I would like to make a toast, to my stunning, extraordinary, incomparable bride."

A chorus of excited cheers rose.

"Deja," he said, "appeared at a time in my life when I had forgotten what it felt like to love and be loved by a woman. I didn't even think it was possible for me anymore. I thought I couldn't do it. I didn't remember how. And Deja," he said with tears in his eyes, "believed. She believed when I didn't. She believed for both of us. She believed for me, until I learned how to believe myself again. And because of her, with her, I have a life I never imagined I could have. Because of her I am grateful to wake up every morning. And because of her I am a better man than I ever thought I could be. Thank you, my love," he said.

Mike's father was crying. Deja was crying. Kristen and

Emily were crying. Even Zachary had stopped fidgeting and was hugging his Elmo doll tightly. Kimmy and her fiancé were crying, though David pretended it was allergies. Grace had tears streaming down her face. She stood and clapped, dragging her husband to his feet, which prompted the entire room to join in.

Hoping that no one would notice, Mike took the opportunity to slip out into the hallway outside the kitchen. She flattened herself against a wall to stay out of the way of the endless stream of busboys. She was out of tears, she was too tired to cry. She just wanted to escape.

This was where Gunther found her, and without being asked he held her and said nothing. When she pulled away, he took her hand and looked at the floor like a child waiting for his punishment. The careening busboys took barely any notice.

"We're not them, Gunther," she said.

"I know that," he answered.

"I'm not interested in having you fix me," she said, "and I'm not here to be a proud memory of the time you were brave enough to go for it."

"That's what you think I want," he said. Hurting him was suddenly all she knew how to do.

"We're not them," she repeated.

He squeezed his eyes shut for a moment and exhaled, then opened them and looked down at her. She watched him searching for the magic words that could bring this dying thing back to life. But they'd said everything.

"Why won't you try?" he asked, even though he knew she wouldn't answer and she didn't.

She observed the wrinkle that appeared between his eyebrows when he didn't know what to do. She stared at his irises and tried to memorize the color. She took in the feeling of having his huge form next to hers because she knew she was losing him and she couldn't stop.

"Apologize to Deja and your dad for me, will you?" he asked. He sprinted up the stairs. It was the first time he'd ever turned away from her.

HEAD FOR THE BORDER

Gerry and Deja took off for Italy the morning after the wedding. They were too happy to notice that Mike wasn't, and she wasn't going to make it obvious anyway. She wasn't someone to whom life simply happened. She strode through it, she made choices and then she owned them. So she told herself.

Gunther hadn't left her. She'd asked him to go. She didn't know when he would board a plane and she didn't care. She only hoped it would be soon.

Mike knew you were supposed to float in quicksand, that you'd only sink more quickly if you struggled and flailed against the inevitable. She chose not to consider the fact that at the rate she was going, no one would be there to hold out a branch when she needed to be pulled out.

Since her quiet breakdown, the Life Skills girls had been tender and concerned with Mike. They didn't argue with her or speak out of turn. Kinara left a packet of nut-free trail mix on her desk, Sadie a copy of Dr. Phil's new book. And Talia smiled. At least once a day.

Her stepsisters, and that was how they referred to themselves, called twice after the wedding to check in on her.

"Seriously," Kimmy said to Mike's voice mail, "come for dinner. We need to party while our parents are away."

Mike appreciated the care. She just wasn't ready to reach out for that branch.

She had begun to avoid the mirror. Cheryl caught her at school and suggested she not wait much longer to begin moisturizing.

"I'll give it some thought," Mike promised.

"Mike," Cheryl began to say, "why don't you just—"

"I have class," Mike said. She didn't want to know the rest.

She was walking again. Blocks and blocks around the city, out of her way, to nowhere in particular. She never seemed to get closer to or farther from anything. She was going in circles. A series of right turns that were always somehow wrong. She told herself they were both better off. She ignored the feeling that his absence was a chasm widening beneath her feet, a hole big enough to fall through.

And then one night, even after ordering Thai food and watching her fill of undersea mammals, she realized she wasn't remotely tired. She wouldn't be able to think about sleep for hours. The empty apartment seemed to echo around her. She tried to lose herself in a program about fighting sharks, but even the enormous teeth and rippling blood in the water failed to distract her. It was after midnight. She slipped into her jeans and threw on her jacket.

She listened to the sound of her boots striking the pavement and when she looked up she was almost at 60th

Street. She turned right on 59th. She crossed below Central Park. Even as she made her way toward Columbus Circle she pretended she was just walking.

She never for a moment considered it a good idea. Just an overwhelming need to get as far away as possible from reality, as quickly as she could.

"I knew you'd come back," he said when he saw her standing in the hall.

"Can I come in?"

He stepped aside and made way for her. She stood in the foyer, suddenly shivering. She hadn't realized she was so cold.

"There's a limit to the number of times you can show up at a man's door and expect him to control himself," he said, but he kept his distance as she kicked off her shoes and made her way into the living room. She let him stare. It was what she'd come for after all.

When she didn't say anything he said, "Good timing, in any case. The apartment's been rented. This time next week I won't be here."

He stood in the living room doorway, nowhere near her. She looked out the window at the glittering view. She regretted that she'd taken so long to get here. Every moment had been so exhausting for so long and with Brian everything was easy. Everything. She didn't have to move. She just had to stand here.

He poured her a scotch. She heard him set it down on the glass coffee table behind her.

"Just tell me now if I'm going to get my hand slapped again," he said.

"No," she told him. "You're not."

He still stood across the room. She knew that he was waiting for her to look at him but this felt better. Just looking out the window. There were so many other little windows, so many other people making their own mistakes. If she focused on them she could remember she was small and then it didn't matter how awful she was. She couldn't be the worst. Out of all those tiny windows she couldn't be nearly the worst.

"I know I shouldn't ask," he said.

"You'd have to be an idiot."

He laughed quietly. "That I would," he said. She heard him set his drink down and then he was behind her. He slid his hands around her waist and she felt him kissing her shoulder blades. She remembered how short he was.

"Why are you here?" he whispered into her back.

She didn't want to talk. Talking was thinking and she wanted to put her brain to sleep and to let her body be useful.

"Hmm?" He ran his fingers over her shoulder.

"Because you and I are the same," she said, quietly and firmly.

"Yesss." He hissed the sound into the smooth skin of her back and she felt herself finally giving up and sinking into the depths. Floating had taken so much work and she wasn't meant for it. She was too dark and too heavy, she belonged at the bottom.

She didn't need the drink he'd poured. She was underneath him on the sofa and he was kissing her and devouring her like a hungry hyena. It wouldn't even be sex, she knew, it would just be feeding some unspeakable self-destroying need that lived in them both. She didn't owe better to anyone.

As he kissed her she allowed herself to disappear, little by little. She felt herself melting into the leather sofa, as if she were becoming part of the upholstery, so by the time he was finished she wouldn't even be there anymore and that would truly be a relief.

Suddenly he stopped. He pulled back.

"What's wrong?" she said. If he made some kind of declaration she would fall apart. She was here for one thing and one thing only.

"What did you eat tonight?" he asked.

"What?"

"What did you eat?"

"Are you kidding me?"

"Fishy," he said.

She was mortified. "I can't believe this," she said. "You spend months trying to get me in bed and now we're quibbling about my breath?"

He opened his mouth and moved his jaw back and forth as if he had something stuck in his throat.

"Did you have shrimp?"

"Unbelievable." She slithered out from underneath him and he sat back on the couch, his hands at the sides of his throat. "You are just unbelievable!"

"Michaela, have you eaten shrimp tonight?" he demanded angrily, and the sound of her full name jogged a memory. "My mouth itches."

"Oh, God," she said, because he wasn't worried about her breath. Shrimp pad thai. Shellfish allergy. "Oh, God, Brian, I did. Yes, I did."

"Shit," he said, still clutching at his throat.

"I didn't even think—"

"Shit," he said again, and she knew that his throat was beginning to close up.

"You have an EpiPen! Where is it?" He could inject

himself with epinephrine and halt the allergic reaction. He could keep ahead of anaphylaxis long enough to get a taxi to the hospital.

"Don't have it," he said.

"What?! You keep one here!" She remembered it. She'd seen it in a kitchen drawer, she thought, or maybe in the medicine cabinet. She began to rush toward the bathroom.

"It's gone," he said, "I've boxed it up and sent it to Scarsdale. I was hardly going to be here. Throat's closing."

"I'll call 911." She fumbled for the cell phone in her coat pocket.

"Hospital," he said quickly. "They'll never get here in time."

By the time they were in a taxi he was making wheezing noises.

"It's okay," she told him. "You're okay."

He couldn't answer, or at least he didn't, and she wondered if maybe he wasn't okay. What if they didn't make it in time? How much time did he even have?

"You have to go faster." She leaned in to the cab driver and tried not to sound too desperate. Somewhere she remembered that panic would speed the progress of anaphylaxis. Her Life Skills CPR training would do no good at all if she couldn't even get air into his lungs.

He was starting to look slightly purple. "Brian," she told him, "we're almost there."

He nodded slowly.

She was the wrong person for this. She was the wrong person to be in this taxi with this dying man who was married to someone else. She didn't know how to do this.

She felt something brush against her and she looked down to see that he was groping for her hand. Still looking straight ahead, gasping and turning blue, he was reaching out for her. For someone who tore down lovers and abraded friends and made plants wilt just by looking at them. He was asking her, he was begging her to show up. Just that. Just show up.

It didn't matter to him that she didn't know how. It only mattered that she took his hand then.

"I'm here," she said. "I'm here."

"Okay, get out of the cab!" the driver shouted. They were in front of the emergency entrance at Mount Sinai. "Get out!" he shouted again. No one wanted a dead man in the back of his taxi. The driver began to honk. Mike could hear herself shouting for help and suddenly there were people in scrubs with a stretcher and they were taking Brian away. They were asking her questions and she was talking as fast as she could about the shrimp and the kissing and the packed-up apartment with no EpiPen. They wheeled him around a corner and she couldn't see him anymore. A triage nurse was shoving forms at her and asking questions whose answers she didn't know. She wasn't his wife.

Mike sat and waited. Any minute now the Worst Possible Choices Awards committee would be showing up to hand her a giant check. She wondered if she would scream and fall to her knees like all those people who were visited by Ed McMahon. Instead there was a doctor, who looked too young to be a doctor, explaining that Brian was resting. He was going to stay overnight.

"You should call his wife," she said. She watched the doctor taking in her age and the abashed look on her face. "She should be here."

"Do you want to see him?" the doctor asked.

"No," she said. "Just call his wife. And do you think... could you skip the details?"

"We'll leave that to the patient," he said, and turned away.

She sat in the waiting room and wondered how long exactly it would take for Ursula to get there from Westchester. At least an hour, she thought. Mike would recognize Ursula from the photos on Brian's desk, but Ursula had never laid eyes on her. What was the proper etiquette for this situation?

It would have been easiest just to leave. He was going to be fine, there was no reason for her to stay. But she thought of Brian's gray head lying on a pillow, alone in his hospital room and she wanted to know that someone was there with him. A few walls away, yes, but there. In case he asked.

He didn't.

Mike sat in the waiting room for nearly two hours. The Ursula who rushed in, breathless in Burberry, was too thin, and muscled in a way that suggested too many training sessions and not enough joy. It was nearly four AM, but Mrs. Bentley had taken the time to put makeup on. Or maybe she never took it off. Her tennis bracelet flashed under the fluorescents. Mike wondered if Ursula knew that it had been a freebie from a client, a South African diamond merchant. Probably not.

If she kept sitting here, she knew, the nurse would eventually raise a finger and point in Mike's direction. Ursula would turn toward Mike, and the blood would drain from her stretched and tightened face as she understood that everything she had certainly suspected of him was true.

Mike slipped out before that could happen.

As the chilly, early morning air hit her face, it occurred to her that she had done something right. She had taken care of someone, except he wasn't the one she wanted to waste it on. He wasn't the one whose hand she wanted to hold. Wrong accent, wrong everything.

If she wanted to be someone who made choices, someone who acted instead of being acted upon, now was the time. Suddenly, finally, she wanted to be brave and she wanted to make someone proud and she wanted to know that she could lose someone in the most unthinkable and grotesque way possible and that it would still be worth it.

She figured she could be in Brooklyn before six.

CAN YOU HEAR ME NOW?

So there was a too late after all. You could wait too long, stay silent too often when you should have spoken. Said nothing when you should have said, *Please don't go.*

She'd rung Gunther's buzzer five or six times before realizing that something was wrong. She'd awakened his neighbors one by one until someone had been foolish enough to buzz a stranger into the building. She took the steps to his apartment two at a time, and when at last she was standing in front of his door, she understood why he hadn't answered. There was a hole where the dead bolt should have been. She stared as if it wasn't real, checked the number on the door three times, spun around hoping an explanation lay somewhere in the tile floor of the hallway. She tried the door and found it unlocked. Stepping into his apartment was like entering a ghost town. She closed the door gently behind her and remembered slipping out through this same door, slipping through his hands when he'd tried to hold her. Everything was gone.

Mike slid down the blank stucco wall of Gunther's empty apartment in Brooklyn and sat on the floor until the sun was high in the sky. How could a person disappear so completely from your life so fast? He had said it would be soon and she should have listened. Some editor in Sydney had been smart enough to nail him down right away then, and now there was no more time. There were dust bunnies in the corner and a fuzzy outline on the wall where a photo of Uluru had hung but there was no more time.

She was getting good at this crying thing. If only Gunther could have seen her being ushered out of his bare apartment by an impatient super while tears rolled down Mike's cheeks, would he have understood then all the things she couldn't say? He had wanted her, broken and incomplete and malfunctioning, and she'd been ready to throw herself on the scrap heap and say no thank you. Asking him to stay seemed like the easiest thing in the world, now that she would never have the chance.

Yes, there was a too late and a too far and a just forget about it, it's over. But there was also someone who could tell her what she needed to hear, if only she could get him to say it to her face.

She walked to the subway crying while the Park Slope mommies looked on in horror. (They were just so glad to have settled down and been *done* with all that drama!) She rode the train crying and the schoolkids whispered and laughed because it didn't seem right to scream and carry on as usual with some lady crying all over the F train.

She cried as she walked home and she cried as her computer thrummed to life. She cried as she searched the Web for the information she needed, and all through her shower and the whole time she was getting dressed. As evening fell, she cried on the way downtown. She walked through Chelsea crying and sympathetic gym-goers peered out at her from above their muscle shirts and thought, With that face, how bad can things be? And when she reached her destination, she stood outside and waited. Crying. She had more than twenty-five years worth of reasonable crying to get through, and now she had a reason. She was a fucking girl, for fuck's sake, and occasionally every girl needed to have a good cry and if New York didn't like it it could shove it! She was crying, but she was still Mike.

She waited more than half an hour. Her nose was red and her eyes were puffy and guilty men in suits or knit caps or fancy Ben Sherman shirts that were expensive enough to look scruffy still passed her and wondered whether they could make her feel better, 'cause they sure would have liked to try. She noticed that none of them stopped to talk though, and thought maybe she should save this crying thing for the bars.

She somehow missed the moment when the man she was waiting for pushed through the door and out onto the sidewalk, but suddenly he was standing across the street from her. And any fear she'd had that he wouldn't see her dissipated immediately because he was staring straight at her. He stood for a moment and shook his head slowly from side to side, as if he couldn't believe she was there. He crossed the street to stand in front of her.

"Jesus," he said.

"Hi," she said, and she sniffled.

"Are you crying?" he asked, utterly incredulous.

"It's new," she said.

"Apparently."

They stood and looked at each other, waiting for the

three-year gap to close so they could stand in the same place and speak.

"Are you going to ask me what I'm doing here?" she said finally.

"I kind of assumed we'd get to that," he said. He was almost smiling. She tried to remember the last smile he'd directed at her but she couldn't.

"You look good, Jay," she said, because she was practicing what nice people said to each other and because he did.

"Thanks," he said. "I don't need to say that to you, do I?"

She offered him a small, wet laugh.

"Okay, what are you doing here?" he said. "Don't keep a turkey in suspense."

And now she knew she had to fess up to being a creepy stalker and that he would be insanely weirded out and she'd just have to stand there and take it. She needed him now. After all these years she finally needed him. "I've been coming to see your shows. I've been sneaking in and sitting in the back and then running away before you came out. I've been doing it for months."

He smiled at his shoes for a long moment. "I know," he said.

"You what?"

"I know." He looked at her shyly, as if he were flattered.

"I don't understand."

"Mike, these clubs are like the size of my bathroom. You look into the audience before you go on. Everybody does. And to be honest, you're kinda hard to miss."

"Oh, Christ," she moaned.

"By the way, you're pretty popular with these guys, so if you're ever looking to date another comic…"

"I can't believe this."

"Yeah, you'd make a lousy spy, just FYI."

"You think I'm crazy," she said.

"No, hey, I used to be in love with you, I know you're crazy."

She couldn't believe how even he seemed. Like he didn't even mind that she'd been skulking around in dark corners pretending she was invisible every time he got up on stage. Like he didn't hate her anymore.

"I mean, it was a little weird at first. I don't usually do material about people to their faces, but it was kind of cathartic in a way. At least you were showing up, which was a step up from where we used to be."

"You have to tell me what it is, Jay."

"What what is?"

All of a sudden it was hard to find the words. It's not easy to say, "Tell me why you fell out of love with me. Tell me what I did wrong so I can learn to do it better. Tell me now because I've just been left again and I know it's all my fault." She tried to take a deep breath but it caught in her throat as a sob.

Jay began to shift his weight back and forth. He shoved his hands in his jacket pockets and cleared his throat. Ah, she knew this routine. This was nerves. This was the moment before he'd asked her out. The moment before he'd asked her to move in.

"Listen, Mike, about the jokes…"

Oh, no, she thought, this was the moment he was going to apologize.

"Jay, no—"

"No, I need to say this—"

"I'm telling you, you don't—"

"Three years and you still can't listen!" he shouted.

"Okay," she quieted. "I'm listening."

He cleared his throat again. "About the jokes. They're not...I mean...the way that I write...they're not really you."

"I know," she said.

"I mean, obviously you didn't really do all that stuff."

"I did enough," she admitted.

"Yeah, but...I just don't want you to think that you were, like...horrible or...It's exaggerated."

This was what Gunther had been talking about. This was one of those chances. One of those moments where even if you couldn't fix everything, you could make a few tiny things a whole lot better and it would be worth it.

"I was though," she said.

Jay looked at his shoes.

"I shut you down, Jay. And I knew I was doing it. I made you go away because that was what I wanted. I wanted you to go away and so I made you do it."

"Are you trying to make me feel better? Because this is..."

"I don't know," she said. "I just...I guess it's been long enough that I've let you think it could have been different and it couldn't. I couldn't."

"Wow," he said.

"No kidding," she said.

They said nothing, but Mike had stopped crying.

"You really want to know?" Jay asked her.

"I really do."

"So you cry now," he said, after a moment.

"I told you, it's new."

"You know, Gunther always said one day you'd grow up and that that was worth waiting for."

Mike felt a tightening in her chest.

"I always told him he'd been punched by one too many

kangaroos," he went on. "Maybe he got you better than I did. You still talk to him?"

She didn't know how to answer that and he didn't wait. "I always thought he was in love with you, you know."

Mike kicked at the pavement with the toe of her boot. "I need your help," she said, because she couldn't say any of the other things she was thinking.

"Am I dying?" he asked. "Isn't this what happens when you die? You get to see miracles?"

"I'm serious," she said.

"So am I." He smiled. "Mike Edwards shows up crying and asking me for help. It's like Christmas."

"You're Jewish."

"Well, this is how I imagine Christmas."

She smiled. "Can we go somewhere and talk?"

"There's a diner down the street. Let me just call my girlfriend and tell her I'll be late."

"You gonna tell her you're with me?" she asked.

"Full disclosure," he said, extracting his cell phone. "Works a lot better."

Over a cup of coffee, Mike listened patiently while Jay explained the various ways in which she'd broken him down and pushed him out the door.

"Your new girlfriend," she asked, "she's . . . softer?"

"She's a girly-girl," he confirmed. "But not when it counts. She's cool. You'd like her."

"I don't really want to know her," Mike said truthfully.

"You know that's not your problem, right?" he said.

"What?"

"It was never about being ladylike or something. It was just . . . it was kind of like dating Dirty Harry. You could stand to let somebody in."

She nodded.

"Honestly," he said, "you're a beautiful girl, you know that. But the way that men look at you . . . you use it to keep them away. I felt so lucky when you gave me a shot."

"Yeah, right," she said, "if you'd only known."

"I did, Mike. I'm serious. I was like, honored or something. And I kept figuring I'd get at whatever was in there when you thought I deserved it. But I never did. So there I was, feeling like I'd won the lottery and you never exactly tried to convince me otherwise."

"You deserved better than you got," she said.

"I was no dreamboat."

They laughed.

"Can I ask," he finally ventured, "what brought on the need for this long-delayed postmortem? I mean, I didn't think we were ever going to speak again."

She exhaled slowly and decided partial disclosure might be best. "Because I loved somebody," she said, "and I didn't deserve him. And I'd like to be someone who does."

DRIVERS WANTED

She was being punished and she deserved that. So she didn't try to call Gunther. She didn't send an e-mail. He had made his choices and probably they were the right ones. He would be better off without her.

She threw herself into teaching. Her lessons were more elaborate, more inventive than they'd ever been. She showed up early and stayed late. She reorganized her desk. She cleaned the whiteboard.

One morning, when Mike arrived at school to prep, Grace was waiting in her classroom. A skinny, frail-looking young man in a sweater vest leaned against Mike's desk. He wore a cast on his leg.

"Good morning," Mike said tentatively. She clutched her paper cup of coffee.

"Michaela," Grace said, "this is Derek Luce."

"Hello," he said. He reached out his hand but Mike had to cross the room to reach him. She felt something bad coming. "Pleased to make your acquaintance," Derek Luce said.

"Yeah," Mike replied. "How's the leg?"

"Much better. Much, much better."

"Derek is recovering faster than anyone expected," Grace said.

"Great," Mike said.

"Wonderful," Derek Luce said.

"He's ready to come back, Mike."

Mike looked at Grace. "When?"

"Immediately," Derek Luce said. "Monday."

"Today is Thursday," Mike said. "I committed to another three weeks. That was what we agreed on, Grace." She couldn't believe what she was saying, that she was actually asking to stay on longer. But to lose her days with the Life Skills girls suddenly seemed like more than she could take.

"It's Derek's class," Grace said gently.

"I know," Mike said. "I know, but you're … don't you want to heal? It's a lot of work, teaching this class."

"He knows," Grace said.

"I've been teaching it for six years."

Mike looked from Grace to Derek Luce and back again. This was the wrong time to lose her job, her class. They were the only people she looked forward to seeing when she got up in the morning. She didn't want to go back to lonely, aimless days that stretched on endlessly into purgatory.

Mike sat heavily on one of the chair-desks. "I didn't teach your curriculum," she said defiantly to Derek Luce.

"I explained," Grace said.

"Subs always change things," Derek Luce said.

"They don't raise their hands anymore."

"We'll deal with the changes." Derek Luce was calm. He looked prim and persnickety. Mike disliked him intensely. He was taking her girls away.

"Monday?" she said plaintively.

"Let's take a walk to my office while Derek gets himself organized," Grace suggested. She put a protective arm around Mike and led her out of the classroom and down the hall.

"I left my coffee in there," Mike murmured.

"It's okay," Grace said.

"He'll drink it."

"No, he won't."

Grace settled Mike in a chair in her office. "I'm sorry," she said. "I know it's sudden."

"We haven't even covered everything."

"That's the thing with children. You never get to cover everything."

Mike sulked. She pouted. She slumped in her chair.

"Michaela, you're not a teacher."

"I know," Mike grumbled petulantly.

"You've done a magnificent, slightly crazy job with a class you were never meant to teach. And those little girls are better for it."

Mike looked up.

"They're better for it," Grace repeated. "But it's time to let them go, and go back to what you do best."

Mike snorted. What she did best was no longer available to her. It had been weeks since she'd missed her real job. She wasn't even sure if she wanted it anymore, and you had to want it. You had to want it worse than anyone else.

"I don't have anything to go back to," she said.

"Yes, you do," Grace said. "I sent your video to the national office."

"My parents' night video?"

"They want to buy it from you. And they want to meet with you about a job in the marketing department. Regional director."

Mike stared at Grace dumbly.

"Close your mouth when you go for the interview. You look like an idiot," Grace said sternly.

"Thank you, Grace."

"You thank me now. You get this job, who do you think you'll be answering to? You won't be thanking me then."

"I might."

"Nobody likes a suck-up, Michaela. Now go thank those little girls for putting up with you."

For her last day of class, Mike made cookies for the Life Skills girls. She watched their little faces twist and scrunch as they attempted to chew and swallow the leathery disasters.

"They're not good, are they?" she asked.

They smiled pitifully at her, their cheeks bulging.

"Spit 'em out," she said. They all did. Every last one. "Sorry," Mike explained, "I suck at baking."

"It's okay," Sadie said. "You have other gifts."

"When will you know if you have the job?" Brooklyn asked.

"Couple of weeks, maybe."

"Don't forget the firm handshake," Jahia said.

"And keep your answers short and to the point," Fenice added.

"You guys," Mike said, "I taught that to you. I know."

"It never hurts to be reminded," Asia said.

"Good point," Mike said.

She looked around the room. They looked so much older to her than they had seven weeks ago. When she'd first seen them they were a mob, a sea of shrill voices and cardigan sweaters that were there to defeat her. And now they were eleven little women with their own personalities and ideas and habits. It must be terrifying to be truly responsible for making one of these, she thought, and she hoped her father and Deja were soaking up the Italian sun and drinking Chianti.

They each hugged her on the way out, but Talia hung back so she could be the last one out. She hoisted her pink backpack over one shoulder and stood with her other hand on her hip.

"I don't like Mr. Luce," she said.

"Good," Mike replied.

Talia smiled. "You'll really be upstairs?"

"If I get the job, I'll be upstairs from ten to six, five days a week."

"Does it pay okay?" Talia asked.

"Okay enough." Mike smiled at her. "Aren't you gonna be late for your next class?"

Talia paused. "My mom's coming home," she said. "In two months. She might have to go back again but she'll be home at least for a while. You wanna meet her?"

"Talia, my friend, I would love to meet your mom."

"I'm your friend?"

"Yeah." Mike thought for a minute. "You're my short friend. I should get some girlfriends."

After Talia had gone and Mike had cleared the last of her stuff out of the desk, she flicked off the light switch and shut the door on her classroom, Deja's classroom, for the last time. She had one more thing to do.

As Mike rounded the corner by the gymnasium, Cheryl appeared out of nowhere in a flowing pink and blue caftan. Her blonde curls were piled in a high cascading fountain on top of her head.

"Oh, you're still here." Cheryl seemed awkward, uneasy.

"Almost gone," Mike said.

"Well, good luck then. I heard you might be joining the worker bees upstairs."

"I might, thanks."

"Well, it's been nice getting to know you," Cheryl said and extended her hand. This all seemed terribly formal and unnecessary to Mike, but she shook it anyway.

"Thanks for helping me out in the beginning," Mike said, even though she wasn't sure exactly what Cheryl had done. It seemed like the right thing to say.

"Can I be honest?" Cheryl said. "The more I get to know you, the less I understand."

"Huh," Mike said genially, "that makes two of us. Take care, Cheryl." She moved on and left Cheryl standing mystified in the hallway. "See you around," Mike called over her shoulder.

She found her way eventually to the library. The stacks seemed humorously low to the ground, like everything was scaled for hobbits. The librarians seemed to tower sleepily over their empire. Mike addressed the nearest adult, a middle-aged man leaning over the card catalog.

"Excuse me," Mike whispered. "I'm a sub here, and I'd like to make a donation to the library. Who should I speak to about that?"

"You can talk to me," the man said. "What have you got?"

From her bag, Mike pulled four slim hard-backed books. There were quirky illustrations on the covers, each featuring a strange-looking furry animal with a rodential head, short legs, and a long tail. She handed them over.

"*Edwina the Mongoose,* by Caroline Edwards," the man read. "Any good?"

"Yeah," Mike said. "Really good."

"Thanks," the man said. "I'll catalog them."

"My pleasure," Mike said. And that, at least, was true.

YOU'VE COME
A LONG WAY, BABY

Three and a half months later, Mike Edwards woke up knowing that her mother was nearby for the first time in nearly thirty years. She could look south from her new one-bedroom apartment and just make out the gothic spires of Green-Wood Cemetery climbing into the sky. She missed the enormous television, but she no longer felt the need to watch so many commercials. She missed the spinach scrambles, but had promised herself she'd try to cook once every month. She missed her family. But at least she had one.

Outer-borough life was not the frontier trial she had expected. They had restaurants, and yes, Deja proved to be a font of useful information in this regard, though no Moroccan cuisine had surfaced as yet. The commute wasn't nearly as bad as Mike had expected. She found that she liked the coffee she could buy from a cart on Fourth Avenue before she boarded the subway every morning. She missed wearing jeans to work, but supposed business casual was a small price to pay for the title of Regional Marketing Director, March Schools, Inc.

Her office was one floor above Grace's, and she liked to stop what she was doing and listen when she heard strains of phone conversation floating up through the defunct pneumatic mail tubes. She'd begun to find Grace's tirades inspiring. She popped by the Life Skills class to give the occasional guest lecture when Derek Luce had physical therapy.

Every Friday afternoon, Mike took yoga. Basic yoga, nothing too strenuous, no human pretzel-making. But she worked up a sweat and felt like she had a neck when she left. She rarely spotted Cheryl, at the studio or at school, but she no longer ran and hid when it happened.

Kristen and Emily had begun to host the family dinners every few weeks, in their refurbished limestone house in Carroll Gardens, and Mike was almost used to the laughter and the noise and the warmth, though she drew the line at babysitting. She hadn't spoken with Jay since their night at the Hollywood Diner. There wasn't much left to say and anyway they were ex-lovers, not friends.

She'd had no word from Gunther.

She thought of him though. In the morning when she stared at Australia on her map-of-the-world shower curtain. When she ate her toast and watched the morning news. When she saw a man opening a door for someone. When she heard an accent on the street. When she passed her old classroom. When her father bit his lip and didn't ask. When she drank whiskey. When she held still. When she was alone. When she was with people.

This was her sentence, she knew, for learning the lesson too late and hurting him one too many times. She liked to think that maybe someday she'd buy a ticket and board a plane and show up on his doorstep, but she knew she never would. To pick up the phone or type a message would have been to say she was ready to hold another human being like an egg in her hand and she didn't trust herself yet not to drop him or crush him or let him roll away.

She didn't visit the Drunk. It wasn't on the way from anywhere to anywhere she went anymore and besides, she'd decided not to drink alone. But in what Mike regarded as the ultimate concession to her X chromosomes, she'd developed a fondness for hot chocolate. Sometimes with mint or cinnamon, but most often with cayenne pepper. It was like dangerous chocolate.

She'd developed a Saturday ritual. She bought the *New York Times* and walked to Cocoa Bar on Seventh Avenue and she pumped herself full of sugar and worked on the crossword. She liked that she knew no one in Park Slope, now that Gunther had gone. She liked to sit and be left alone.

One early fall Saturday, she arrived with her paper to find that her usual table had been occupied. Applying pink lip gloss next to two empty coffee mugs was Cheryl, who started when she saw Mike.

"Oh!" Cheryl said. "Hi!"

"Hi, Cheryl." Mike smiled. She tried to think of something to say that wasn't "Get out of my neighborhood." "I thought you lived—"

"—In the East Village, I do!" Cheryl seemed nervous and overly bright, like a paralyzed chipmunk.

"Well, you're clearly here with a friend so I'll let you—"

The bathroom door opened, and an enormous Australian filled the doorframe before ducking his head to step out.

"Oh, my God," Mike said softly.

"Oh, my God," Gunther replied.

"Oh, my God," Cheryl concurred.

"You're not in Manhattan." Gunther looked at her, astounded.

"You're not in Australia," Mike said.

"You first," he said.

"I live here. I got a place. South Slope."

"In Brooklyn?" He didn't seem able to quite wrap his mind around it.

"I like the neighborhood," she said. "Now you."

"I was in Australia."

She waited, but he had stopped. "And . . ." she demanded.

"It didn't work."

"The job?"

"It just . . . didn't feel like home anymore. My family said I've gotten cynical. Everyone is so damned optimistic there."

"We ruined you," she said, and quickly added, "New York." Just so there was no confusion.

"Maybe." He laughed. "Maybe."

"I'm sorry," she said.

"Don't be," he said. "The *Herald* has me reporting from New York. For the moment."

"They hired you?"

"For the moment," he said. "They think there's a series of features in this Murdoch bit. We'll see."

"That's great."

"Yeah."

"It's terrific!" Cheryl added, though neither of them listened to her.

"Your apartment was empty," Mike said.

"Yeah, I had to move. The company rents it. Belongs to the next sucker now."

"Oh," she said. She could barely speak. He'd been here all the time.

"You went to my place?" he asked.

"While ago," she said, failing to sound nonchalant.

"I meant to call," he said, looking at his shoes.

"No, you didn't," she said. "It's okay. You were right."

"I guess you can only give a guy the flick so many times…" He meant it as a joke, but neither of them found it funny.

"He's got a great new place!" Cheryl piped up and Mike and Gunther both remembered she was there.

"I'm subletting from a friend of Cheryl's," he said hastily.

"Cobble Hill," Cheryl chirped, though no one noticed.

"I can't believe you're here," Mike said.

"Yep, we're all here!" Cheryl reminded them.

So her place had been taken, Mike thought. This was how it was. She'd leapt out a window and Cheryl had come through the door. She supposed it made some twisted sense.

Mike needed to go. She needed to get far away from the way Gunther was staring at her. "I've interrupted you," she said quickly. "I've gotta go."

"Okay," Cheryl said.

Gunther remained silent, standing there like an enormous monument to missed opportunities.

Mike made one final attempt at calm. "It was good to see you," she told him.

"Yeah," he said.

"See you Monday!" Cheryl said merrily.

"Monday," Mike said. She turned to make her escape. And she was almost at the door when she stopped.

Second chances are wasted on people too foolish to take them.

Mike turned back.

Gunther was still standing, staring as if she were a mirage, as if he'd blink and she'd disappear. Quickly, before she could change her mind, Mike marched back and faced him. All that stood between them now was Cheryl, still seated and staring up at a very tall tennis match.

"I miss you every day," Mike said to him. "I miss you so much that sometimes I think I'll stop breathing. It hurts, it physically hurts, do you know what I mean?"

He nodded.

"I know I'm shit. I know you fought for me and I fought against you. But I was lucky for every moment you wasted on me. And I did know it then. I just didn't know how to do *this.*"

People were looking. Cheryl gaped like a large-mouthed bass.

"What do you want me for?" Gunther asked quietly.

"For everything," Mike said. "For anything and everything you'll give me."

"For this?" he asked. Slowly, deliberately, and with an entire café full of silent people watching, Gunther stepped around Cheryl. He took Mike's face in both his hands and he kissed her. He kissed her for a long time and she let him. So long that uncomfortable murmurs began to wend around the room and the curious manager poked his head around from the bar to see why everyone was so quiet.

"This is like the story of my life," Cheryl said to no one in particular.

"For that?" Gunther asked Mike when he finally pulled away.

She didn't care who was watching. She didn't care what anyone thought. She only cared that he was there and that this was a chance she hadn't let slip by.

"Oh, yeah," she said. "What else you got?"

And from a silver frame above a fireplace on the Upper East Side of Manhattan, Caroline smiled and winked and said, "'Atta girl."

ABOUT THE AUTHOR

Ellen Shanman is a graduate of Northwestern University. She lives and writes in Brooklyn, New York.

ACKNOWLEDGMENTS

Thank you to all of my wonderful teachers, in school and out.

I owe a debt of gratitude to all of the following people for their advice and support, and for my relative sanity: my agent, Annelise Robey, and my editor, Shauna Summers. Also at Bantam, Katie Rudkin and Jessica Sebor. For excellent counsel, David Korzenik. Friends/readers/advisors Jessica Arinella, Jen Jafarzadeh, Kate McGovern, Mark Sage, Sara Sellar, Micahlyn Whitt, and Meredith Zeitlin. PG Kain, for the phone calls and the indispensable lunches. My very old friend Cheryl Conkling, who lent me her name but certainly not her likeness. The entire extensive Schumacher clan, who have made me one of their own from the beginning, but especially Janie and Doug, David and Amie, Darrell and Shirley. My mother and father for all they've given me and all they continue to teach me. And Jon, for whom there aren't adequate words to say thank you the way I mean it.

Sometimes the right book is just waiting for the right time to be discovered.

Entertaining, intelligent, and lively books
by fascinating storytellers
you won't want to miss.

New voices. New choices.

AVAILABLE IN SUMMER 2008	COMING IN FALL 2008
Garden Spells	*Swim to Me*
The Wedding Officer	*Thank You for All Things*
How to Talk to a Widower	*Good Luck*
Everything Nice	*The Pre-Nup*

Enter to win a year of
Bantam Discovery novels! For more details visit
www.bantamdiscovery.com.